Love Me
or
Hate Me

STEPHANIE ALVES

This book contains detailed sexual content and graphic
language, as well as some other topic which might be
triggering to some.
You can see the full list of content warnings on my website
here: stephaniealvesauthor.com

Happy Reading!

Also by Stephanie Alves

Standalone

Love Me or Hate Me

Campus Games Series

Never Have I Ever (Book #1)
Spin The Bottle (Book #2)
Would You Rather (Book #3)

For all the people who want someone to see them at their worst and still love them.

Playlist

🟢 ·||||··||·||·||·||·|||·

In your eyes – The Weeknd ft Doja cat
Wasted times – The Weeknd
Pov – Ariana Grande
Up at night – Kehlani ft Justin Bieber
Hate that I love you – Rihanna ft Ne-Yo
Never knew I needed – Ne-Yo
Honey – Kehlani
Breathin – Ariana Grande
Best part – Daniel Caesar ft H.E.R
As you are – The Weeknd
Every kind of way – H.E.R
Feels – Kehlani
I know a love – Trey Songz

One

Melissa

This can't be happening.

There's no way this is happening.

This has to be some kind of sick joke or a prank. Right?

I blink away the confusion, and Zaria's face gradually comes into focus as I make an effort to open my eyes. Seeing as we share a wall, when her phone rang in the middle of the night and jolted me awake in the process, I had no choice but to get out of bed to wake Zaria up, since she sleeps like the dead.

Now, in hindsight, I wish I had just stayed in bed.

"You're joking."

"I'm not," she replies, reaching up to wipe at her tired, heavy eyes hidden behind the curtain of her thick lashes.

Zaria has this natural ability to catch everyone's eye when she strolls down the street. It's just impossible not to notice her – with her long curly hair, her wardrobe bursting with vibrant colors and perfect style, and that infectious bright smile of hers.

Even at four in the morning, she's still beautiful. Her warm brown skin, flawlessly pampered by the ten-step skincare routine she swears by before bedtime, has this gentle glow. But, there's something different this time. Her eyes, usually filled with cheer, now carry a hint of remorse.

I shake my head, struggling to make sense of what she's telling me. "What do you mean Gabriel's moving in?" I ask, secretly praying that I misheard her.

"He said he needed a place to move into," she says with a deep sigh. "I guess something happened between him and Lucy, and they broke up."

My eyes widen in surprise. Gabriel and Lucy hadn't been dating for long, but it's still a shock to hear, especially since the last time I saw Lucy, she seemed smitten with him.

"I told him he could stay with us in the meantime," she says, causing my stomach to plummet even further.

A bitter laugh escapes me. Zaria's words linger in the air, echoing in my brain as I struggle to come to grips with it. "If this is a prank, it's not a very funny one," I mutter, shaking my head, but my smile is completely wiped when I see the serious expression on her face.

"I knew this would be a problem," she admits, pressing her hand against her forehead in exasperation. "But Gabriel assured me you two could be civil with each other."

I can't help but release a scoff. What a load of bullshit. Gabriel and I can't spend more than a few minutes around each other without going at each other's throats. It's been that way ever since we met ten years ago. We never got along. Ever. He loves to torment me, and irritate me to the core.

It's bad enough that we argue whenever we see each other, which wasn't all that often, but now I would have to see him every day, and live with him.

In the same house.

There's no way we can be civil with each other, no matter how much Gabriel fed his sister that line.

My brows knit together involuntarily as I picture what living with him will be like. Just the thought of him turning my life into a living hell, enjoying every moment with a mocking laugh, intensifies the knot in my stomach.

A weight settles on my chest, and instinctively, I raise a hand to steady it, attempting to alleviate the pounding of my heart. Just the mere thought of his arrival is enough to make me freak out, and he hasn't even set foot in the door.

I try to keep calm, and practice what my therapist tells me to do. *Deep breath in, hold it for ten, deep breath out.*

Fuck that.

It's not working.

"It's just for a while," she says, her hand gently gliding up and down my arm in a reassuring gesture. Her eyes soften when they meet mine and she gives me a tentative smile, but Zaria's attempts to console me do little to crush the rising anxiety.

"What exactly constitutes as a while?" I ask her, dropping my hand from my chest.

"About a month?" she says in a wince as my eyes widen in response.

"A month?" I cry out. I thought he'd maybe stay here one, two weeks tops. But four whole weeks, in the same apartment with the guy who has makes it his mission to annoy me every chance he gets since high school? I won't survive it.

Maybe I should consider adapting Zaria's ten-step skincare routine, because I can already feel the onset of some wrinkles.

She sighs, her frustration evident in the subtle shake of her head. "The idiot went ahead and signed a lease with the girl," she says, her eyes rolling as she folds her arms across her chest. "I told him not to move in with her, but..." Another sigh escapes her, dripping with irritation. "Gabriel, as always, does whatever he wants."

"Doesn't he have any money saved up?" As much as I don't like the guy, he isn't stupid. I'm sure he has savings he could fall back on if he needed.

"We don't really talk about that kind of stuff," she says, wrinkling her nose. "He asked if he could stay over, and I said yes." Her brows tug together, and she lifts her shoulder in a shrug. "He's my brother, M. Family helps family."

Dropping my head, I pull my bottom lip between my teeth. Of course. They always helped each other out. No matter what. I, however, couldn't relate to their close knit family dynamic. The closest thing I had to a family were Zaria and her parents.

"He didn't even tell you why they broke up all of a sudden?" I ask her, a little intrigued. Gabriel's relationship caught me off guard when Zaria told me about it. Back in high school, he was a known player. Every girl wanted Gabriel Anderson, and that hadn't changed when we graduated and he left the state to go to college.

I had to admit, even if I hated the thought, and as much as I tried to deny it, Gabriel Anderson was an attractive man. And worst of all, at the mere age of fourteen, I had become just like all the other girls, and developed a crush on him. It ended just as briefly as it started when I found out what an asshole he was, though.

The first time I ever laid eyes on him, was after Zaria invited me over to her house. Gabriel was walking down the stairs, and I still remember how my breath hitched in my throat at the sight of him. His chiseled jaw was covered in stubble, which was now a short, trimmed beard, and his pouty lips were glossy as he ran his tongue over them.

I remember how he introduced himself, and how I was a blabbering mess, unable to stop drooling as my eyes drifted to his arms, the muscles, his dark skin, glistening from just coming out of the shower.

But I also remember all the times he teased me over the years, and how no matter how handsome he was, and is, I won't let myself go there ever again. There was no denying the man was unbelievably gorgeous, but would I ever admit that to anyone? Hell no. Especially not to Zaria. I don't even want to think about what she would do if she ever found out I once had a teeny, tiny crush on her big brother.

"No, he didn't tell me." She shrugs. "He just mentioned the break up, and that he need a place to crash for a while."

I wonder why he didn't tell his sister. Gabriel and Zaria have always been close, so what could be the reason behind him not confiding in her about the breakup?

"Can you promise me, Melissa?" she asks, her eyes pleading with mine. "Can you promise you'll at least try to get along?"

How do I do that? How can I make such a promise when the mere thought of spending over thirty days with Gabriel under the same roof already has my heart racing out of my chest?

How can I forgive him for everything he's said, and done throughout the years? It wasn't just that he didn't like me for some unknown reason, but it seemed like I was the only person he didn't like.

Everyone always loved Gabriel. He was charming, happy and charismatic. With everyone except me.

A deep sigh leaves my lips. "I'll try," I tell her, holding my hand up when she starts to smile. "But I can't promise anything."

"That's all I can ask for," she says, with a grin that makes me think she definitely misinterpreted my statement. "You're like my sister, M, you know that." My eyes soften at her words. "I just don't want a war going on between you two."

She's right. If he was going to be staying with us, then the least I could do try to make the best out of the situation.

"I'm going back to sleep," she says, crashing onto her bed, before pulling the covers over her body. "I only have tomorrow off, and then I'm back at the hospital."

I let out a laugh at the sight of her drifting off to sleep so fast. I envy her. It always takes me hours of tossing and turning before I can finally find some resemblance of rest. "When will he be here?" I ask her, bracing myself for the inevitable.

"Noon," she mumbles, already halfway asleep.

I shake my head, a smile tugging at my lips, and turn around, making my way into my bedroom.

Pulling the covers over my head, I let the dark engulf me, begging myself to fall asleep. I'll need to be well rested if I have to deal with him, but sleeping seems impossible. Not when the situation has me wide awake making my brain works overtime about everything that could go wrong.

I wonder how Gabriel felt about our living situation? He promised Zaria we could be civil, but what did that mean, exactly? We have never once been civil with each other, so the thought of that happening now seems improbable.

I just know he must be hating the fact that he has to live in the same apartment as me.

Letting out a frustrated groan, I force my eyes closed, attempting to bury myself deeper into the bed. Hopefully a good night's rest can prepare me for what's about to happen tomorrow. Maybe it won't even be that bad.

Who am I kidding? It's going to be a nightmare.

Two

Melissa

The sudden knock on the door startles me, making my breath quicken. I strain to hear the distinct sound of Zaria's footsteps, echoing throughout the apartment.

He's here.

The door swings open, and Gabriel's deep voice, accompanied by a few chuckles, reaches my ears. I force myself to take a deep breath, the realization sinking in that I haven't seen him since the day after Christmas. Nine whole months have passed since we last saw each other.

"Thanks for helping me out," I hear him say. "I promise as soon as I can, I'll get out of your hair."

"Don't worry about that, you idiot," Zaria replies. "You know I'd do anything for you."

"Aww. You're getting soft, sis."

"Shut up," she jokes. "You know I can throw a punch if I need to."

I hear his scoff through the thin walls as I sit up on my bed, engrossed in their conversation. "And break a nail? I doubt it."

I let my eyes fall to the ground. I've always admired their relationship. I love how close they are. Being an only child sucks, especially when my mother up and quit being a parent, leaving me and my dad alone.

"So…" Gabriel says, his teasing tone making the hair on my arms rise. "Where's Trevi?"

I roll my eyes. Trevi. The god-awful nickname Gabriel decided to give me a few weeks after we met. He's called me that for the past ten years, knowing I hate it when he does. A mix between the Trevi fountain, and my last name Trevisano. So original, seeing as he teases me every chance he gets over my inability to cook, whilst also being Italian.

"Don't start," Zaria says.

"What?" he replies. "I didn't even do anything."

"Yeah, but I know you." I smile, knowing Zaria's got my back, even though he's her brother. "You tease her and annoy her until she can't take it. This is her apartment, Gabriel. I don't want you guys to kill each other." She lets out a heavy sigh. "I told her I'd talk to you about it, so that's what I'm doing."

"I promise," he says. "I'll be on my best behavior."

My eyes roll. I doubt it.

Sucking in a deep breath, I lift myself out of my bed, and head toward the door. I guess there's no point in trying to delay the inevitable. My hand wraps around the door handle, pulling it open. Two heads turn to look my way, and my eyes drift to Gabriel who's sporting a grin at the sight of me.

"Trevi," he says, his deep voice making my skin shiver, as he looks me up and down, tilting his head at my lazy Sunday outfit. "Nice outfit."

I press my lips together as I fist the hem of my oversized t-shirt in my hands. I'm not trying to impress anyone, less of all him, so I'm not embarrassed about his obvious sarcasm, or the way his eyes drift down to my pink sweatpants as he lifts an eyebrow.

"Was that an attempt at an insult?" I ask.

He feigns hurt, placing his hand against his chest. "I would never insult you."

I scoff. "Dumped and a liar. Not off to a great start, are we?" I tilt my head, catching sight of Zaria shaking her head as she sighs. I know, I know. I broke my promise to her in less than thirty seconds. Guilt racks through me at the disappointed look in her eyes.

Gabriel's eyes glint with mischief as he takes a step closer to me. "For someone who claims she can't stand me, you really do seem to be preoccupied with my relationships." He licks his lips, a teasing smile playing on them. "Do you have a little crush on me, Trevi?"

I shoot him a narrowed glare. As if I'd ever stoop that low ever again. "You think too highly of yourself," I retort.

"And you, clearly think too much of me." He shakes his head, sighing. "Hate to break it to you, but you're not my type."

My nostrils flare in irritation, and I clench my t-shirt tighter between my closed fists. I silently plead with myself not to react to his words, not to let him under my skin. I shouldn't care what Gabriel thinks of me, but for some infuriating reason, I do.

"My heart's breaking," I quip, dripping with sarcasm. "Like I'd ever be hopeless enough to want to be one of your desperate conquests."

His laugh makes my heart race even faster. The asshole actually enjoys this, doesn't he? "The only one desperate here, is you. Don't be jealous, Trevi. It's not a good look."

I let out a scoff. "Jealous?" I repeat. "Of what exactly? You go through girls so fast you probably don't even remember their names." I tilt my head, teasing him as I watch his eyes narrow at me. "Is that why your girlfriend left you?" I ask. "Never did imagine you to be the loyal type."

Gabriel's eyebrows tug together, and instead of answering, he scoffs, turning around to grab his suitcases before walking into our office, is now his bedroom for the time being.

The door slams shut with a harsh thud, and I pull my lip between my teeth, a twinge of regret settling in as the sound echoes through the room, realizing that I've gone too far.

"Well, that went well," Zaria says dryly.

I let out a groan, running a hand down my face. "I'm sorry, Z. I told you I would try, and I did the complete opposite the first change I got."

She sighs. "Maybe this was a bad idea," she says. "I knew you two couldn't stand each other and—"

"No," I interrupt, not letting her take blame for my mistake. She's helping her brother out, the least I can do is not argue with him – at least not while she's around to witness it. "I can do better," I tell her, determined to make this work. "I'll try. For real this time."

Doubt swims in her eyes as she narrows them, and I can't even fault her for it. "Are you sure?" she asks me.

I nod. "It's just going to be harder than I thought," I admit. "But I can handle it," I lie.

"I'll try to talk to him again." She sighs, the subtle shake of her head a clear expression of her frustration. "I know he makes it hard, but you weren't trying either, M."

My stomach churns, the guilt eating me up. "I know," I agree, letting out a groan. "He just infuriates me."

She chuckles. "I can see that." Her finger pokes at my cheek. "Your face is so red I'm tempted to check your blood pressure."

I roll my eyes at her. "Don't go all nurse on me. I'm fine. I'm just flushed with anger." I force a smile, reassuring her that there is nothing to worry about.

"C'mon," she says, linking her arm with mine. "Get dressed. We're going out for some ice cream."

"Your my favorite best friend, you know that?" I joke, nudging her on the arm.

"I'm your only best friend."

This time, the smile on my face isn't forced as we head into my room, and start to pick out some clothes to wear. I've always had a theory that ice cream can solve anything. It can help with loneliness, sadness, or even a heartbreak. But tonight, I need comfort; the kind only a pint of strawberry ice cream could provide.

Three

Gabriel

It's been less than twenty four hours since I moved in, and I already have a 5'4", brunette attacking me.

Honestly, I don't know what I expected. I should have known she wouldn't make this easy. I didn't expect Melissa to sit back and take it.

She's a vixen, this girl. Always fighting me, always trying to one up me in the insults I've grown accustomed to throughout the years.

Little does she know, I like it. I like seeing her angry, I like her eyes wild with fire, I love it, and today is no different.

Luckily, my sister isn't here today, or else Melissa would be the well behaved girl she promised my sister she'd be.

Yawn.

I don't want that.

I want her riled up.

It might sound fucked up, but Melissa has always been the quiet one. The good one. The observant one. But with me? She loses all of that, and becomes a version of herself no one but me sees.

I fucking love that.

"Give me the remote," she yells for the umpteenth time.

"I want to watch the game."

"Ugh," she groans, reaching for the remote again. "I want to watch my show."

I tut, shaking my head. "I was here first, Trevi. Where are your manners?" I joke, loving the flushed color on her cheeks. God, she's pretty. She's somehow gotten prettier in the last nine months since I last saw her.

It's fucking unfair how beautiful she is.

It's unfair I can't do anything about it.

With a huff, she stands and places her hands on her full hips, making my eyes drop to them. *Don't fucking look at her.* "You know, this is my apartment," she says, her eyes narrowed as she scowls at me. Even with a scowl, she's still so fucking beautiful. I run my hand over my mouth, trying to get those thoughts out of my head.

"Nothing gets past you, Trevi," I joke, wanting to move past the millions of thoughts I have of her throughout the years. I don't know why I thought I could handle being in the same space as her when I've struggled immensely since I fucking met her. Maybe I just like to torture myself, because sitting here with her right in front of me, and having to tease her when all I really want to do is stop time so I can just fucking look at her, sound like torture to me.

"You know what I mean," she says, her brows tugging so adorably. "You can't just barge in here and demand things go your way."

I rip my eyes away from her, staring back at the tv. I could leave, I could get out of the house, or go to my room, and let her watch those dumb reality shows she loves so much, but if all the time I get with her is when we're arguing, then I'll take it.

"You're welcome to sit and watch with me if you want, but I'm not leaving." I shoot her a grin, wanting one back, but it would probably be a cold day in hell until I got so much as a smile from Melissa.

But being the stubborn woman she is, she does the opposite and stands in front of the tv, blocking the view. I almost laugh, almost tell her how I don't even care what's on the tv, that I'd much rather just sit here and look at her all day if she'd let me,. But then she'd know how I really feel about her. And I can't let her know that.

My eyes narrow at her. "Get out of the way, Trevi."

She straightens her shoulders. "No," she says, chewing on the inside of her mouth. My pulse starts to race seeing her nervous tick. I don't like that she's nervous. I like her fire, yes, but I never want her to be nervous.

I lift an eyebrow. "I can move you."

She lets out a scoff, ever so stubborn. "I'd like to see you try."

I let out a groan when I lift myself off the couch and approach her slowly. Her head lifts to look up at me, our height difference a big one, ever since we were teenagers, and she presses those pink lips together.

I don't remember the last time I was this close to her, and neither does she by the heavy breathing leaving her lips. Her brows start to quiver as she wonders what I'm going to do.

A grin spreads across my face as I snake a hand across her waist. I revel in the way her eyes widen and before she can think, I lift her up and throw her over my shoulder.

She lets out a cross between a shout and a whimper as I hoist her up on my shoulder. "What are you doing?" she yells. "Put me down."

My chest rumbles with a laugh as I wrap my arms around her legs when she attempt to kick. "You offered me a challenge. I took it."

God damn. From this position, I can smell her. The sweet scent of strawberries invades my nose every time she moves and I stifle a groan. This girl. This damn girl.

"I didn't mean this," she says, kicking her feet again.

"You're pissing me off, Trevi. Stay still, I'm trying to watch the game."

"Then put me down, asshole."

I chuckle. "Are you going to be a good girl and do as I say?"

She stops kicking, her body going stiff in my arms. My eyebrows raise, wondering if she's going to do just that, but that's wishful thinking when it comes to Melissa.

"You're crazy if you think I'll ever listen to you," she retorts.

"Then you're staying here," I tell her, watching as she starts kicking again. "It doesn't bother me."

"It bothers me," she says. "Seriously, Gabriel. How many squats do you do?"

I chuckle, looking behind my shoulder. "Are you checking out my ass, Trevi?"

She lifts her head, rolling her eyes. "There's not much else to look at when I'm flung over your shoulder like a child. Put me down."

I tut, shaking my head. "I'll put you down if you stop acting like a brat."

Her mouth drops open. "Did you seriously call me a brat for wanting to watch a show in my own apartment."

"I was here first."

"I lived here first," she quips.

"I'll make you a deal," I tell her, smiling when she narrows her eyes. "Watch the game with me, and we can watch those dumb shows after."

Her eyes widen. "I'm not making a deal with you."

See? Stubborn. Would it kill her to sit here with me for an hour? "Why not?"

She attempts to push me, groaning when it doesn't work. "What am I going to do here? Sit and knit?"

I let out a laugh. Melissa would never knit. "It's not like you have anything else to do," I joke.

But from the wince on her face, I can tell she didn't like that joke. "What does that mean?" she asks.

I shrug. "I mean, all you do is stay home. It wouldn't hurt to sit and watch a game with me." I grin. "It's called a compromise."

She blinks rapidly as she turns away, and a frown forms on my face. What the hell? She pushes at my arm again, with more force this time. "Put me down."

I drop her to her feet, watching as she reaches up and wipes her eyes. Is she… crying? "Are you ok?" I ask her, reaching for her wrist. My heart thrashes against my chest. What the fuck did I do?

"I'm fine," she mutters, sounding like anything but fine as she pushes my hand off her wrist, and turns around.

My brows furrow. "Wait. Where are you going?"

"Watch your game," she mutters, heading into her bedroom. "You win."

The door slams with force and I'm left staring at the wooden door wondering what the hell I just said to make her mad at me.

Again.

Fuck.

I just wanted to joke with her, have her spend the day with me watching some stupid thing that I wouldn't even be paying attention to, not when she'd be there. I wanted to talk to her without my sister being around, without telling myself all the reasons I shouldn't talk to her.

But I fucked it up.

Again.

I drop down on the couch, letting out a harsh breath as I look up at the tv.

She's wrong. This doesn't feel like winning.

It feels like losing.

Four

Melissa

"M. Are you awake?"

I smile, a relief washing over me at the sound of my best friend's voice as she knocks on my door.

Gabriel's only been here a day, and I'm already questioning if there's any hope left for this living situation.

Gabriel and I never really had much reason to talk before this. Our paths crossed now and then, mostly at family gatherings, but we usually kept our distance. Now, with him living here, avoiding each other has become downright impossible.

Zaria's head pokes through the door as it swings open, and I shoot her a tired smile. "I'm awake," I assure her, though the truth is, it's impossible to drift off when all I can think about is how I'm going to survive the next month with Gabriel if every day is going to be like today.

She drops down on my bed with a sigh, and I glance up at her with hooded eyes, clearly exhausted from her day at work. Given the twelve-hour shift, I'm surprised she didn't crash in her own bed as soon as she got home.

"So, you're both alive," she quips, a playful glint in her eyes. "It couldn't have been that bad, right?"

Rolling my eyes, I can't help but laugh. "You really had no faith in us whatsoever, did you?"

She lets out a scoff. "Please. I've seen your fights first hand. So how did it go today?" she asks.

I suck in a deep breath, wondering if I should be honest with her, or tell her it went well. "It could have been better," I say instead, deciding to keep the details to myself.

"That doesn't sound too promising," she says, narrowing her eyes. She might think there's more to the story, and she'd be right, so I wave her off, wanting to get off the topic of Gabriel.

"Enough about me," I say. "What about you? How was work?"

"Good," she mumbles, a sly smirk dancing on her lips.

"Oh no," I joke, knowing there's more to the story. "I know that look."

"What look?" she teases, her grin giving her away every time.

"You have a crush."

She laughs, realizing I've caught on. "Maybe."

"Do you work with him?" I ask her, intrigued.

"I do," she says, wagging her brows. "It makes for good breaks."

Letting out a chuckle, I shake my head at her suggestive comment. I admire Zaria for being so bold and going after what she wants whenever she wants. I wish I could be like that. Instead I'm the type of girl who stays at home and barely goes out. I'm the type of girl who doesn't go on dates, and barely talks to guys. What Gabriel said earlier might have hurt, but he was right.

"I was thinking recently," she says. "That maybe... I'd like to settle down."

My eyebrows shoot up. "Really?" I ask her. "With this guy?"

She shrugs, a smile on her lips. "If it goes well," she says. "We'll see. Maybe he has a friend." Her brow raises. "For my friend."

I roll my eyes. She already knows I have no interest in dating. I haven't done since things went south when I was in college. I don't crave any of it. Not the cuddles, kisses, or hugs and definitely not sex. I hate the idea of having to depend on someone else, having to open up and share everything about yourself with that other person.

"I know, I know." She sighs. "I was just hoping you'd change your mind."

"I missed you today," I say, reaching out to hug her.

"I know." She lies her head on my shoulder with a breath that lets me know how exhausted she is. "I missed you too." When she pulls back, she has a smile on her face. "Maybe when I have a day off, we can catch up on 'Love Oasis' if you don't finish the episodes on your own."

I let out a groan at the mention the name of our favorite reality show to watch. "If Gabriel keeps hogging the remote like he did today, then that won't be a problem."

"He did?" she asks with a chuckle.

I narrow my eyes at her. "Traitor. Who's side are you on?"

"Yours, M," she says with a laugh. "Always yours."

"Good. Because I'm going to need an alibi if I do end up killing your brother."

"Can I suggest any other possibility before you end up with murder?" she asks, lifting a brow.

I sigh, dramatically. "I'll think about it," I tease.

She shakes her head, a laugh bubbling out of her. "This is going to be interesting," she says, lifting off my bed. "Anyway, I need to go to bed. I'm up at four tomorrow." Zaria buries her head in her hands, letting out a muffled cry. "Goodnight."

I chuckle, watching as she heads out of my room. "Night."

When the door closes with a soft click, I let myself fall into bed, pulling the covers up to my chin.

I let myself close my eyes and hope this month flies by, but ultimately I know it probably won't.

Five

Melissa

"What's up with you today?" Allie asks, scrunching her brows as she gnaws on her sandwich. "You're acting weird."

"Gabriel's in town."

She gulps, her eyes so wide they look like they're about to pop out of her head. Other than Zaria, Allie is the only other person I feel comfortable enough around. She and I have become friends ever since we started working at Maplewood middle school together three years ago. Which means she also knows how much I despise Gabriel.

"You're joking." Her blue eyes stay focused on me as she reaches for her coffee, taking a sip. "How long has it been since you last saw him?"

"Since Christmas," I tell her, thinking back to that day. "I left the morning after when we had an argument."

After my father died, I spent every holiday with the Andersons. They became my second family when my first had vanished. Except for Gabriel.

As much as I tried to avoid him as much as possible, it didn't always end up working, especially when he would do whatever it took to annoy me. It was a game to him, fun even, but to me it was not.

Holidays were, and still are hard to get through, especially Christmas. I still remember my dad waking me up with hot chocolate with only pink marshmallows—my favorite—and dressing as Santa to open presents with me. Even when I was eighteen, and he was a shell of the man I used to know, he still kept those same traditions until he was gone.

I never told any of them that I would spend the mornings at my father's grave, only that I was going to go for a walk. I thought keeping my grief to myself would be easier, since the thought of seeing pity on their faces made me want to crawl inside my skin. I hated people pitying me.

So when I got back, they were all still asleep, and I headed toward the backyard where they had a huge pool. I loved their pool. Loved it since the first time I ever saw it. It was quiet here. Peaceful.

It didn't take long for Gabriel to find me however, and it wasn't long until he sat beside me on the pool deck.

"You weren't here this morning," he said, zipping up his jacket.

My eyes caught on his pajama bottoms and I frowned. "What are you doing here?" I asked him, turning my head away so he didn't see my puffed up lips and red eyes.

"Came to check on a stubborn girl who thinks sitting by the pool in December is a good idea. Especially when you had disappeared this morning."

My shoulders slumped, and I turned my head to look at him. It almost sounded like he was… worried about me.

"Well she's fine," I told him, my chin quivering as I tried my hardest not to cry. I was the furthest thing from fine, but I wouldn't let him know that. "You can leave now."

But he didn't. Instead, he stood up and made his way closer until he was stood in front of me. I lifted my head, and instantly he frowned. "It's Christmas. Why are you upset?"

I shook my head, lowering my head back down. "Gabriel. Just leave me alone."

"C'mon, Trevi." His hand reached out, wrapping around my wrist as he pulled me off the pool chair. "You want to go for a swim?" His brows wagged as he twisted me around until I was a couple of inches away from the pool.

"Gabriel," I gasped, clutching at his jacket. "Don't."

He let out a laugh, pulling me back. "I'm just kidding, Trevi." I let out a heavy breath when I move back away from the pool. "I forgot how fun annoying you is."

"And you just left?" Allie asks.

"I stayed for Christmas day, but the next morning I got on a plane and came back home," I admit. "I just couldn't spend another day pretending everything was fine, and having to deal with Gabriel on top of that."

"You get so worked up over him," she says with a smirk. "Are you sure you don't still have a crush?"

Allie is the only person that knows I had a very brief, embarrassing crush on Gabriel when we were teenagers, and I regret telling her every single day.

"Very positive," I say, dryly. "Why did I ever tell you that?"

"Because you love me," she says, shooting me a kiss. "And you're sure he isn't flirting with you?" she asks, raising a brow. "Because it sounds like flirting to me."

I let out a laugh. "Definitely not. You don't know him, Allie. The man hates me. He lives to make my life a living nightmare. And besides, he's not attracted to me."

Allie scoffs. "That's bullshit."

"I'm serious. He told me point and blank that I'm not his type." I don't even know why I care that I'm not Gabriel's type. I've seen the girls he's dated before. Long legs, beautiful skin, glamorous, confident. Something I'll never be.

Sure, I know I'm somewhat attractive. I have my father's tan skin, and green eyes, full lips and a body that my nonna once described as being 'perfect for childbearing'. But I'd be stupid if I thought that compared to any of the girls I've seen Gabriel with before.

"So, how long is he in town for?" she asks, wiping the corner of her mouth.

I let out a deep sigh, letting my eyes fall closed. "A month."

"What?" Her eyes widen.

"He broke up with his girlfriend, and he moved in with us until he can find a place."

Allie lets out a laugh. "So, what you're saying is that he's single?"

"Allie," I chide. "This is serious. What the hell am I going to do? How am I going to manage living with him when he drives me crazy?"

"I hear hate sex is great," she jokes.

"Forget it." I slump in my chair. "You're no help."

26

She chuckles. "And what did Zaria say about this?"

I wince, breathing out a sigh. "I kind of told her I'd try to get along with him."

She scoffs. "Good luck with that. Guess you'll have to kiss and make up… emphasis on the kiss."

I narrow my eyes. "Hilarious."

She shoots me a smirk. "You'll have to act like a good girl for Mr. Anderson."

I scrunch my nose with disgust. "Mr. Anderson is what I call his dad. Please don't call him that."

"Fine." She grins. "You'll have to be a very good girl for Chef Gabriel then."

"I'm regretting our friendship as we speak."

Six

Melissa

After a long day at work, surrounded by kids, the last thing I want is to come home to the apartment being covered by boxes everywhere.

But of course, that's exactly what happens.

"Gabriel," I call out, wondering why the hell his whole wardrobe is spread out across the apartment. Seriously, how many clothes does this man own?

I hastily step over the mass amounts of cardboard boxes, reaching his closed bedroom door. "Gabriel," I call out again, knocking on the wooden door. He has to be here right? He wouldn't just leave his stuff all over the place and then leave.

The door swings open, and Gabriel stands under the door frame, making my eyes drift to his bare chest. My mouth drops open as my eyes connect with his dark skin, glistening with sweat, his muscular chest more chiseled than the last time I saw him shirtless.

When I hear the sound of his throat clearing, I stiffen, realizing what I was just doing before I lift my eyes to meet his.

His lips twist in a teasing smirk as he crosses his arms. "Were you checking me out, Trevi?" he asks, chuckling.

I take a step back away from him, mentally slapping myself for unknowingly ogling him. "What is all this?" I ask, gesturing toward the scattered boxes,

"My stuff?" he says, lifting a brow.

"You know what I mean," I retort, narrowing my eyes. "Why is your stuff all over the place?"

He lifts his shoulder in a shrug. "The rest of my things got delivered, so I took the day off to put it away," he explains, walking over to pick up a box. "You're welcome to help if you want."

I let out a scoff. "The last thing I would do is help you." Help him? After all the years of shit he gave me? Yeah, right.

He chuckles, shaking his head. "Always so charming," he says.

"I am charming," I tell him. "Just not to you."

He drops the box in his room with a thud and turns back to face me, placing a hand on his chest, making my eyes drop to it once again. *Get it together.* "Wow. I feel so special."

"Trust me, you're not," I say, narrowing my eyes. "You're just someone who pisses me off any chance they get."

He chuckles, again. "And you're such a brat. Do you realize you were the one who started an argument this time?" His brows lift in question.

My lips drop into a frown. He's right. I hate that he's right. He didn't even do anything this time, and somehow he still gets under my skin. "Jackass," I mutter, feeling my face grow hot with frustration.

"I heard that."

I press my lips together in a fake smile. "You were supposed to."

He shakes his head, a smirk on his lips. If I didn't know better, I would think he actually likes when I insult him. "You really know how to dig the knife deep, Trevi," he mocks.

"Please," I say, rolling my eyes. "Like you haven't said worse."

"Only to you," he laughs, unpacking another box.

A scoff escapes me. "How chivalrous of you to let me know I'm the only person in the world you seem to despise."

He lets out a laugh, glancing up at me. "You sound jealous, sweetheart."

My heart thumps against my chest so loud I'm scared he'll hear it as I shoot him a scowl. "Don't call me that. And I'm not jealous."

"Your loss," he says, leaning down to pick up another box. I try not to let my gaze linger on how his biceps flex when he lifts the heavy load.

"Of what exactly?" I ask with a laugh. "Of the fact that you sleep with a new girl every night?" I shake my head. "You probably leave the poor women unsatisfied."

He drops the box in his room, turning back to face me with a raised brow. His tongue darts out to lick his bottom lip, and he lets out a dark chuckle. "Is that another challenge?" he asks, the question hanging in the air.

The last time I made the mistake of challenging him, he followed through on his promise. Red alerts go off in my head, and I take a step back, my ass hitting the kitchen counters. My throat feels like it's closing as I force a gulp.

"Whatever," I mutter, trying to make my pulse return to normal. "I'm going to my room. Make sure you clean all of this up," I tell him before turning around and heading toward my bedroom.

"Sure thing, sweetheart," I hear him mutter with a dark laugh before I enter my bedroom.

Closing the door behind me, I take in a deep breath, trying to calm myself down, and without hesitation, I pull out my phone and search for the only person who will be able to understand.

Melissa:

Is it too late to change my name and move to a different country?

Allie:

Trouble in paradise?

Melissa:

More like trouble in hell

I drop my phone onto my bed and rip off my shirt, eager to get into my pajamas and into bed. I knew this would be hard, but I didn't realize just how difficult it would be to be around Gabriel all the time.

Especially since the attraction to him hasn't gone away no matter how much I want it to. He might be an asshole, but damn it, he's a hot asshole. And I hate to admit that.

My head snaps to the side when my phone buzzes with a notification.

Allie:

> Maybe you can figure out a way to stay away from him until he's gone.

My eyebrows raise. That's not a terrible idea, but how would that work when I live with the guy? I quickly change into my comfy clothes, grab my notebook, and climb into my bed, determined to make this situation work.

No matter what.

Seven

Gabriel

"You're home."

I lift my head, finding Melissa in front of me, holding a notebook in her hand.

"Missed me?" I tease, offering a smirk as I reach up to wipe a bead of sweat from my forehead.

"No," she says with an eye roll. "It's just later than usual, that's all."

"I went to the gym," I explain, noting her eyes briefly dipping to my shirt clung to my body. I went straight to the gym after work, needing to clear my head before returning home to the most beautiful girl I had ever seen, and pretend like I couldn't stand her.

Right now, I kinda wish I had stayed longer at the gym, maybe taken a shower there or something, because, damn it, that workout did nothing to erase thoughts of her from my head. Especially when she's right there, looking so damn beautiful.

"So, I've been thinking," she starts, chewing on the inside of her mouth.

"That's never good, Trevi." I lean on the back of the couch, arms crossed, and stare at her. My gaze fixates on the notebook clutched in her hands. Why is she so nervous?

She lets out a sigh. "I think we should set a schedule."

My brows knit together. "A schedule?" I repeat. "For what, exactly?"

"For the apartment," she clarifies. "I think it's best we find a way to live together without actually… seeing each other."

My frown deepens as I stare back at her. "You're serious?" I ask her, my heart racing out of my chest. What the hell? She made a whole fucking schedule so she can avoid me?

"I think it's for the best, Gabriel," she says with a heavy sigh. "The arguing, the fighting, it's just too much." My chest tightens and I stop fucking breathing. "That way we won't see each other as much until you leave."

She's fucking kidding. She has to be. I mean, I know we joke, and bicker, but I never thought it was this bad. Was it this bad for her? It must be if she'd go to these lengths to avoid seeing me.

Coming here was risky, I know that. Especially when I tend to forget all rational thoughts whenever I'm around her. I've always put walls between us, kept our communication to a minimum. If she didn't like me, then that would be another reason not to go there with her. But this? This fucking kills me. Have I really been that bad to her? Does she really not like me that much?

"Fine," I spit out, trying to sound like I don't give a shit, when in fact I hate this dumb plan of hers. "Show me."

"What?" she asks, her brows furrowing.

"The schedule." I hold my hand out, gesturing to the notebook still in her hands. "Show me it."

She reaches out, handing me the pink, lined notebook, and I stare down at her handwriting, scanning the dumbass schedule that means I don't get to see her for the next few weeks.

"This is fucking stupid," I mutter, looking down at the paper.

"At least I'm trying, Gabriel," she says, crossing her arms. I lift my head to look at her, hating how my body warms at the mere sight of her when she feels the complete fucking opposite. I really have shot myself in the foot when it comes to her. "Do you have any better ideas?" she asks.

I narrow my eyes at her, dropping the notebook on the counter. "How about we act like adults and try to get along?" I tilt my head at her.

She lets out a laugh. "You're kidding right? Because that's worked out so well for us so far."

My shoulders slump. I know she's right. And I'm the cause of it. But fuck, I don't want this. I shake my head. "Do you really hate me that much that you'd rather be alone in your room for hours than spend a few hours with me?"

I don't want her to reply. I don't want to hear her say yes, because it'll break my fucking heart. I warned myself away from Melissa a long time ago. Ever since I formed a little crush on her back in high school, I told myself it's not worth it. She was just a girl, my sister's best friend. It was too risky. Too messy for something short term. But then she stuck around. She became more than a friendly face, she became part of my family, and the complications grew, as did my feelings for her.

And now, I've buried myself so deep I don't see a way out.

She doesn't say anything for a while, but the silence isn't comforting either, it's just as torturous. "We argue all the time, Gabriel," she finally says, shaking her head. "If we stay out of each other's way, we won't have to see each other, and we won't argue."

My jaw ticks as I feel my whole body tighten.

"I promised your sister that I would try," she continues. "This is the only way."

Zaria. She's the reason I stayed away from Melissa in the first place. I'd do anything for my sister, even if it means staying away from the one person I didn't ever want to leave.

"Fine," I mutter, hating myself for agreeing to this.

Her brows shoot up, a shocked expression painted on her face. "Really? You're on board?"

"Yeah." I straighten off the back of the couch. "If you hate me so much that you'd make up this fucking schedule to avoid seeing me, then the least I can do is stay out of your way."

I pick up my gym bag, and headphones and turn around, heading into my bedroom.

"You hate me too," I hear her say, stopping me in my tracks. I turn, looking back at her. Her lips are pursed, and her brows are tugged together. "This is beneficial for both of us."

Wrong. She's so fucking wrong about everything. I don't hate her. I never fucking did. That's the goddamn problem.

A scoff escapes me before I can stop it as I scan her from her head to her toes. It might be the last time I see her for a while, so I soak her in. My favorite sight in the world, and it's being ripped away from me. "I could never hate you."

I don't wait to hear her reply, or see the expression on her face. Turning back around, I head into my room and close the door behind me, leaning up against it. Fuck. I wipe a hand down my face, groaning into my palm.

Why the fuck did I say that?

Eight

Melissa

It's been three days since Gabriel and I agreed to the schedule, and ever since I haven't been able to forget Gabriel's words. They've been playing on a loop in my head, making it hard to focus on anything else.

I could never hate you.

There are so many moments when I'm tempted to knock on his door almost desperate to understand what he meant by those words. But I don't. He agreed to the schedule, and giving in to the temptation would feel like admitting defeat. And that's not something I'm ready to do anytime soon.

Especially since the schedule is working.

Kind of.

While we're avoiding seeing each other, which in turn results in us not being able to argue, Gabriel has managed to find a way to still communicate with me.

At first I was confused when I saw a Tupperware filled with chicken alfredo, and a pink sticky note attached to the wall.

Made extra. Go crazy.

I thought he left it for Zaria at first, but when I remembered she doesn't like alfredo pasta, I knew he had left it for me. I shouldn't have been so touched by the thought of Gabriel leaving me some food, but no one had ever done that before.

Zaria cooked here and there, but more often than not, we'd go out to eat. I, however, had no knowledge, or interest in cooking. My meals mainly consisted of takeout. My dad hardly ever cooked either, so I never really learnt how to. I always wondered if my mother knew how to cook. Would she have taught me if she did?

The next day, a smile slid on my face when I came home from work, and I saw another pink sticky note stuck to the tv this time.

I gave one of those reality shows you like so much a go.

I rest my case.

They suck.

This time, I did leave a reply, grabbing one of my yellow sticky notes.

Let me guess, you like movies with naked girls and violence?

But when I woke up this morning, there was no reply from Gabriel. I don't know why I thought we were somehow putting our past behind us and trying to move on, but clearly Gabriel has no intention of doing so.

I try to put it out of my mind, and decide to take a bath instead, wanting to relax after the hectic week at school. I sink into the tub, feeling the warmth surround me, letting my muscles unwind. It's one of the reasons I picked this apartment. Sure, the bedrooms aren't huge, and since Zaria and I had just graduated and decided to live in San Fran together, we were on a budget, but when we saw it had an island and a tub, it made it instantly better by tenfold.

My ears perk up when I hear the front door close, knowing it was probably Gabriel leaving. I quickly step out of the bath, and dry myself off before slipping into my comfy clothes.

Steam trails behind me as I leave the bathroom, and my eyes sweep across the apartment in search of more sticky notes. But I still don't see any.

"M?" My attention darts to the front door as Zaria walks in, looking as gorgeous as ever, whereas I opt for comfort over style. "Why are you wearing sweatpants?" she asks.

"It's Saturday." I pull the towel off my head, letting my hair air dry.

"Which means we need to go out," she says with a grin on her face.

"Zaria," I groan.

"Come on," she pleads. "I need a night off from work, and I know you need to blow off some steam too, especially with Gabriel here." Her brow lifts. "We'll have a few drinks, dance a little. What do you say?"

I hate crowds with a passion, and I especially hate nightclubs. They're loud, and sweaty, and reek of alcohol and cheap cologne, but Zaria's right.

I need this. I need a night where I'm not buried in work or sat at home watching a cheesy rom com I've already seen multiple times. I need a night where I can stop thinking about Gabriel.

"Who else is coming?" I say with a sigh.

"Really?" she asks, her eyes widening.

"Yeah." I chuckle at her expression. "You're right. I need a distraction from Gabriel."

"I can invite Allie and her wife," she says, pulling out her phone. "I can't believe you agreed."

"Am I really that boring?" I joke, feeling the sting of my own words.

She looks up at me, tugging her brows together. "You're not boring, M. You just don't like going out into crowded places, and that's okay." She reaches out, tugging me on the arm when I look away. "Hey, if you want to back out, it's ok. I don't mind. I just thought we could have some fun."

"No." I blink away the wetness in my eyes, hating that I miss out on so much because of my social anxiety. "I want to go."

"Are you sure?" she asks, a touch of concern in her eyes.

I give her a confident nod. "I'm sure. It'll be fine."

"Just let me know if it's too much for you, and we'll leave, okay? I just want you to have fun." Her understanding means the world to me, and I nod again, silently grateful for a best friend who gets me.

"Thank you," I mumble, feeling the warmth of her support.

"You don't need to thank me. I'm here for you, M. Always." She gives me a warm smile. "I'm going to go take a shower. Get ready," she says with a narrowing gaze. "We'll leave at eleven."

"That's ten hours away," I say with narrowed eyes.

"Exactly," she sighs. "No time at all."

As she heads into her bedroom, I let out a laugh, which turns into a sigh as the reality of what I just agreed to sinks in.

Nine

Melissa

"I'll have a pornstar martini," Zaria shouts over the loud music.

The bartender winks at her, before turning to me. "What about you, sweetheart?" he asks, his heavy British accent prominent.

"Do you have anything sweet?" I ask him, cringing from the earlier taste of the tequila shots Zaria had ordered for us.

He smiles, grabbing a glass. "I have something I think you'll like."

I reluctantly glance around the dark nightclub, the strobing lights making me squint. Zaria sways her hips to the music, a soft laugh escaping her when a guy comes over to talk to her.

"Here you go sweetheart." I twist my head, seeing mine and Zaria's drinks on the bar.

"Thanks." Zaria reaches into her purse, but the guy she was previously talking to, stops her.

"It's on me," he says, pulling out his wallet.

Zaria doesn't argue, she just shoots him a flirtatious smile as she sips on her drink. I shake my head in amusement, averting my gaze to the pink colored drink in front of me. "What is it?" I ask the bartender as I pick it up.

"Strawberry daquiri," he says. "It's pretty much strawberries and rum."

Swirling the straw around in the drink, I take a sip, feeling the burn of the alcohol in my throat as the sweet flavor coats my tongue.

"Thanks for the drink," Zaria says to the guy as she wraps her arm around mine. "Come on," she whispers in my ear.

Heading through the busy crowd, I'm grateful that Zaria's holding on to me, because if I was alone here, I know I'd be overwhelmed.

As soon as we reach the booth where Allie and her wife Charlotte are sat, we drop down on the booth, shuffling inside. My skirt begins to ride up, making me regret my clothing choice for tonight. My corset top, and leather skirt are a much tamer choice, however, compared to Zaria's mini, flame colored dress that compliments her dark brown skin tone well.

Zaria tumbles over as she sits, making Charlotte reach out and grab her before she falls to the ground. "Don't tell me you're drunk already," Charlotte says with a laugh. "You had two drinks."

"Three," Zaria says, with a grin as she holds up three fingers.

"Four," I remind her, gesturing to the drink she's holding.

"And some shots," she adds as she takes a sip of her drink.

I groan at the reminder. "God, they were the worst. I'm never drinking tequila again."

Allie laughs, with a nod. "I agree."

"I don't know," Charlotte says. "I kind of like them."

"I'm with her," Zaria says, nodding as she sips on her drink.

The music changes and Charlotte leans into her wife. I let myself admire them, and the way they need each other so much, the way they look at each other. I've always been fine on my own, it's the way I preferred it, but seeing Allie and Charlotte so in love right now is making me wish I could have that feeling.

"We're going to dance," Allie says, as Zaria moves out of the way so they can leave the booth. "Don't wait up."

They both chuckle as they make their way to the dance floor, and I smile at how happy they are.

My eyes catch on a tall guy walking through the crowd. I squint, realizing it's the same guy from the bar who bought Zaria her drinks, and if I'm not mistaken, he's coming right over—

"Hey."

Zaria snaps her head to the left, glancing up at him. She shoots him a smile, her eyes slightly widened. "Oh hey."

He flashes her a grin, his white teeth visible in the dark room. "You ran away from me back there."

"I did?" she teases, tilting her head.

I lean back in the booth, sipping on my drink as I watch her flirt. Ever since I met her, she's always been the complete opposite of me. Fun, confident and a huge flirt, which is why this is so fascinating to me. I have been in two dates in the last four years, and they've both ended with the guy having to 'leave because of an emergency'. I could never talk to a guy like she does.

"You know you did," he flirts back. "Was I not obvious about being into you?"

"You were."

"Hmm, then what about a dance?" he asks her.

Zaria smiles, but then it slips as she looks back at me, her brows tugged together. "Maybe another time."

"Zaria," I chastise, knowing she's blowing him off because of me.

She shakes her head. "I told you I'd be there for you, and I intend to do that."

I let out a laugh. "You're not my babysitter. I'm fine."

"M," she says, reaching out her hand. "I'm not going to ditch you."

"I can come back later," the guy says.

"No," I tell Zaria, narrowing my eyes at her. "She'd love to dance with you."

Zaria's frown deepens but then she retracts her hand. "You're sure?" she asks, scanning my eyes for any hint of hesitation.

I nod, a faint smile on my lips. "Go."

"I'll be right back," she says, lifting herself out of the booth.

I watch as she heads onto the dancefloor, the guy wrapping his hands around her hips as they dance to the music.

I let out a sigh, looking away as I pull the straw from my drink, downing the rest. The alcohol leaves a burn in my throat, but I'm hoping it'll kick in soon, and maybe quiet the chaos inside my head.

"Damn. Tough night?" I raise my head and spot a tall man standing a few inches above me, hands snug in his pockets. I find myself appreciating his perfectly styled brown hair, and the muscles accentuated by his white t-shirt.

He arches an eyebrow, and it hits me that I've just zoned out.

"Um…" I stumble over my words, staring up at him. God, I'm terrible at this. I just watched Zaria flirt first-hand, and I still don't know how she did it.

"Made you speechless?" he jokes. "I hate to see you here all alone, mind if I join you?"

Swallowing all the nerves, I decide to try to be more like Zaria, and nod. "Sure."

He takes a seat opposite me on the booth and leans back. "So, can I ask why you're here on your own?"

"I, uh, came with my friends, actually, but they're dancing." My fingers toy nervously with the rim of my glass.

"Ah, I see." His brow lifts. "And you didn't want to join?"

"They were paired up," I confess, the corners of my lips turning up with a laugh. "I can't exactly dance on my own."

He grins, a playful glint in his eyes as he leans forward. "Then aren't you glad I'm here?"

"Why's that?" I ask, meeting his gaze.

"Because I'd love to dance with you," he says with a charming smile, and my eyes widen in surprise.

"You would?"

He nods. "If you'd like." His lips curve, and he runs his tongue over his bottom lip subtly. It reminds me a little of Gabriel, and I tell myself to push those thoughts away. The whole point of coming out tonight was to stop thinking about him.

I steal a glance at the dancefloor, and then back at him. I find myself unconsciously chewing on the inside of my mouth. "I don't even know your name."

"That's an easy fix," he says with a shrug. "My name's Thomas. What's yours?"

"Melissa," I reply.

His smile makes my body warm, or it might be the effect of alcohol. "Well, Melissa. I'd love to dance with you, if you'd like," he says, tilting his head. "Or we can just hang out here if you prefer. What do you say?"

A million thoughts race through my mind, but I blink them away. The last thing I need is to overthink everything as usual. Tonight, I just want to have fun for once.

I stand up in response, and his smile widens as he joins me, his hand resting on the small of my back as we make our way to the dancefloor.

His hands wrap around my waist as he turns me around so my back hits his chest. Normally I'd be thinking about any and everything, telling myself why this is a bad idea, wondering who this guy really is, but right now I don't care. I just want to dance, and let all thoughts fly out of my mind.

It's only when I sense his arm brushing against my stomach that I realize he's holding onto me tightly, his hand gradually descending lower and lower over my leather skirt as he draws closer, enveloping me. My skin breaks out into goosebumps when I feel his hard length press against my ass, and I stiffen, freezing in his arms.

I try to shift, to push him away and create some distance, but his grip tightens, holding me in place. He leans down, his lips brushing against the shell of my ear. What's wrong?" he whispers, his tone sending a chill down my spine.

"I… I want to leave." I push at his arm, wanting to get out of here, away from him, but he tugs harder, eliciting a gasp out of me.

"We're having fun, Melissa. What's the problem?"

The scent of alcohol on his breath invades my senses, and I shake my head. This is all wrong. I don't want this. "I want to leave," I repeat, louder this time, as I tug harder at his arms wrapped around my waist. My eyes scan the crowd for any sign of Zaria or Allie, but they're nowhere in sight.

"C'mon," he sneers. "No woman comes to a club dressed like that if she doesn't want to get laid." I shiver with disgust when he presses himself into me even more.

"Let me go!" I yell, kicking his leg, hard enough to make him groan, his grip on me slipping until I can get out of his reach.

I hear a thud and a collective gasp comes from the people around me. The crowd closes in, and I turn just in time to see Thomas grabbing his face. "Fucking prick." He leers at the person who punched him. I turn my head, and see…

"Gabriel?"

His head snaps to me, his brows tugging together. "Are you okay?"

I don't get to answer because Thomas rears his fist back and throws a punch, hitting Gabriel's face.

"Gabriel," I gasp, reaching for him.

"Who the fuck are you?" Thomas asks, spitting out blood.

Gabriel cracks his jaw before grabbing the front of Thomas' shirt, and punches him right in the face. "You fucking touched her," he says, his lips curling into a sneer. "And she told you to let her go."

Thomas scoffs. "Is she your girlfriend or something?" he asks, more blood pouring out his nose and mouth. "Because she hit on me first, dude. Too bad she's a fucking prude."

Gabriel lets out a grunt, before he swings his fist directly into his chin. "Watch your fucking mouth."

"Alright. Break it up." The crowd opens as security head through, grabbing both of the guys. "You're going to have to take it outside," they tell them.

"Fuck this," Thomas spits, curling his lip in disgust. "She's not fucking worth it." He moves out of the security guard's grasp, and walks off.

"If you cause any more trouble, you're out," they tell Gabriel. He nods, watching as they leave.

"What the hell, Gabriel? What were you thinking?"

His eyes lock on mine and his jaw ticks. "I saw what he did to you," he says. "I couldn't just let him get away with it."

My breath catches in my throat as I stare back at him. I don't know whether I should thank him or yell at him for getting himself hurt. "What are you doing here?" I ask instead.

He runs a hand through his hair. "Zaria told me you guys were going out."

"So you came to spy on her? She's a grown woman, Gabriel."

His lips twitch. "Something like that." His smile slips, his eyes zoning in on me. "Why did you agree to this?" he asks. "You hate this type of place."

My lips part in shock. "Because you know me so well?" I ask.

"I do," he agrees, no ounce of a joke on his face. "Zaria, I get. She loves places like this, but you?" He shakes his head. "Why did you come here, Melissa?"

I chew on the inside of my mouth, deciding to be honest with him. "I was trying to avoid you," I tell him.

He scoffs. "Even more than you have been?" His brows tug, and he takes a step closer. "Is that why you didn't reply to my note today?"

I purse my lips. "What are you talking about? There was no note."

"What? Mel—"

"There you are." We turn our heads at Zaria's voice. "Where have you—Gabriel?" She asks, blinking. "What are you doing here?"

He releases a sigh. "Came to pick you guys up," he says, the muscles in his jaw tensing when he glances at me. "Let's go."

"Where's Allie?" I ask Zaria. I haven't seen Allie or Charlotte since they went to dance.

"They went home," she slurs, her steps off balance. "They're soooo gonna bang."

I chuckle when I see Gabriel groan at how inebriated Zaria is. "Seeing your sister drunk is never fun," he mutters to himself.

"Like I haven't seen you drunk before," she says, narrowing her eyes at him. "M, tell him he's ruining our fun."

Gabriel glances at me, raising an eyebrow. I smirk as I say, "You're ruining our fun."

My eyes drift to the curve of his lips as he shakes his head. "You won't be saying that tomorrow."

Ten

Melissa

I'm never drinking again.

Waking up this morning was pure agony, which explains why I'm still buried in bed, hating myself for accepting those shots, and the extra drinks. Who knew something so sweet could get you so drunk?

With a valiant effort, I manage to drag myself out of my bed, attempting to stay upright long enough to make the room stop spinning.

God, my throat feels so dry. Pulling on my door handle, I swing the door open, freezing when I see Gabriel standing in the kitchen. Aside from yesterday, I hadn't seen or talked to him since we had agreed on the schedule.

It was foolish of me to think that it would work, because as much as I hate to admit it, I'm glad he came out last night. If he hadn't, who knows what Thomas would have done.

He turns around, his eyes locking on mine, and I instantly notice the cut on his lip, wincing when I remember what he did for me.

"Fun night?" he teases.

"Shut up," I mumble, sitting down on the stool. "You're enjoying seeing me in agony, aren't you?" My eyes catch on the cut on his bottom lip and I swallow. "Does it hurt?" I ask.

His lips curve into a teasing smirk before he sighs. "So much. Kiss it better?"

"Funny," I deadpan, lifting my eyes, seeing his arms crossed as his eyes remain stuck on mine. "Why are you staring at me?" I ask.

The corner of his lips raise in a small smile. "Just trying to see if you're going to throw up or not. Are you hungry?" he asks, making my face contort with disgust. The last thing I want right now is food. He lets out a laugh, nodding. "Got it. No food." He heads toward the sink, and when he turns around, a full glass of water is placed in front of me. "Here," he says, his deep voice making me shiver. "Drink this."

I hesitantly lift my head, meeting his gaze before I drink the cold water, relaxing when it soothes my dry throat.

"Better?" he asks.

I nod, placing the empty glass back on the table. "Thanks."

"What was that?" he asks, sounding surprised. "I must have misheard you. I could have sworn you said thanks."

I roll my eyes. "I feel bad enough without your gloating."

"You're welcome, Trevi," he says with a smile that makes my skin tingle. I tried so hard to avoid him these past few days but now I'm struggling to remember why.

Because we always argue.

Though we're not arguing now.

"You're thinking quite a bit over there." Gabriel's voice pulls me from my thoughts. I blink, glancing up at him. "What's up, Trevi?" he asks, filling up a glass with water

I take a deep breath before admitting, "I made a mistake."

"How so?" Gabriel asks, taking a sip of water.

A heavy sigh escapes me, hating that I have to admit the schedule was a stupid idea. "About the schedule. You were right, it was stupid to think it would work."

His brows shoot up as he swallows down the water, and then his lips curl into a smirk. "So, you miss me?" he asks, his tone so smug it makes me want to take my words back.

"You're an asshole."

He laughs, shaking his head. "Don't worry. I miss you too. You're the only one who calls me an asshole, where else would I be greeted with such kindness?" He gives me a warm smile. "We can forget all about the schedule if you want," he says.

I do want that. I hate to admit it, but trying to keep my distance from him was harder than I thought possible. "But what if we end up arguing?" I ask him. The whole reason I came up with the schedule in the first place was to avoid that happening, and while it was hard, it worked. We didn't argue because we didn't see each other. So, if we go back to how it was and we start arguing again, I'm not sure I can take it.

"We won't," he says, sounding determined. "I can lay off teasing you if you can do the same." His brow lifts, waiting for an answer.

My teeth tug on the inside of my mouth. "I can do that."

"Are you sure?" Gabriel asks, tilting his head. "Because I'm not going back to that schedule, Melissa. No way in hell."

A laugh bubbles out of me. "Was it really that bad?"

His jaw ticks as he stares back at me, not saying anything for a while. "It was."

I frown, wondering what he means by that, when Zaria's door flings open. She tumbles out of her room, her clothes, and makeup from last night still on.

"Shit. Zaria." I lift off the stool, hurrying over to her. "Are you okay?"

She smiles, a sleepy warmth in her eyes. "Great. I had so much fun last night," she murmurs, clearly still half asleep. "Thanks for coming out with me, M." A little yawn interrupts her words, and I can't help but smile when she leans into me.

"Anytime," I tell her, even though the idea of going back to that club makes me want to puke. But if it makes her this happy, then I'll go with her every weekend.

"God, I need a shower," She winces, pulling out of my reach as she walks over to the bathroom. "And some takeout," she calls out.

"Already on the way," I tell her, knowing how she loves greasy food when she's hungover.

When the door closes, I turn back around to see Gabriel stare at me with his arms crossed. "You're a good friend to her," he says, his forehead pinching together.

"She's been my best friend for so long," I tell him with a smile on my face. "I can't imagine my life without her."

An expression crosses his face that I don't understand but it vanishes as fast as it came when he nods. "I'll be in the gym today," he says, downing the water before washing the glass in the sink.

My shoulders tense, wondering why he's trying to leave. Did I say something wrong? "Gabriel," I call. He turns around, and lifts his brow in question. "Are we good?"

His lips curve into a smile, but it's all wrong. "Of course, Trevi. Why wouldn't we be?"

Eleven

Gabriel

"Heading home?" Thomas grins, his eyes following as I take off my apron.

"Don't start," I glare, slipping into my jacket.

"You told her yet?"

I flip him off, hearing his laughter. "You know I haven't."

Not many people know about my feelings for my sisters best friend, but Thomas has been like a brother ever since I started working at his restaurant two years ago. He's watched as I grew as a chef, improving every day in the kitchen until he gave me the position as his sous chef.

"Never met a guy who purposefully moves in with the girl he can't have," he mutters, crossing his arms. "It's almost like you like to torture yourself."

Being around Melissa isn't exactly torture. Or so I thought before we started hanging out every day. The schedule she set up was fucking agony, but at least I didn't have to see her, look at her, smile at her.

Ever since the day after the club, her and I have been getting along. But after years of telling myself not to go there with her, and pushing her away, it's way too easy to fall back on the promises I made to myself.

"I didn't *purposefully* move in."

"I offered you my guest room."

My jaw ticks, knowing he's right.

I didn't even think before calling Zaria and asking her if I could crash with her and Melissa. The truth is, I wanted to see her.

I hadn't seen her since last Christmas, and I had the perfect opportunity to. It was just a couple of weeks until I got my stuff in order, and could find a place of my own, but I figured it wouldn't be that big of a deal. Of course that was before I saw how much she hated me.

I've got to say, it was like a knife to the heart when she handed me her notebook, and I saw how much she wanted to stay away from me.

But luckily we got over that, and now I have a new obstacle to conquer.

Not revealing my feelings for her.

It's harder than I ever thought possible, but not completely unattainable.

"Have you found a place yet?"

"Wouldn't be living with my sister if I had."

He scoffs. "Since the girl you're crazy over lives there too, I highly doubt it. But I actually meant for your restaurant."

Frustration courses through me knowing he's probably right. I haven't even begun to start looking for an apartment. the truth is,. I don't really want to go back to how things were between Mel and me.

"No," I reply, a reminder as to why lingering in the back of my mind. "I'm still trying to work some things out."

"I thought you had the place you wanted picked out" he asks.

"I do," I affirm. "It's just a little more complicated than I originally thought."

"You always have a job here," he says with a genuine smile.

I nod, grateful for him allowing me to pursue my dream. "See you tomorrow," I say to Thomas before heading for the back exit, dying to get home.

"Have fun." He laughs behind me, probably thinking about how much of an idiot I am for putting myself in this situation.

By the time I get home, my heart pounds at the thought of seeing her again. And when I open the door, and see her sat on the couch, covered with a blanket, I press my fist to my lips to stop my smile.

Fuck. She's just so *pretty*.

I'm so fucked.

"Hey, Trevi."

She turns away from the papers she's holding and she gives me a warm smile that's brand fucking new.

Fuck me.

I like it a lot.

"You're home." Her tone catches me by surprised. It almost sounds like she's happy I'm home early. Or maybe that's just my hopeful imagination.

"What are you doing?" I ask, gesturing to the stack of papers she has beside her.

"Grading papers," she replies with a sigh.

"You sound like you need a distraction," I say, kicking my shoes off by the door. Her head tilts back as she glances at me, and I have to fight the urge to tell her beautiful she is.

It was so easy to forget how much I wanted her when we barely saw each other. But right now, It's so fucking hard to remember exactly why I can't have her.

"Yes, please," she breathes out, the sound warming my body.

She moves the papers out of the way, and I drop down on the couch beside her. I was planning on taking a shower, maybe even getting a workout in, but I take one look at her and all of my plans go out the window.

"What do you want to watch?" I ask her, grabbing the remote.

"Anything," she sighs. "My brain is pure mush. I need something easy and fun." I start scrolling through the options, and she stops me. "That one," she says when I stop on one with a dog.

I let out a scoff. "Of course you'd pick a movie with a dog."

"I like dogs," she says with a shrug, crossing her legs on the couch.

"I remember," I tell. *I remember everything about you.* "You used to go crazy over Sadie."

Her eyes brighten at the mention of my old dog. I know how much Melissa loved her. She bawled like a baby when Sadie passed a few years ago.

"God, I miss that dog," I admit, shaking my head. I even fought with Zaria over the name for a while, but in the end, I caved, and Sadie stuck.

Clicking play, we both sit back and watch the movie. But my eyes keep drifting over to Melissa. She pulls the blanket over her body, only her head poking out as her eyes remain locked on the screen. It wasn't that long ago that we were fighting over who got to watch what, and I wish I could have told myself back then that it wasn't worth it.

Arguing with her, teasing her, making her angry wasn't the way. Not anymore. Making her smile, having her beside me. That was way better. Even if it was fucking torture.

My phone buzzes in my pocket, and I pull it out, seeing my sister's name on the screen.

Zaria:

Are you behaving?

Gabriel:

Don't worry. She's still alive.

Zaria:

I'm more worried about her killing you.

I snicker, shaking my head at how dramatic my sister is. She's been there through all the arguments Mel and I have had, and she's seen how bad it's gotten. It doesn't shock me that she doesn't trust what I'm telling her.

Gabriel:

I'm alive too.

Zaria:

Proof?

How do I know this is you?

Idiot. I smile, nudging Melissa on the arm. "Take a picture with me?"

She sniffs, her eyes brimming with tears. "What?"

"Are you crying?" I ask her, worry filling my veins.

She shakes her head, wiping away the tears down her face. "Have you not been watching the movie?"

No. I've been watching you. "It's just a movie, Trevi. You don't need to cry," I tease.

"Shut up," she mutters with a laugh. "Why do we need to take a picture?"

"Zaria doesn't believe I'm alive." When her brows furrow with confusion, I elaborate. "She's having a hard time believing we're actually getting along and thinks you've killed me."

She shakes her head, a laugh on her pretty lips, and she sits up. "Fine," she says. "Take the picture."

I pull up the camera on my phone and point it directly at us. I flip the camera off, and Melissa smiles sweetly. A smile pulls at my lips at the picture, and I save it before I send it to Zaria, who replies immediately.

Zaria:

Ok. I believe you.

I shake my head, and pocket my phone, looking up at the TV when Melissa interrupts. Or more accurately, her stomach does.

"Hungry?" I guess.

She nods. "I wanted to get my work done as soon as I got home." She reaches for her phone. "I'll order some takeout."

"I'll cook dinner," I offer instead.

She lifts her head, frowning. "You don't have to do that."

"I want to," I assure her.

Her teeth tug at her bottom lip. "Are you sure? Because I don't want to bother you."

I scoff. "Nothing you do bothers me, Trevi." She doesn't know just how accurate that statement is.

She nods, a soft smile on her lips. "I'd love that."

I walk toward the kitchen, unable to stop smiling. I love cooking, I always have, but cooking for her? It makes it a million times better.

It's not long until she joins me in the kitchen, sitting at the island, while I finish cooking. "It smells good," she says, swelling my chest with a sense of pride.

I plate up, and grab a couple of wine glasses, filling them with white wine.

"I'm not really a big drinker," she laughs, shaking her head.

I'm brought back to when she was hungover as hell after the club, and I chuckle. "Trust me," I say. "White wine goes well with salmon."

I sit on the stool beside her, my attention fully focused on her taking a bite. Her eyes close, savoring the flavors, and then she lets out a sweet little moan.

Oh fuck.

"That's probably the best meal I've ever tasted," she says, going in for another bite.

I can't even appreciate the compliment she just gave me, because I'm trying, desperately not to get hard over the little moans she's making while eating.

"That's... great." I pick up my wine glass, downing half of it in one go.

She moans again, shaking her head. "Seriously. You're so talented."

"Yeah." I swallow, begging myself not to get hard right now.

How would she react if she looked down and saw me sporting an erection? I'm guessing not very well.

She takes a sip of her wine, washing it down. "Have you ever thought about opening your own restaurant."

"Yeah, I've thought about it," I admit. It's practically the reason I'm here. I take a bite of my food, hoping she doesn't make any more noises that make me want to rip my hair out.

"And?" she asks, intrigued.

I really don't want to get into it, not when she's finally let go of her past hatred for me. "Nothing to tell," I say instead, swallowing down the food.

Thankfully Melissa lets it go and takes another bite. I sneak glances at her, smiling when she finishes her whole plate. "That was so delicious," she says before sipping on her wine. "Thank you."

I shrug, acting like it's not a big deal when in reality, I want to cook for her every single night. "It's no problem, Melissa." I pick up both our plates, dropping them into the sink. "You feel like dessert?" I ask, already knowing the answer as I pull out the strawberry ice cream from the freezer.

"Always," she mutters with a huge grin on her face. Her eyes shift to the carton in my hands and her eyebrows tug together. "What's that?"

I glance down at the note I left on the lid of the ice cream back when she made the schedule. "You didn't see it?"

She shakes her head when I rip off the note. "What is it?"

"I left it here after your last note," I admit, sliding it toward her.

"I thought you didn't reply," she says, glancing down at the note, reading it. "You wanted to watch a movie with me?" she asks, reading the note where I told her I bought her favorite ice cream and she could eat it while we watched whatever she wanted. It would probably have been an episode of Love Oasis, but if I was with her, then it wouldn't have mattered.

I just wanted to see you. "Yeah. I uh…" I reach up, running my hand over the back of my neck. "I wanted to apologize for making it hard to be around me."

"Wow." She blinks, the corner of her lips lifting slightly. "I wish I had seen it before I apologized," she teases with a smirk.

I chuckle, scooping some ice cream out into a bowl before sliding it toward her. "You're so stubborn. Just eat the ice cream, Trevi."

She eyes me warily. "You're not having any?"

I shake my head, my face scrunching with disgust. "Hell no. I hate strawberry ice cream."

She narrows her eyes at me, wrapping her lips around the spoon. "Have you even tried it?"

I lift my eyebrows. "No, actually. I haven't."

She scoops some more ice cream on her spoon, and holds it out to me. My eyes drop to it, and I hesitantly lean forward, and bring the spoon to my mouth. I keep my eyes on her while I taste the ice cream. Her eyes dip to my lips, and I beg myself to have some control.

"You're right," I say, licking my lips as I look at her, trying to get the rancid taste of the ice cream out of my mouth, but also trying to keep the taste of her lips. "It's the best thing I've ever tasted."

Twelve

Melissa

There's something wrong with me.

That's the only explanation as to why I can't stop thinking about Gabriel.

It used to be so easy before he moved in, seeing as he lived on the other side of town, I barely saw him. Especially since I hadn't visited his parents' house since last Christmas.

But now, he's everywhere. *Everywhere.*

And while my plan to avoid him was stupid, and didn't work, I'm debating whether this is better.

Since the nightclub last week, he's been different. Funnier, thoughtful, nice. I don't think I have ever used any of those words to describe Gabriel before. This past week has been a massive step forward in building an actual friendship with Gabriel, but instead, my stupid brain decides to overthink everything he said and did. I catch myself staring at him a lot, wondering why he keeps staring back, wondering what he thinks when he looks at me, if he thinks about me when he's not at the apartment.

I know he doesn't. I know those looks mean nothing, and these foolish thoughts are nothing but that. Foolish.

But... I can't help it.

"And then we got kicked out," Allie says with a laugh, snapping me out of thoughts about Gabriel.

I blink, shaking my head slightly to get myself together. Shit. What was she talking about? I force a smile, and nod along, but Allie's eyes narrow, reading through me.

"You didn't hear a single word of what I just said, did you?" she asks.

My eyes fall closed. "I'm sorry," I sigh, shaking my head. "I just got lost in my thoughts."

She nods sympathetically, sipping on her coffee. "Gabriel still giving you a hard time?"

I press my lips together, leaning back in my chair. "Not exactly," I say, trying to hide my guilty face with my mug.

Her eyes widen, and she leans forward, placing her coffee on the table. "Interesting. So there's been some development with Chef Gabriel. Details, please."

I roll my eyes, a laugh bubbling out of me from the huge grin on her face. "Don't get your hopes up. We're just getting friendly, that's all."

"That's all?" she asks. "That's the only reason why you're blushing like a teenager?"

I am? "I am not." I lift my hand, pressing my palm, and lo and behold, my face is heating up. "This is just because of my hot tea," I lie straight through my teeth. "I told you it's not like that. Besides, we couldn't even stand to be in the same room as each other a few weeks ago. We're just making the best out of the situation."

Allie smiles, knowingly. "Okay," she says, leaning back in her chair. "I won't pry."

"He still manages to annoy me," I tell her. "But now it's just… less."

"Who annoys you?"

I turn my head, spotting Mason standing beside me, with his arms crossed over his gym whistle.

I wince, hoping the bell goes off soon because I'm not ready to be hit on again, for the umpteenth time.

His grin creeps me out as he sits down on the empty seat beside me. My body stiffens at the feel of his thigh pressed against mine. He really doesn't know how to take no for an answer, does he?

"No one," Allie and I say in unison.

"C'mon," he says, brushing a hand through his dirty blond hair, as he leans closer to me. "I like gossiping too. I won't tell."

"It really is no one," I say, wanting him to get away from me.

He does the exact opposite and smiles instead. "So, Melissa." I press my lips into a tight smile, wishing he'd just leave me alone. "Are you going to the staff party on Friday?"

The staff party was an event the school held every year to thank the teachers for the hard work they did. And while, usually I attended, I was considerably debating whether or not I should. "I don't know," I tell him, trying to ignore Allie's side glance beside me.

She always attended. Her, Charlotte and I would make a day of it, getting our hair done, our nails and then we'd get drunk on the open bar and watch as other people attempted to dance. Although after last week at the club, I don't think I'm going to get drunk anytime soon.

"C'mon," he goads, nudging his elbow against mine. "It will be fun. I'd love to take you as my date."

Another reason not to go. "Mason," I start, shaking my head. "I don't think—"

"We've worked together for years now, Melissa. I'd really like to get to know you better."

Mason isn't exactly ugly per se, but he definitely isn't what I want. His smile makes me uneasy, and the fact that he's persisting this hard when I've made it clear to him that I'm not interested makes my skin crawl.

"There are no anti-fraternization polices," he reminds me.

"Mason—"

"She has a boyfriend."

My head snaps to Allie who smiles sympathetically at him. Why the hell did she just say that? I definitely do not have a boyfriend, which Allie knows, so why—

Oh.

She shoots me a look with her eyes, and mine widen, realization hitting me.

"Really?" Mason asks, his brow raised in suspicion.

"Yes," I lie. "I have a boyfriend."

"Huh. Well, that sucks." He leans back into his chair, watching me with intrigue, a smile slowly curling on his lips. "You should bring him."

What?

"I'd love to meet the lucky bastard who shares a bed with Melissa Trevisano."

My insides churn at the thought of him thinking about me in a bed, or thinking about me at all.

"I'm sure he's busy," I say, trying to imagine what the hell a fake boyfriend who didn't exist could be doing on a Saturday night.

"I'm sure he can make it," he says, crossing his arms. "Who would miss a chance at taking you out?"

Damn it. He wasn't letting this go. While I appreciate Allie for trying to make Mason back off, this isn't exactly ideal, either.

"Sure," I relent. "I'll ask him."

"Great," he says, lifting off his chair. "I can't wait to meet him." He grins before turning around and heads out of the teachers' lounge.

Once he's out of sight, I turn to Allie and let out a groan. "A boyfriend?" I ask her.

"It was the first thing I could think of," she says with a wince. "I didn't think he'd want to meet the guy."

"It's Mason," I say, dryly. "Of course he would."

"Fuck, I'm so sorry, babe," she says, my eyes softening at her apologetic expression.

Letting out a sigh, I straighten in my seat. "It's fine. I mean, it worked, I guess."

But how the hell am I supposed to make it work? I don't have a boyfriend. I'm not even close. I can't just show up without someone though, because then Mason would get suspicious and know I'm lying. He'd never give up if he found out the truth.

"You could try an online dating app," she suggests, making me burst out into laughter. There is no way I'm joining a dating app to try and find someone to take to the party on Saturday.

"Alright," she concedes. "They'd probably want something in return anyway."

"I am not sleeping with a stranger so he can attend the staff party as my date."

She shrugs, knowing I'm out of options. I mean, where do I even find someone willing to help me? I don't have any friends who are men, or even a cousin or—

"Wait." My head snaps to hers. "You have three brothers. Surely one of them could help me out, and be my fake date?" I ask, hope building in my chest.

She shakes her head. "They're all married or in relationships, babe."

I shoot her a look. "Emphasis on the fake. I'm not looking for a husband, only someone to scare off Mason."

"I know, Melissa," she says with a smile. "But do you want to be the one to explain to their wives that a hot single girl wants to take them out on a 'fake date' to scare off a guy at work?" She shakes her head, holding her hands up. "I don't want to get my eyes clawed out by my sisters-in-law."

Damn it. She's right.

The only other person I can think of with a brother is Zaria and… Nope. Not going there.

"I'm sorry I got you in this mess," she says with a frown.

"I know," I sigh. "I'll figure it out."

I have no idea how I'm going to ask someone to be my fake boyfriend, but I'd figure something out.

Hopefully.

Thirteen

Melissa

I caved, and I hate myself for it.

Online dating is the absolute worst.

Not only are the pictures eye roll worthy, but the bios are atrocious.

Most of them list their height, or how much they can bench press, but the worst contender? The list of desirable attributes they're looking for.

List after list of things they want from women, letting everyone else know they're not good enough if they don't fit the description.

My eyes glaze over with boredom, as I glance up at the time, noticing I've been sat on the couch for over an hour trying to find someone decent enough to take as my fake boyfriend on Saturday.

No options yet.

I was so adamant about not using a dating app, and yet here I am, disgusted when the messages start to roll in. Sexual joke after sexual joke that makes my skin crawl.

This is hopeless. Throwing my phone down onto the couch I groan into my hands.

"Woah." I turn my head, seeing Gabriel smile at me at the front door. "Someone's upset."

"You're off from work already?" I ask.

"You sound delighted to see me," he jokes, letting out a laugh.

A heavy sigh escapes me. "I didn't mean for it to come out that way, I just… never mind."

"No," he says with furrowed brows as he drops down onto the couch beside me. "Tell me. What's wrong?"

"You don't want to know." My cheeks heat up at the thought of telling him I'm currently trying to find a date. I don't know why that's so embarrassing, but it is. "Trust me."

"If that was supposed to turn me away, it did the opposite," he says with a grin. "Tell me. I'm intrigued now."

No way. Reaching for the remote, I turn on the tv, and scroll through the movie catalogue. "Want to watch a movie?" I ask him.

"You're deflecting." His eyes narrow beside me, and I force myself to turn away from him. I don't know what the hell this fluttering feeling in my stomach is whenever I look at him, but I don't like it at all.

"I'm tired, Gabriel," I say with a sigh. "I just want to relax and watch something. I don't really feel like talking about work."

"So it's something to do with work?"

Turning my head, I squint at him as his eyes roam all over my face. "You're not going to drop this, are you?"

"Do you want me to?" he asks, his lips dropping into a frown.

I gulp. "Yes."

His brows knit together, but then he lets out a sigh, and turns his head to the TV. "How about a horror movie?"

I don't even have to look at him to know he's probably smiling cunningly, knowing I hate horror movies with a passion. "Don't," I warn him. "You know I hate them."

"You know it's fake right?" he asks, smirking. "It's only a movie. It won't hurt you."

"I'm serious, Gabriel." Zaria was also a horror movie fanatic, and it drove me crazy whenever she would watch one. I was living with psychopaths.

"C'mon, Trevi," he says, wrapping his arm around my shoulders as he plastered me to his side. "I'll keep you safe."

My stomach plummets as more of those fluttering feelings roam all over my body. I am not going there ever again. I force myself to shift away from him, craving his body heat that I only felt for a second. "You can watch it on your own if you want," I say. "I'll just go to bed. I'm feeling pretty tired."

His brows dip and before I can get up, his hand encircles my wrist. "No," he says. "Stay." His intense stare burns into my eyes and I force myself to swallow. "Please."

"Gabriel," I sigh. "I really don't want to watch a horror movie."

"I'll put something else on." I try to ignore the way his thumb rubs circles over my wrist, but it's impossible when my heart's in my throat. My eyes drop down to where his hand is holding me, and I watch as he rubs the skin again. "I want you here with me."

I suck in a deep breath, slowly pulling my arm from his reach. "Ok," I say, my voice hardly audible. I shuffle closer to him, careful to keep my distance. While being pressed up against him was nice, it was too much for me to handle.

He picks up the remote and scrolls through, landing on an action movie I haven't watched in a long time. I smile, leaning back. "My dad and I used to watch this all the time," I say, remembering our movie nights. God, I missed him so bad.

"Yeah, I remember him telling me about it." I turn my head to glance at him, seeing his sympathetic smile. I always forget how close our families always were. While Gabriel has managed to make my life a nightmare for the past ten years, he was always there. At family gatherings, holidays, birthdays, and even at graduation when my dad was no longer here, and couldn't be there for me. Gabriel was.

"It was his favorite film," I say, watching as the opening scene for The Godfather appears on the screen. "We used to watch it religiously every year." I gulp, my throat starting to close up. "I actually haven't watched this since he um…." Tears fill my eyes, and I blink them away.

"Hey," Gabriel says in a gentle tone, his hand running up and down my arm. "I can put something else on if you want."

"No." I shake my head, wiping my eyes. "Don't. Please."

"Okay," he says, removing his hand. "I won't." The corner of his lips lift slightly. "You know, it's kind of nice hanging out with you. We could have been doing this for a long time if you weren't such a brat."

My forehead pinches together. "If you hadn't driven me crazy every chance you got, then I wouldn't have to be a brat."

"Don't lie, Trevi." I feel his smirk all the way through my body. I really need to keep myself in check. "You loved getting under my skin just like I did yours."

Our eyes lock and I track his movements when his tongue darts out to wet his bottom lip. When I look back at him, he's not smiling anymore. He's just watching me instead, heavy, charged, and nothing like I've ever witnessed before. Gabriel's never really looked at me. Not like this.

Ding

Ding

Ding

The noise forces us apart as I try to look for my phone, wondering where the hell I put it.

The question is answered when I see Gabriel glaring down at my phone while notifications keep going off.

"Who is it? I ask, wondering what has his expression so weird. I've never really seen him like this before.

"Why the fuck are you on a dating app?" he asks, his brows pinched together.

"What?" I repeat, my eyes widening when I realize what messages he must be reading. "Gabriel, give me my phone."

He continues staring down at it. "Who the fuck uses pick-up lines anymore?"

Oh god, this is so bad. "Gabriel," I call, trying to get his attention. "Give me my phone."

He turns his head, his gaze meeting mine as he hands me my phone, and I let out a breath of relief, before scanning down the messages.

I wince at the myriad of sex jokes, and ridiculous pick-up lines, knowing Gabriel read them.

"Why are you on there?" he asks. "It doesn't seem like you."

I scoff, dropping my phone onto my lap. "Why? Because according to you, I never go out?" I shake my head, humiliation flooding me. "Well, I'm trying to change that, ok?"

"What?" He reaches for me. "Melissa, I didn't mean that in a bad way. You don't have to change anything about you. Ever."

When my head lifts, and I meet his eyes, I can see his sincere expression and I sigh. "Whatever. We both know it's true."

"That doesn't mean you need to go out with every guy you see."

I roll my eyes. "I'm not interested in any of these guys," I admit. "I just needed... Never mind. It's none of your business."

"I've told you before, you can make it my business if you want. I don't mind whatever it is when it comes to you."

His words make my pulse race as I swallow harshly. "You're being nice to me," I point out. "Stop that. It's weird."

He laughs, shuffling closer to me. "I'm serious. If you need help with something, maybe I can help," he offers with a lift of his shoulders.

"No." I laugh, shaking my head. "No, you can't help me."

"Why not?" he asks, raising his brow. "I'm thinking of every worst case scenario right now, so you might as well tell me."

I lean back into the couch, blowing out a breath. I know I'm probably going to regret this, but… "I need a date," I blurt out.

"You just said you weren't interested in any of that."

"I'm not," I admit. God, am I really going to confide in Gabriel about Mason? "I'm not looking for a date, just someone who can pretend to be my boyfriend for the staff party on Saturday."

"Why?" he asks.

My teeth graze the inside of my cheek, and I look down at my fingers nervously fiddling in my lap. "There's this guy at work," I start, letting out a slow breath. "He just can't seem to understand that I'm not interested. No matter how clear I've been in the past, he keeps pushing. So, when he asked again, Allie blurted out that I have a boyfriend. And now he wants to meet him.

"Which guy?"

I lift my head, meeting his murderous gaze. "What?"

"Which fucking guy is it? Give me a name, and I'll teach him the word no."

"You don't need to do that," I say, laughing at his clenched jaw. "I just need to find someone who will come with me and pretend to be my date for an hour or two, just to convince him and hopefully make him back off." I sigh, glancing down at my phone. "I tried online dating, but that's a dud."

"I'll go with you."

My eyes widen. "You're joking."

"Why not?" he asks with a shrug. "Got any other options?"

No, and he knows it.

"Gabriel. You work late on Saturdays."

"I can take a day off."

I laugh. "You're not serious. You can't just take a day off."

"Sure I can. If you need me, then yes, I can."

My mind spins, wondering if I entered an alternate dimension where Gabriel suddenly stopped being the guy who I couldn't stand to be near. "I can find someone else," I tell him. "Or I'll just go alone, either way, I can figure it out."

He leans back into the couch as he groans into his hands, sounding frustrated. "You are the most stubborn woman I've ever met," he says, snapping his head to me. "I'm offering to help you, Melissa. Why not accept it?"

Why am I saying no? He's right. I have no other options, and here Gabriel is, volunteering to help me on a night where he's supposed to be working. "You really want to go?"

His shoulders slump as a lazy smile crosses his face. "Yes, Trevi. I want you to know if you ever need anything, I'm here."

"This is so weird," I say, narrowing my eyes at him. "Shouldn't you be insulting me?"

A soft chuckle escapes him, and suddenly, my insides tingle as a subtle warmth spreads within me. "Not anymore," he says. "Don't worry. You'll get used to it." He leans back, and drapes his arm around my shoulders. "This is going to be so fun."

This is going to be anything *but* fun.

Fourteen

Gabriel

"Finally, you're home."

I lift my head to see Melissa standing by the couch, a slim hand propped on her hip. My gaze drift to where they always want to go whenever she's in the room. Her eyes. The lime green of them so intoxicating. I swear it's what drew me to her in the first place.

"Well, this is a nice surprise," I joke as I slip off my shoes. "You were waiting for me?"

She raises an eyebrow, and I figure I've said the wrong thing. It always seems to be the case around her. "You should have been home two hours ago. Where have you been?"

I smirk, my heart pounding at the knowledge of Melissa waiting for me, anticipating me, wanting me around. "You've been keeping track?"

She rolls her eyes, frustrated as hell, but honestly it just makes her that much hotter. Fuck. I've really got to stop ogling my sister's best friend. It's going to do me no good.

Ah fuck it.

It's not like this is the first time I've let myself picture her pretty, pink lips or the soft brown of her hair wrapped in my fist, or even—

"Gabriel."

I blink, snapping out of a million and one thoughts of Melissa. "Yes, sweetheart?"

"Don't call me that," she says, shooting me a glare. "You promised you'd help me out, remember?"

"Of course I do." Like I could ever forget that I'm taking Melissa out on a date. Sure, it's not real, and I'm just there to scare off the guy that won't stop harassing her, but let a guy dream.

I've got to say, it took everything in me not to find out where the motherfucker lives and break his skinny ass legs. But that's not what Melissa asked for, and whatever she wants, I'll do.

She just doesn't know it.

"The party is tomorrow, Melissa."

"I know that," she says with a sigh. "But we haven't had time to get our story straight. Mason's not going to be the only person who's surprised I brought someone with me. What if they ask questions and we don't know the answer?"

I scoff. "That won't happen."

"How can you be so sure?"

Because I know everything about you. "Because I'm good at thinking on the spot. We've got this, Mel. There's no need to worry."

She blinks, and I realize my mistake of letting a nickname slip. We don't really do the nickname stuff apart from me calling her Trevi all of those years, but this… this is different.

Shaking her head, she drops down onto the couch. "I like to be prepared," she says like it's news to me. "So, can you do this for me, please?"

Fuck. Hearing her say please so sweetly, caves me in. "Sure, Trevi." I let out a sigh and drop down beside her, my eyes going straight to her long legs in her little jersey shorts. I didn't realize how hard it would be to be around her all the time when she hardly wears bras, and is constantly strolling around in cute loungewear that makes me hard as a fucking rock.

I wish she knew exactly what she did to me. I wish she knew the effect she had on me, and why I had to stay very far away from her.

"I don't know anything about you," she admits with a frown. "Like, what's your favorite food, favorite color, favorite place?"

A laugh bubbles out of me. "Who is going to ask all that?"

"You never know," she says with a shrug. "I don't want Mason to know I'm lying."

That's not happening. If he thinks Melissa is available, he will stop at nothing to get her, and seeing how uncomfortable she is around him is enough for me to straighten my shoulders and take this seriously.

"Blue."

"Huh?" she asks, her brows knitted together.

"My favorite color," I clarify. "It's blue. My favorite food is probably my mom's chicken stew, and my favorite place…" I rub a hand over my chin. "I don't have one," I admit with a shrug.

She watches me with intent. "Blue, huh?" she asks with a smirk. "That's so basic."

I love when she goes right back to teasing me. I grin, keeping my eyes on her. "Your favorite color is pink, Mel," I point out, noticing how her eyes widen at the new nickname. "What's more basic than that?"

She frowns. "Pink isn't basic. Misogyny made women hate pink because it's associated with being weak and fragile. Pink is a powerful color, and I won't be ridiculed for liking it."

Well damn.

"You're right, sweetheart." A red tint coats her fair skin, and it make me want to take a bite out of the apple of her cheek. So supple, so soft, so fucking beautiful. "I'm sorry."

"Why do you like blue?" she asks.

I shrug, leaning back. "I don't know. I guess it reminds me of the beach. I used to hang out there a lot. It's quiet. Peaceful."

I swallow, looking back at her to find her eyes locked on mine, intrigue swimming in them. "Wow," she says, shaking her head. "That's actually... deep. I didn't think it was possible with you."

My chest shakes with a laugh. "Yeah, well, we already know you don't know me. There's more to me than just a hot bod," I say, flashing her a huge grin.

"And modesty is, for sure, one of them," she says dryly.

"Exactly." I nudge her arm. "See, you know me."

"Favorite film?" she asks instead, needy for information about me. Don't know why I like that so much, but I really do.

I smile, looking away from her. I just know she's going to tease me about it.

"What?" she asks. "Why are you embarrassed?" She gasps, placing her hands over her mouth as she grins. "Don't tell me it's something girly like Legally Blonde?"

I let out a laugh. "No, it's not that." I run a hand over my beard. "Promise you won't make fun of me?"

"I'll do no such thing," she says with complete honesty.

I let out a laugh, knowing she's going to tease the hell out of me, but if she really wants to know me… "It's Ratatouille," I admit with a sigh.

Her forehead wrinkles with confusion. "Why would that be embarrassing?" she asks, but then a light bulb goes off, and her smile widens as she puts the pieces together. "Are you telling me you became a chef because of Remi the rat?"

"No," I say with a scoff, knowing I'm lying out of my ass. "Fine, maybe I did," I admit, pinching the bridge of my nose when I hear her laugh. "This is exactly why I didn't want to tell you."

"No, I'm sorry," she says, in a fit of laughter that I can't look away from. Never really seen her laugh around me, not like this. Fuck, I love it. I'm such an asshole for being the reason it's taken her ten years to be like this around me.

The crappy thing is, it makes this crush even fucking bigger. I don't think I can even call it that. This isn't a crush anymore. It hasn't been for a long time, and I don't know what the fuck to do about it.

"Continue," Melissa says, attempting to stop laughing.

"It might have been the reason I wanted to start cooking, but my mom taught me everything I know. I always loved helping her in the kitchen."

She smiles, but it's not the warm smile she had on a few minutes ago. It's strained, forced. "That's so nice," she says, glancing away. "I never learned how to cook."

I figure she's thinking of her dad, and I want to grab her, and wrap my arms around her. "Trust me," I joke, wanting that smile back. "I know."

Pressing her eyes closed, she blinks away the tears, and lifts her head, her forehead pinched together. "How did we meet?"

I notice the change in attitude, and decide to move on if she really wants to. I have no idea how it feels to lose a parents, and Mel has no one, except us. And I'm the reason she hasn't been around since last year.

"In real life, or…"

"No," she clarifies. "If anyone asks. How did we meet?"

If they wanted the real version, I'd tell them I was completely blindsided by my sister bringing home her friend. I'd tell them I couldn't take my eyes off her dainty blue dress. I'd tell them I couldn't get her bright green eyes out of my mind even after knowing it was a bad idea to think of her. I'd tell them I haven't stopped thinking about her ever since.

"You watch movies, don't you?" I ask her, knowing the answer. The girl is a pure romantic.

"Yeah."

"Then think of a meet-cute. Something you'd love to happen, and we'll go with that."

She thinks for a while, tapping her pink pen against her plump lip. "I can tell them we both reached for the same caramel filled donut, and you gave yours up for me."

Is that what she wants? If so, I'll leave right now and get her a dozen donuts. "Wow," I say, shaking my head. "You really don't know me. I hate caramel."

She shakes her head, those gorgeous lips curling into a smile. "Fine, any ideas?"

"Just be honest," I tell her. "We met through my sister, and it's been a long time coming. You only realized your feelings for me recently." I shoot her a grin, those words hitting very close to home. I wonder if Melissa has any feelings for me. I know she used to be attracted to me back in high school, it was hard to miss her wandering eyes and cute little smiles, but now, after everything? Does she want me like I want her?

I doubt it.

"Are we done?" I ask her, wanting to get in the shower and wash away all these thoughts about her. It won't work, though. It never does. She consumes me day in and day out. "You know everything there is to know about me, now." Well, not *everything.*

"Almost," she says. "You should know some things about me, too."

I stare at her for way too long. I can tell she means well, but seriously? Half my brain is filled with knowledge on Melissa. I doubt anyone but Zaria knows her like I do. Even then, my sister doesn't know Melissa's nervous tick she does, or how when she's quiet, it usually means she just doesn't know what to say. My sister doesn't know how much Melissa overthinks, but I do. I can see it, every thought rambling in that head of hers, thinking, thinking and more thinking. The girl does nothing but think.

"I know you," I tell her, wanting her to drop it.

But Melissa, doesn't drop it. She laughs, instead. "Bullshit," she says. "You don't know anything about me."

She's so fucking wrong.

"I know you, Mel," I repeat. "I've known you for ten years."

"Okay then." Her hands clasp on her lap as she narrows her eyes at me. "What exactly do you know about me?"

Don't do it. Don't let her know how much you think about her.

She keeps looking at me, waiting, hoping, and the words tumble out of me.

"You say your favorite movie is Home alone, but you've watched Clueless the most. Your favorite ice cream flavor is strawberry, and you eat it whenever you're stressed or upset. You hate when people interrupt you but you never say anything because you hate confrontation." Her mouth drops open, and her eyes widen, but I can't seem to stop, even though I know I should. "You bite the inside of your cheek when you're nervous, or embarrassed. You love watching proposal videos, and you cry at every single one of them."

I might hate myself tomorrow for admitting that to her, but right now, seeing the expression on her face? It's fucking priceless. I know Melissa doesn't think anyone pays attention to her, or even cares to learn these things about her, but I've been trying to unlearn everything about this woman for ten years, and it's impossible.

It's impossible for me not to take note of her, and see things no one else can, because whenever she's near, I feel pulled to her, like a moth to a flame.

"How?" She shakes her head. "How do you know all of that?"

"Mel, c'mon." I run a hand over my face. "I've known you since you were fourteen. You spent days, nights, weekends over at my house. Of course I know you."

Her parted lips close as she leans back. "Wow."

"I've never seen you speechless before," I joke. "It's kind of nice."

Those gorgeous green eyes turn into slits as she shoots me a glare. "You just ruined it."

"Glad to be of service." I lift myself off the couch needing to keep my distance from her. I told her way too much just now. I just hope she doesn't read too much into it, or else, I'm fucked. "Can I go now?" I ask. "I need to shower."

"Yeah," she says with a sigh. "I think we're good."

"Don't worry," I tell her. "We'll make everyone know you're off limits."

Even to me.

Fifteen

Melissa

"This better work," I mutter to my reflection, applying another layer of lip gloss. Stepping back from the mirror, I glance at my body in the mirror, adjusting the long sleeve, black dress Zaria made me buy over a year ago. She told me it would be helpful in case I had any dates to go to, but unsurprisingly, it's been shoved in the back of my closet for months.

"Trevi, c'mon." Gabriel groans, knocking on the door for the tenth time tonight. "It's been over an hour."

"I'm almost done."

He sighs from outside of the door. "I know when women say almost, it means not even close."

I roll my eyes, a slight smile forming on my lips. Fixing my straightened hair, I take one last look in the mirror before I open the door to the melodramatic, impatient guy outside.

"Are you happy?" I ask when I swing the door open.

He turns around at the sound of my voice, and his jaw slackens as his eyes make their way down the length of my dress, and then back up to my face. The look on his face makes my body grow warm and I start to doubt myself.

"Is something wrong?" I ask, wondering why the hell he's acting so weird. "Is it too much?"

He shakes his head, rubbing the pad of his thumb over his bottom lip. "No," he says, his voice thick. "Definitely not too much."

I let my eyes fall down the length of his body, my breath quickening at the sight of him in a white button-down shirt, black jeans, and a black blazer.

Holy hell.

I swallow harshly, forcing myself to stop ogling him, but when our eyes lock, his lips are curved in a cocky smirk. "Like what you see?"

"What?" I take a step back, my eyes widening. "No. Of course not."

Gabriel laughs, his gaze dipping back to my dress. "It's ok if you find me attractive, Trevi. I won't tell."

God. I hated how he knows exactly what's going on in my head. It's embarrassing as hell for him to know how much I'm attracted to him right now when he straight up told me I'm not his type.

I told myself I wouldn't fall back into the high school crush I once had on him, and here I am, drooling at the sight of him.

"Whatever," I murmur, my cheeks burning up. "Let's just go." I push past him, or try to, but I don't get very far when his hand wraps around my wrist and spins me around until my back is plastered against his chest.

"What—" I gasp, feeling the hard muscles of his peck against the thin material of my dress

"Don't play with me, Melissa," he says in a deep husky voice I've never heard from him before.

"What are you talking about?" I ask, feeling his breath an inch from the sensitive skin of my neck.

"You know exactly what you're doing, wearing that dress." His thumb rubs circles over my wrist and I glance down at his hand wrapped around mine.

"What does that mean?" I ask him, my heart racing out of my chest. "What am I doing?"

I lift my head to look at him, and at the sight of my expression, he pulls back, confusion written all over his face. With a groan, he lets go of my wrist and runs a hand over his face. "Fuck."

"What's wrong? Are you backing out?" I ask, hesitantly, praying that wasn't the case. "Because you were the one who offered. I could have found someone else, or —"

"No," he interrupts, shaking his head. "Just drop it. It's nothing." He turns around, and heads toward the door.

"Are you sure?"

A heavy sigh leaves his lips. "Yes. I'm sure. I told you I would help you, and I plan on doing just that."

His lips are saying all the right things, but the way he's acting makes me a little wary. "You can still back out," I remind him. "I can come up with something. I don't want you to do something you don't want to do."

He shakes his head, taking a step closer to me. "I want to do this," he emphasizes. "I promised you I would go with you, and I don't break my promises, Melissa. You're not going in there alone."

I nod, grateful that he didn't decide to back track on his promise. "Okay. Let's go." Walking toward the front door, I start to wince. It's been a very long time since I wore heels, and tonight's going to be a long night.

"Is that what you're wearing?" Gabriel's voice stops me, and I turn to look at him, seeing his eyes locked on my heels.

"Yeah. Why?"

He shakes his head, pressing his lips together in a smile. "You're going to regret that," he says.

"I'm sure I'll be fine." He might be right, but I'm not one to accept defeat.

He sighs, pulling out his car keys. "Get in my car," he says, handing me the keys. "I'll be right back."

Sixteen

Melissa

"Close the windows."

"I like to have them open," Gabriel says, looking at me for a second before he turns his attention back to the road. "It's too fucking hot in here."

"And I'd like to show up not looking like I was in a fight." My eyes widen when I open the mirror in the sun visor, and see my hair all wild and frizzy. So much for attempting to look decent tonight.

"You look fine," he mutters.

"Fine isn't exactly what I was going for."

"Why?" Gabriel asks, rolling up the windows before glancing at me. "Is there someone you're trying to impress?"

"No."

"Really?" His eyes roam my dress once again. "You seem to care a lot about what you look like tonight."

My eyebrows tug together as I glance at him, seeing his hands clutching the steering wheel with a tight grip. "Would I bring you as a date if I had someone I was interested in?"

He scoffs out a laugh. "I feel flattered, Trevi, really."

"You know what I mean," I say with an eye roll. "If I actually had an interest in someone from work, I wouldn't be on dating apps, or asking you to pretend to be my date. There's no one," I admit.

Gabriel doesn't reply, he just keeps driving until I see the school come into view. My pulse races the closer and closer we get, until he parks the car. I feel my heart stuffed in the back of my throat. This is never going to work. No one is going to believe I suddenly have a boyfriend whom I never mentioned before.

They'll all see through it. Mason will see through it, and then he'll never leave me alone. They'll all know I'm a liar, a fraud, a—

"Stop." I snap my head to face Gabriel, concern painted on his expression. "Get out of your head, Trevi," he says, making me frown. How the hell does he know what I was thinking? "It's going to be fine."

My teeth tug on the inside of my cheek, shaking my head. "How do you know that?"

He sighs. "Because I'll be with you every step of the way," he says, making my shoulders slump with relief. I'm glad I'm not doing this alone. "If you start to feel overwhelmed, or want to leave, just tell me, and we'll leave."

"Really?"

He smiles, making my eyes drop to his lips. "Really. If there's any reason at all, you just let me know, and I'll get you out of there."

A breath of relief leaves my lips and I smile up at him. "Thank you."

He shrugs. "That's what I'm here for." He opens the car door, and steps out. "Let's go. We have some pretending to do."

As soon as I step out of the car, Gabriel's right beside me, holding out his hand. My eyes drop to his palm reaching out for me, and my stomach spins at the thought of doing something so intimately with Gabriel. Sure, hand holding isn't a big deal to most people, but this is Gabriel.

We've been arguing for years, and now I'm going to pretend we're dating.

I really hope this works.

Reluctantly, I step forward, and slide my hand into his, sucking in a breath when his fingers interlock with mine.

"You ready?" he asks, squeezing our hands together.

Our eyes meet when I lift my head, and I get lost in his gaze, in the way he smiles, in him. I blink, trying to get myself together and nod, breaking eye contact. "Yeah. I'm ready."

His hand reaches out and pushes open the door, the music booming from inside. I'm relieved I'm holding onto Gabriel right now, because at this moment, I'm depending on him for balance as my heels click on the ground, digging into my feet.

"Are you good?" he asks.

"Yep," I lie, feeling like an idiot for wearing these heels I knew would be uncomfortable. No way am I telling him that, though. I'll just have to power through, and hope my feet aren't dead by the end of the night.

The music gets louder and louder as we walk inside, and I spot Allie dancing with Charlotte in middle of the room.

I let out a laugh at how bold she is, even as some of the older women throw glares at them. I love how unapologetic she is about the love she has for her wife.

My smile, however, disappears when I see Mason by the bar, his eyes locked on me. A shiver runs down my spine at the creepy smile plastered on his lips as his eyes drop to my figure.

I hate how earlier tonight I felt good in this dress, and right now all I want to do is cover myself up.

I squeeze Gabriel's hand and he immediately turns his head. "What is it?" he asks. "You want to leave?"

I shake my head. "No, that's not it."

"Then what?"

I subtly gesture toward Mason who's walking toward Gabriel and me, with a drink in his hand. Gabriel turns his head, and spots him, straightening as soon as he realizes who that might be.

"Melissa," Mason slurs, the reek of alcohol wafting from his breath. "You made it." Great. He's drunk. "I was beginning to think you were lying about having a date tonight," he says, leaning closer to me. He laughs, and the sound makes my stomach churn as he looks down my body once again. "You look fucking great," he mumbles, swaying slightly. "Big improvement from what you usually wear." His eyes stay glued to my chest, making me wish I had never worn this dress.

I squeeze Gabriel's hand again, thankful that he's with me, and press myself closer to him. "This is Gabriel," I explain, wanting him to back off. "My boyfriend." That word feels funny in my mouth, but I try not to think about it, smiling cautiously at him, hoping he believes it.

Mason's gaze switches from me to Gabriel and he gives him a once over, before holding out his hand. "Well, at least I know she wasn't lying," he says, laughing again. "Nice to meet you."

Gabriel reaches out his other hand, still clutching mine with the other and greets him. "Nice to meet you," he says, in a deeper voice than normal. Damn, he's good at playing the overprotective boyfriend card.

"Tight grip," Mason says, wincing as he pulls out of Gabriel's hand. "How long have you guys been together?" he asks, taking another swig of his drink. "Melissa never mentioned a boyfriend before last week."

"We only got together recently," Gabriel says, going off the script we planned yesterday. "But it's been a long time coming."

I lift my head at his words, that damn fluttering feeling back in my stomach. He dips his head, his eyes connecting with mine and I can't seem to look away. I don't *want* to look away.

"Well that's too bad," Mason says with a grin. "I've been trying to get her to go out with me, but I guess you got there first." With a laugh, he nudges me on the shoulder, and I've never been less attracted to him than I am right now.

"Listen. I'd appreciate it if you weren't constantly hitting on my girlfriend." My eyes widen and I look up at Gabriel who's scowling at Mason. "If you're acting like a fucking asshole when I'm here, I don't even want to know what she has to put up with when I'm not."

"Excuse me?" Mason asks, shooting Gabriel a glare. "Who do you think you're talking to?"

Gabriel's eyebrows lift. "I'm talking to a scumbag who thinks it's ok to pressure a woman even after she's denied you multiple times. She said no. Once should suffice."

"Gabriel," I whisper. "What are you doing?"

"What I should have done when you told me about this guy," he says, his eyes swimming with concern before he turns his focus back to Mason. "If I hear that you hit on her, or touched her, or even looked at her wrong, you best believe I will come and find you. Got it?"

Mason gulps back the rest of his drink. "Yeah, I got it."

"Good." Gabriel straightens his jacket, tugging me along with him. "See you around Rudy," he says, heading away from him.

"It's Mason."

"Yeah, whatever," Gabriel mutters, tightening his grip on my hand. He heads toward the back table, groaning when he sees most of the food is gone. "I'm fucking starving."

"There's a slice over there." I gesture toward the singular slice of pizza on the back end of the table.

He eyes me, carefully. "You don't want it?" he asks.

I shrug. "Not really."

He must change his mind because he sighs, turning around from the table. "Are you okay?" he asks. "I didn't realize how bad he actually was, but fuck it was agony not to punch him right there."

"I'm fine," I say with a laugh. "The plan was just to act like we were dating, not to act like an ass."

He scoffs, crossing his arms. "He was an ass," he says, leaning back into the wall. "The way he was looking at you made me want to snap his skinny legs." With a shake of his head, he breathes out a sigh. "Fuck, Mel. Why didn't you tell me how bad he actually was?"

Mel.

He's only called me that a few times before, but every time he says it, my heart does backflips.

And I'm not sure that's a good thing.

"He was worse today," I admit. "He's not usually this... forward." I wince, remembering all the nasty remarks Mason made today. "It must have been the alcohol."

"I fucking hated hearing him talk to you like that. Especially with me standing right there."

I smirk. "Possessive, are we?"

The corner of his lips lift as his eyes narrow in on me. "I just want him to understand you're off limits."

I can't help but smile, which he takes note of as his eyes drop to my mouth. *Gabriel is looking at my mouth.* It probably doesn't mean anything, but my heart doesn't seem to understand that because it's beating out of control.

He breaks eye contact first, looking behind me, and I frown, turning around to try and see who he's looking at. When I see a group of women laughing, staring right at me, my body heats.

"What's their deal?" he asks.

I sigh, turning away from them. "They're like the mean girls of high school who never grew up," I tell him. "They love to gossip, about everything and anything, and I guess tonight, it's about us."

His eyes turn back to mine and he moves closer, sliding his hands to my waist. I suck in a breath. "What are you doing?" I ask, feeling the weight of his big hands wrapped around my body. I've never been held, not like this.

"Giving them something to talk about," he whispers, leaning down into me. "I thought that's what you wanted." The cold air of his breath hits my cheek and my eyes flutter closed, a warm feeling building in my core. "To prove to them that I'm your boyfriend."

"N-no," I stutter, forcing my eyes to stay open. The thought of Gabriel kissing me makes my legs turn to jello. I don't think I realized how bad I wanted him to until his lips were a few inches away, and his hands were wrapped around my body. But I don't want it like this. I don't want it to be fake. I want him to kiss me because he wants to, because he wants me. But that's never going to happen.

"I don't want you to kiss me," I manage to say, my voice thick and breathy. I pray that he doesn't pick up on it, that he doesn't know how much he affects me. "I just wanted you to get Mason to back off."

His brows tug together, and his lips drop into a frown, but then he drops his hands and moves away from me, letting out a sigh. "You're right," he says, running a hand down his face. "It would have been a terrible idea."

Ouch.

I swallow harshly, feeling the sting of his words. I know it wouldn't have been smart to kiss Gabriel, especially when all of these feelings are coming back, but it still hurt to know he doesn't want me.

"Yeah," I breathe out, wanting the ground to open up and swallow me whole.

"Hey, babe." I turn my head, seeing Allie and Charlotte heading toward us.

"Hey," I say, embracing her, and Charlotte in a hug. Allie knows the relationship with Gabriel was fake, so I didn't have to pretend with her.

When I pull back, Allie's lips are tugged in a smile as she looks at Gabriel. "And who's this?" she asks. While I always talked her ear off about Gabriel, she had never actually met him.

"This is Gabriel," I tell her, nervous about whether or not she'd blurt out that I had a secret crush on him. My eyes widen, trying to send her signals so she won't say anything.

"Gabriel, huh?" she muses, with a smirk spread across her face.

"Yeah, nice to meet you…"

"Allie," she finishes for him, greeting him. Her tongue runs over her teeth as her eyes travel down the length of Gabriel's body. She shakes her head, a chuckle leaving her lips. "Wow. Melissa's told me so much about you."

Gabriel turns to face me. "You've been telling people about me, sweetheart?" His voice makes me shiver, but when I turn to Allie, the expression on her face makes me sweat. She's enjoying this too much, and I have to shut it down. Or else she'll never stop teasing me about it until I crack and tell her my feelings for Gabriel are back.

"Allie knows this is fake," I tell him, not wanting him to put on an act anymore. It was fine while Mason was questioning us, but every time he touches me, or calls me a sweet nickname

I let myself slip deeper and deeper into delusion, believing that this is real.

"Yeah, *sweetheart*," Allie says with a smirk.

"Oh," Gabriel says with a laugh. "Sorry. I just wanted to make it convincing."

"Oh, it was convincing, alright," Allie murmurs, turning to her wife. "Wasn't it, *sweetheart*?"

Charlotte nods, laughing at Allie's attempt to tease me.

I narrow my eyes at her, releasing a sigh. "You're never going to let this go, are you?"

Allie shakes her head. "I'm afraid not. This is just too good."

"Great," I mumble.

"So, did it work?" Allie asks. "Did Mason buy it? He left, so he must have believed it."

I nod. "Yeah. Gabriel even threatened him if he ever hit on me again."

Allie's eyes widen as she turns to Gabriel. "You did?"

"Of course," he says with a shrug. "He made Melissa uncomfortable. It was the least I could do."

"That's so sweet," Allie says, dropping her head onto Charlotte's wife. "You have the best fake boyfriend ever," she tells me, humor dripping from her tone.

I narrow my eyes at her, praying her to let it go. She might think there's more between Gabriel and I than I'm letting on but the truth is, the only reason he came with me tonight was because he feels guilty over what he did for the last ten years. I'm his sister's best friend, and he probably felt it was his duty to protect him like he would his sister.

It doesn't matter what Allie thinks, because I know what this is, and I won't let myself get my hopes up. Not again.

An hour later, and I'm drained from having to speak to people I don't usually talk to. Though I'm not doing much of the talking, seeing as they're mostly interested in Gabriel.

"It's getting late," I whisper to Gabriel when we're finally away from everyone. "We should probably go home."

Gabriel's head turns toward me, his dark eyes locking onto mine. "You want to leave" he asks.

I shrug. "We've been here for a while now, and I'm tired," I admit, admitting defeat. "I'm hungry, and my feet hurt and I just want to go to bed." I sigh, pleading him with my eyes. "We proved to Mason that my boyfriend was real, and after you threatened him, he'll probably never talk to me again."

"Good." Gabriel's eyes burn into mine. "He doesn't deserve to."

I smile at his protectiveness, but it turns into a wince as a shooting, burning sensation crawls over my feet. "Can we please leave now?" I beg.

"Sure, Trevi." He chuckles, grabbing my hand in his. I don't even care that Mason's no longer here, and technically, it's unnecessary. His hand is warm, and I like it. "Let's go."

"Thank God," I breathe out as he interlocks his fingers with mine and leads the way out of the gym, heading into the parking lot.

A breath of relief leaves me when we finally reach his car, and I lean against it, wanting these shoes off.

"Are you ready to admit those shoes were a mistake?" Gabriel asks, watching me as he leans against the car with his arms crossed.

I glance at him. "Don't make me say it," I plead. "I don't want to prove you right."

He laughs, shaking his head. "You're so stubborn. Just admit they were a mistake, Melissa."

"Fine," I concede, breathing out a harsh sigh. "They were a mistake. You win. Now can you please open the car so I can take them off?"

He smiles, a soft laugh leaving his lips, but instead of opening the door, he heads to the trunk of his car, unlocking it. When he returns, he's holding a pair of sleek black pumps in his hands.

"I knew you would need these," he says, handing me the pair of shoes.

My heart thumps so loud against my chest, I'm afraid he'll be able to hear it. Sucking in a deep breath, I glance down at the shoes. "You brought these for me?"

"Those heels might look good," he says, his eyes dipping down my legs. "But I knew it would kill your feet."

"Thank you," I say, quietly, unable to believe he would ever do something so thoughtful.

He nods, and leans down to take off my heels, placing them in the back seat. While I slip into the pumps he brought me, he opens the passenger door, holding it open until I get inside.

A few hours ago, I was terrified about how this night would go, but with Gabriel standing beside me, it wasn't that bad.

"Are you hungry?" he asks, putting the car in drive.

I drop back against the headrest, and turn my head to look at him. "Starving."

Seventeen

Gabriel

"Wait, where are you going?" Melissa asks.

"You said you were hungry," I remind her, glancing at her for a second. Just for a second. It's too easy to get distracted by her, especially when she's in my car, in a tiny little dress and those long legs exposed.

I've gotten so used to Melissa always being in sweats and jeans, and tonight she caught me by surprise. She's always been incredibly beautiful to me, but tonight? It was almost impossible to keep all those feelings I have for her bottled down.

"I wanted to go home," she groans, probably tired, and overwhelmed and desperate to get into her own bed.

She actually lasted longer than I thought she would. I was so ready to get her the fuck out of there, especially after seeing the creep who hits on Melissa day in, and day out. She's lucky we had witnesses, or else he wouldn't have left with his jaw intact.

The way he was devouring her, looking at her, wanting her, it made me feel something I haven't felt probably ever.

Jealous.

I don't get jealous.

I've never been jealous with any other girl, so why the fuck does this one turn my head upside down?

The more I tell myself we can't be together, the more I want to rebel against my own rules. Tonight was an example of how she makes me forget all rationale. I almost kissed her. I wanted to so bad. So freaking bad, that I didn't think about the consequences. She's Zaria's best friend. She'd been off limits for so long I forgot what it was like to have something you want.

I had her tonight. I held her hand, I touched her, looked at her. It was everything I'd wanted for so long that I took it too far and almost pressed my lips against her.

I'm glad she stopped it. Really, I am. Because I'd hate the idea of our kiss being

anything but real, and out of need. She didn't want me like that, and I couldn't have her like I wanted to.

But fuck, it was getting hard to keep telling myself that.

"Trust me," I say, wanting to spend a little longer with her. I'm not ready to end the night just yet. She's here, with me, and while she definitely doesn't think so, this is almost like a date.

I can't let go of that just yet.

"I want to make sure you get some food in you first before you pass out."

She scoffs. "I won't pass out. Plus, you're a chef, why don't you make me food?"

I'll make you anything you want. I laugh, instead. "You couldn't afford me as a personal chef, sweetheart."

Her cheeks turn the prettiest shade of pink before she looks out of the window. I don't want to make her embarrassed, or uncomfortable but I love calling her sweetheart. I've spent so long trying to push her away, finding ways I can tease her that it's a breath of fresh air to compliment her.

Of course, she'll probably think I'm just trying to get under her skin.

She groans again, closing her eyes. "So... tired," she mumbles.

I laugh when I see the time, noticing it's still pretty early. For me, at least. "Stop complaining. We're almost there."

A few minutes later, I park the car at 'Grub 'n' Stuff Diner' and wait for Melissa to notice we've stopped.

She blinks, her eyes flicking up to the red neon sign. "I have to walk?" she asks, frowning.

She's so fucking cute. I laugh. "It's less than thirty steps." A groan leaves her lips. "I mean, I could pick you up if you want," I offer, grinning like an idiot when her eyes widen. "Throw you over my shoulder like I did when I first moved in and you were acting like a brat."

She shoots me a glare, and opens the car door, wincing as soon as her feet hit the floor. I know I was joking about carrying her, but right now, I'm tempted to do just that.

Climbing out of the car, I lock the doors and head over to her, allowing her to lean on me as we walk inside the diner. She chooses a booth close to the door, and I sit opposite her.

"Better?" I ask her, once she's seated.

"I will be when I have some food."

"Good evening." I turn, seeing the waitress standing above us. "What can I get you today?" she asks, shooting me a flirty smile.

I sneak a glance at Melissa watching her frown as she watches at the girl flirt with me.

"We're still looking," I tell her. "Thanks." Her cheeks flush as she smiles back before moving away.

The girl's attractive sure, but there isn't an ounce of desire in me toward her, not when Melissa is sitting in front of me. She opens the menu, scanning it and I take that as my opportunity to just look at her. I watch as she bites her lip, deep in concentration as she looks through all of the options. I look at her fingers clutching the menu that felt so soft and warm against my hand. I notice the front pieces of her hair frizzing up making her look so adorable.

God.

I snatch the menu from the table, and open it, trying to get my thoughts in order. The only thing I'm doing, is torturing myself by having these thoughts, hoping that one day I can have her, kiss her, touch her. And I know I can't.

"Are you ready to order?" I look up, seeing the waitress from before, her eyes still on me. How long was I zoning out for?

"I'd like the pancakes with maple syrup and a strawberry milkshake," Melissa speaks up, handing her the menu.

She finally acknowledges Mel, turning her head to look at her, and lifts an eyebrow at her. "Is that all?"

"Um…" Melissa nibbles on the inside of her mouth, frowning. "Yeah, that's all."

"Great." The waitress takes the menu from her, and turns back to face me. "And what will you have?"

"I'll have the burger and fries with the coke." When I see the waitress smirk at me, again, I grow impatient. "My girlfriend has a sweet tooth," I say, stifling a laugh when the waitress frowns. "She'll probably want something savory afterward so I'll have another order of fries. Thank you." I hand her the menu, seeing her smile fade away as she leaves the table.

"What was that for?" Melissa asks, confusion written all over her face. "We don't need to pretend anymore."

Who's pretending, sweetheart? "I'm still on the clock as your fake boyfriend until the clock strikes midnight," I joke.

Her brows tug together. "So, the extra fries and the..." She swallows so harshly, I can hear her gulp from here. "The girlfriend comment?" she asks. "That was all for show?"

Not even close. "Some of it," I admit. "But I also wanted her to stop acting like you weren't sitting right here."

"Why?" she asks. "We're not really dating, and I don't want her to spit in my food," she says, scrunching her nose in an adorable way that makes me want to grab her and kiss her. "She was clearly flirting with you. You can flirt back if you're interested."

What the fuck?

I can't stand looking at anyone but her, and she wanted me to flirt with some random girl right in front of her?

"You really want me to do that?" I ask her, narrowing my eyes. "You want me to flirt with her, and ask for her number, and take her home?"

She blanches, her throat moving as she swallows. "I don't care what you do, Gabriel," she says with an even tone that pisses me off. "You're single after all."

My spine stiffens, a shiver running down my body at her words. Does she really not care?

"Here you go," the waitress says a few moments later, placing down the plates in front of us. "Enjoy."

I look up at the girl, seeing her flash me another smile. Does Melissa really think I want her when the girl I've been gone for is right here in front of me?

"Thanks." I glance at Melissa, watching her take a sip of her milkshake.

"I'm not interested," I tell Melissa once the waitress is out of ear shot.

"Huh?" she asks, a mouthful of pancakes in her mouth.

I want to laugh at the sight, smile at how she's devouring those pancakes, but I can't stop thinking about how blasé she was when she suggested I flirt with someone else.

"I'm not interested," I repeat, trying to keep my cool. "In the waitress."

Her throat moves as she swallows down her bite, staring up at me. "Really?"

The hope in her voice breaks me. "Really," I tell her, wanting her to know I'm not that kind of guy. "How could you think I'd do that to you when you're supposed to be my date?"

She frowns a little. "It's not like it's a real date."

I shrug. "You're right about that," I admit. "If this was a real date, I'd take you home at the end of the night and strip that tight dress off your body like you were my gift to unwrap on Christmas Day."

Melissa freezes, her eyes widening as she tries to make sense of what I've just told her. I should be kicking myself for making my feelings for her so obvious, but I'm sick of denying myself what I want.

"But regardless." I straighten my jacket, before picking up a couple of fries. "Real or not, I'm not interested." I shove the fries in my mouth, keeping my eyes on her.

"Because you recently broke up with Lucy?" she asks, taking a sip of her milkshake.

My ex-girlfriend's name in Melissa's mouth makes me shift in my seat. What would she say if she found out the reason that mess of a relationship ended was because of her? "Because she's not what I want." *Because I want you.*

She dips her head, cutting up her pancakes in little triangles before stuffing them in her mouth, washing it all down with a headache-inducing sweet, strawberry milkshake.

We eat in silence for the majority of the time until Melissa finishes off her milkshake, leaning back against the booth. "I don't think I've ever been this full in my life."

I laugh. "Maybe it's because you ate those pancakes in less than two minutes."

She blushes, the rosy tint coating her pale skin. "I was hungry," she says.

"You ready to go home?"

"Yes," she breathes out, grabbing her purse.

I scoff, reaching out to stop her. "Don't even think about it."

"Gabriel, I asked you to come with me tonight," she says, her brows knitted together. "The least I can do is pay."

"I'm not letting you pay, Melissa. You owe me nothing. I offered to help, and I had a great time tonight," I admit, loving how her eyes brighten. "I'm paying. End of."

She sighs. "I really don't want to fight you on this."

"Then don't," I say with a shrug. "I can afford to take a pretty girl out."

My favorite pink shade is back on her cheeks as she puts her purse away.

I quickly pay for our meal before we head out of the diner. Mel's eyes are heavy and I can tell she's dying to go to sleep.

"We're not going anywhere else, right?" she asks with one eye open when I close the car door.

"No, Trevi," I chuckle. "Let's get you home."

"Good. I'm too tired."

I put the car in drive, and make my way onto the road, sneaking a glance at Melissa to find her already looking at me.

"Thank you," she mumbles.

"You don't have to thank me. It was just a couple of pancakes."

She shakes her head. "Not just for that. For tonight," she clarifies. "I don't know what I would have done if you weren't there."

I gulp, locking in on those big, beautiful, green eyes of hers. "Good thing you don't have to worry about that anymore."

She smiles, closing her eyes as she leans back against the head-rest. A few seconds later, though, she sits up and starts digging around the car.

"What are you looking for?" I ask.

"The fries. I need something savory."

Eighteen

Melissa

I've never really had a family.

All I really had was my dad. And while he always tries his hardest to fulfill both roles of a parent, there was always an empty void within me, wishing, hoping that my mother would come back.

She never did, of course. But I never stopped hoping for it. For her.

So being here, with the Andersons while they talk, and laugh, and have regular family dinner, it makes my stomach hurt. I will never have that. This is the closest I will ever get to having a real family, and it isn't even mine.

"Grab those tongs for me, baby," Terry calls out to Zaria who's lounging by the pool alongside me.

She lifts off the sun lounger, and grabs a pair of tongs from the table, handing them over to her dad, before she sits back beside me. I shouldn't be feeling this emotional from seeing Zaria hang out with her dad, but it just makes me miss my own that much more.

"Hey, pops," Gabriel greets his dad when he steps out onto the yard.

"Well, look who finally showed up," Terry jokes, greeting him with a hug. "Where've you been?"

"I had some work related issue," he says with a sigh. "But I wouldn't miss family dinner. You already know that." He glances at Zaria. "By the way, mom asked for your help."

"For what?"

"Some kind of dessert emergency."

"And you couldn't help her?" she questions with a raised eyebrow. "You're a chef."

"Not yet," he says. "And you know desserts aren't my specialty."

"Men," Zaria sighs, standing up with a groan before she heads inside the house.

"I'm going to grab a beer. Do you want one?" Gabriel asks his dad.

His dad nods, flipping over the meat on the grill. "There's some in there," he says, gesturing to the cooler besides my lounger.

Gabriel heads toward me, and I know he's just coming to collect the beers, but the way his eyes are on me makes my body warm.

"What about you, Melissa?" Terry asks, turning his focus on me. "Do you want a beer?"

"She doesn't like beer, dad," Gabriel says, throwing me a wink as he opens the cooler, and grabs two beers. I hate how he knows me.

Terry laughs, shaking his head. "I hope he hasn't been causing any problems, living with you girls."

Gabriel smirks, lifting his head. "Of course not. Right, Trevi?"

"No," I reply, narrowing my eyes at Gabriel as he chuckles softly. "He's been great, actually."

"Really?" Terry asks. It's not a secret how Gabriel and I used to bicker all the time, so I understand the shock in his voice.

"Yeah," I reply, smiling slightly as Gabriel lifts himself off the ground, looking down at me.

"Hmm." Terry nods. "That's good. There's nothing worse than fights within the family."

A pressure builds in my chest, but this time it's not painful. Hearing those words from him means more to me than he'll ever know. I think a big part of it is that he was close with my dad.

"Here," Gabriel says, throwing his dad a beer. He cracks it open, and takes a sip. "Have you decided what to do with the house?" he asks, making me tense.

"Not yet."

"What house?" Gabriel asks, frowning.

"My dad's," I reply. "He left me his house in his will."

It's been way too long, but I still don't know what to do with it. I think it'd feel too weird moving in without him there, but I also don't want to sell it. That place holds so many memories, and important moments of my life. If I sell it, it would be like losing another part of him.

"I know it's hard to let go," Terry continues, resting the tongs on the side of the grill when he turns to face me with an apologetic look in his eyes. "But your dad left you that house to help you, not hurt you. Whether you want to keep it, or sell it, that's your choice, Melissa."

My dad was a real estate agent, so he knew the market was rising every day. I know Terry is right, and the house wasn't supposed to be a burden, but sometimes it feels like there's a right choice, and a wrong one, and I don't know which is which.

"You still have time," he says. "You're young. You can figure it out. And if you ever need anything, you know we're here for you. Even this one." He gestures toward Gabriel.

My eyes lock with Gabriel's and he smiles. "Yeah, Trevi. Even me."

I let out a laugh, grateful that we no longer hate each other's guts. Gabriel makes his way over to me, dropping down on the lounger beside me. We both sit in silence for a while, the only sounds filling the air being the birds, and the sizzling grill.

"Do you remember when we were last here?" he asks, taking a swig of his beer.

I sigh, thinking back to that day, and how different we are right now. "Things have completely changed since then," I whisper.

"I'm relieved they are."

"You are?" I ask, turning to face him.

His eyes meet mine, and his brows knit together. "Of course I am, Mel. Do you really think I wanted to hurt you that day?"

I shrug. "I don't know."

"You really think that of me?" he asks, a pained expression on his face.

"What do you expect, Gabriel? You hated me for years, and I didn't even know why," I tell him with a frown. "What did I ever do to make you despise me all those years?"

His jaw tightens, and he shakes his head, his lips parting as if he's about to speak, but then Zaria comes outside.

"Is the food almost done?" she asks her dad.

Gabriel groans, turning away from me as he sits up and scrubs his face with his hand.

"Yeah. Help me take all of this inside," Terry tells his daughter.

Gabriel lifts himself off the lounger, grabbing the corn, and I grab the tray from Terry, bringing it inside, and place it on the dining table alongside the rest of the food.

"God, this looks so good," Zaria groans. "I feel like I haven't eaten a real meal in so long."

"Probably because you're always eating those tiny sandwiches at work," her mom says, chastising her. "Are you sure you can't stay longer today?"

She shakes her head. "No, I have to back in an hour."

Her mom sighs, and then holds out her hands. I place one hand in Gabriel's and another in Zaria's, and close my eyes as Naomi says grace.

Everyone starts eating shortly after, and by the time I've had a few bites, I gulp, feeling nauseous as I look down at the plate in front of me. The appetite that was there a few minutes ago has completely disappeared as it always does when I'm on my period.

My stomach cramps up as the pain curls inside of me, and I groan, wishing I'd have stayed home. I usually do when it gets really bad, but it's been so long since I had a meal with the Andersons, and seeing as Gabriel and I are no longer at each other's throats, I wanted to come over again.

"Are you okay?" Gabriel asks, leaning closer to me while Zaria talks to her parents about her job.

I lift my head, my eyes meeting his. "Yeah," I whisper, licking my lips. "I just need some water."

"Are you sure?" he questions with a frown. "I can get it for you."

"No." I shake my head. "I can do it." Standing up from the table, I excuse myself as I head toward the kitchen. Reaching up, I grab a glass from the cabinet, and fill it with water when another cramp hits. Fuck. I should have brought some painkillers with me.

"Cramps?" I turn my head, seeing Naomi enter the kitchen.

"Yeah," I say, drinking some of my water. "I'll be fine, though."

"You barely ate."

"I don't have much of an appetite."

She nods, approaching me. "And how have things been with Gabriel? From what I see, it's been good."

"Yeah, we don't argue as much anymore."

"As much?" she asks. "So you still argue?"

I laugh, lifting a shoulder. "Sometimes."

"You've always… admired him, haven't you?"

My brows tug together as I look at her, wondering what she means, but before I can ask, she beats me to it.

"I see how you look at him," she says with a smile. My eyes widen, and my heart freezes. She does? "And now you guys aren't arguing anymore…" she trails off, lifting her eyebrows at me.

"It's not like that," I say, feeling awkward talking about this to Gabriel's mom.

"So you don't have feelings for my son?"

I blink, feeling my heart in my throat as I swallow. "I don't…" I shake my head, unable to finish my words. The truth is, I do have feelings for Gabriel, and I hate myself for letting it go there again. I told myself it wasn't smart to do, that he's hurt me in the past, that it's pointless seeing as Gabriel isn't interested in me. But I guess I didn't care about any of that, because here I am.

"I thought so," she says with a smile as she grabs some plates.

"Don't tell him," I ask her, pleading her with my eyes. "Please."

"Don't worry," she says, shaking her head. "No one else needs to know."

A breath of relief leaves my lips and I finish off my water, dying to get home so I can get in bed and find some comfort.

"We're having dessert," she says, reaching for a spoon. "With how much of a sweet tooth you are, I'm sure your appetite will return."

I laugh, knowing she's completely right. "I'd love some."

Nineteen

Melissa

"Lie down," Gabriel says as soon as we walk into the apartment. He shuts the door behind him and turns to face me.

My head is pounding, and my stomach is being tortured from the inside out. His smooth, deep voice makes me blink. "Huh?"

"Lie down on the couch," he repeats, grabbing a glass of water.

"Why?"

He shakes his head, a soft laugh leaving his lips. "You're always so stubborn." Holding out the glass of water, he hands me two pills to go with it."

My cheeks heat with embarrassment, and I drop my eyes to his hands, grabbing the pills and the water. "Did your mom tell you?" I ask, feeling mortified over the fact that he knows I'm on my period.

"No," he says, watching me as I take the pills.

"Then how did you know?" I ask, wiping my mouth when I finish off the water.

He smiles, knowingly. "I have a sister, and a mother, Mel. I know what it looks like when it's that time of the month."

"Oh."

"Lie down," he tells me, gesturing with his head toward the couch behind me.

"I need to get changed first. I hate lounging around in jeans." He nods, and I make my way to my bedroom, stripping out of my clothes before putting my sweatpants and a big hoodie on. My mind reels back to what Naomi said earlier, and I can't stop thinking about it, no matter how hard I try.

I have feelings for Gabriel. It's something I've tried to deny, but I can't anymore. I know it, and now so does Naomi.

But if Naomi figured it out, how long will it take until Zaria figures it out? What about Gabriel? I'd hate for him to know, especially when I know he doesn't reciprocate those feelings.

A sigh leaves my lips, desperately wanting those thoughts out of my head. I open my bedroom door, and step out into the living room, watching Gabriel place some pillows and a blanket on the couch.

The sight makes me smile, but I also don't want him to feel obligated. "You don't need to do this for me," I explain, feeling my heart beat against my chest. "I can just go to my room."

He glares at me. "Stop being stubborn and come lie down, Mel."

I step toward him, and lie down on the couch. Gabriel places a heating pad over my stomach, covering me with a blanket, and I keep my eyes on him while he fluffs out the pillows, and fixes the blanket. My stomach flutters uncontrollably as his eyes meet mine. I can't believe he's doing this. Taking care of me. I haven't had anyone do anything close to this since I was a little girl, and I forgot how much I miss it.

"Are you going to leave?" I ask him, swallowing down the urge to beg him to stay here with me.

His lips curve as he drops down onto the edge of the couch, and picks up my feet, placing it on top of his legs. "I'm not going anywhere, Mel."

I let myself nestle deeper into the pillows, and close my eyes, a warm feeling coating my body from head to toe.

My eyes flutter open when I hear soft mumbling coming from the TV.

"You're awake," Gabriel says, making me blink as I turn to look up at him. My legs are still on his. I finally register that I'm still lying on him, and move back, sitting up on the couch.

"How long was I asleep for?" I ask him, wiping the sleep from my eyes.

"Not long," he says, running a hand over his beard. "About an hour, or so. Are you feeling better?"

I swallow, and nod when I remember everything he did for me. "I don't know what to say," I admit, acknowledging how weird of a situation this is when just a couple of weeks ago, everything between us was completely different."

His lips curve into a smirk. "A thank you would be nice."

I chuckle. "Thank you."

He nods, keeping his eyes on me. "Are you hungry? I made you something."

"You did?" I question, surprised.

"Yeah." He lifts off the couch, heading into the kitchen, and when he comes back, he has a plate with a couple of brownies on it.

"You made brownies?" My brows furrow. "I thought you said dessert wasn't your specialty."

"It's not," he confirms. "But I figured I'd learn since my roommate has a huge sweet tooth."

My head snaps up to his, and I'm left completely speechless, realizing he learned for me. *Don't get your hopes up. This doesn't mean anything.* I swallow. "Didn't you say being my personal chef was expensive?"

He laughs, handing me the plate, as he sits beside me on the couch. "Consider this a trial run."

I grab a brownie, and take a bite, groaning when the chocolatey flavor explodes in my mouth. How the hell is he so good at everything?

"Good?" he guesses with a laugh.

"Yeah," I mumble, my mouth filled with the brownie. "Thank you."

"Zaria would inhale chocolate. I figured you'd like it, too."

I nod in agreement. "I do."

"Good." He settles into the couch, and I turn my head to the TV, my eyes widening when I see what's on the screen. "Clueless?" I ask.

"Yeah," he replies with a smile.

"Why were you watching Clueless?"

He shrugs, glancing back at me. "It's your favorite."

He remembers that? I laugh, settling back as I watch the movie. "I'm surprised you're watching this. It's not very manly," I joke, knowing most men wouldn't be caught dead watching a chick flick.

Gabriel scoffs. "I think we both know I don't give a crap about stuff like that. I'm manly where it counts."

His words dip to my core, and I smirk, teasingly. "Yeah? And where would that be?" I taunt.

His eyes drop to my mouth, and he leans in, running a thumb across my bottom lip. My lips part as I stare up at him. He pulls back and sucks his thumb into his mouth, cleaning off the crumb from my lips. "Don't push it, Trevi," he says with a heated gaze. "We both know you don't want to go there."

I gulp, knowing he's right. I don't want to go there, not when he'll shut me down and say I'm not his type again.

But one thing's for sure.

This heavy feeling in my chest isn't anxiety, or nervousness, it's something else I'm not quite ready to admit yet.

I think I'm falling in love with Gabriel.

Twenty

Melissa

How can this be happening?

I can't possibly be in love with Gabriel. He's everything I once despised. Arrogant, annoying, egotistical. But he's none of those things anymore. During the time we've spent together recently, he's become kind, and thoughtful, and he's still so attractive it's annoying.

Shit.

I knew I shouldn't have gotten close to him. Every day we spend together, and every conversation we have makes me fall deeper, and deeper for him. I was only fooling myself thinking the opposite would happen.

My body warms, surrounded by the hot water as I soap up my body, wanting to warm up from the rain storm I was caught in on my way home, and relax. it doesn't last long when I hear the sound of a door closing.

I sit up, reaching for my phone. A groan escapes me when I see what time it is. Gabriel must be back from work.

I step out of the bath, looking around for my towel. I need to get out of here before he finds me. I'm not exactly proud of it, but I've been avoiding Gabriel for the past few days.

Sure, it might seem foolish after I scrapped the schedule, but I'm in over my head over what to do about these feelings. The more time I spend with him, the more they grow, and if Naomi caught on so easily, I don't know what I'd do if Gabriel ever found out.

I just need some time. I'm sure having some distance from him will help me get over this crush. I've done it once before, I know I can do it again.

My eyebrows tug together as I try to find my towel. Where the hell is it? I curse, when I realize I forgot it in my room.

I glance at the hand towel, losing hope when I realize that will cover nothing. The clothes I previously wore are drenched from the rain, and the mere thought of putting them back on makes my skin crawl.

Which means…

"Gabriel?" I call out.

"Trevi?" he asks. "What's up?"

God. I haven't heard his voice in so long, and the sound of it goes straight to my core. "I forgot to bring my towel," I tell him, my body heating from embarrassment. "Can you please bring me one?"

I hear a sigh from him, and then a knock at the door a few moments later. "Open the door, Mel," he says from the other side.

"I'm not exactly decent right now," I reply, struggling to find something to cover myself with.

"I won't look. I promise."

Having no other choice, I reach for the door handle, and open the door, seeing Gabriel facing away from me. I hide my body behind the door, and clear my throat. "You can turn around," I tell him.

His heavy breathing is loud as he turns his head to the side, still not facing me. "I'd rather not."

My brows furrow. "I'm not going to flash you," I promise. "I'm behind the door."

Hesitantly, he turns around, and his eyes scan my face, dipping to my neck, and back up. I lock eyes with him, seeing his throat moves as he swallows, and runs his tongue over his bottom lip.

My eyes drop to his hands, but I don't see anything in them. "Where's my towel?"

"Why have you been ignoring me?" he asks, making me stunned by his question. I assumed he wouldn't have noticed, but my assumptions are always wrong when it comes to Gabriel.

I blink, struggling to find the words. "I um…"

"You've been avoiding me," he says, his eyes narrowed. "Deny it."

I can't. He's right. I have been avoiding him, but I can't tell him the reason why.

"Just give me my towel, Gabriel. I'm soaking wet."

His jaw tightens as his eyes darken on me, and I feel the heat of his gaze all over my body. "Tell me what I did," he asks, his voice thick. "Tell me why you're avoiding me."

"That's blackmail."

"Hardly," he replies with a lift of his shoulders.

"Why are you making this a big deal? I've just been busy."

"Lies," he says, determined.

I shake my head. "Maybe I just don't like seeing your face every day."

"More lies." He takes as step closer. "What did I do, Mel?" he pleads, his expression pained. "Tell me."

I let out a groan. "Please," I beg, not wanting to tell him I stupidly caught feelings for him even with the hundreds of reasons I shouldn't have. "Just… please give me my towel so I can get dressed."

He watches me for a while, his jaw tense, before he sighs, and grabs a towel, throwing it to me.

"Thank you," I mutter, closing the door so I can get dry and covered.

By the time I step out into the hallway, Gabriel's not here. I head into my bedroom, grabbing my clothes and step into them.

I hear noise coming from outside, so I open the door, spotting Gabriel in the kitchen, cooking dinner. He's been cooking dinner for me every night, and even though I've been trying to keep my distance, he always keeps it on a plate for me.

Guilt stabs me in my chest, wondering if he'll do it again today. I need to get over these feelings for him, but staying away isn't helping either.

I reluctantly step out into the hallway, and he turns around when he hears my footsteps. "You're here."

"Yeah." I breathe out a sigh, sitting on the stool at the kitchen island.

He frowns. "So you're not avoiding me anymore?"

I open my mouth to come up with an excuse, but Gabriel cuts me off.

"Don't lie to me," he says. "Please. Just tell me the truth." He steps closer, crossing his arms as he looks at me. "Did I say something to make you feel like you needed to keep your distance?" he asks, his Adam's apple bobbing when he swallows. "If I made you uncomfortable—"

"What?" I interrupt, confused. "No, of course not."

His shoulders slump with relief, but the question is back on his face. "Then what?" he asks. "What did I do?"

"You didn't do anything, Gabriel." None of this is his fault. It's all me. I'm struggling to be around him when these feelings just keep growing, and I don't know how to control them.

"So, why's you been avoiding me?"

"I just… I'm having some personal issues I need to deal with. But it had nothing to do with you," I lie, pressing my lips together.

"Are you sure?" he asks, lifting a brow in question. "Because I'm done with this keeping our distance bullshit, Trevi. I want to see you." He does? "Even if you're having a shitty day, and don't want to talk, we can sit in silence and watch a movie." He shakes his head. "But please don't close yourself off from me again."

His eyes bore into mine, and I smile, my breath catching in the back of my throat. Why does he do this? He makes it so easy to fall deeper for him, when I know it's one-sided.

"I won't," I promise him.

"Good," he says with a smile. "Do you want some food? We can even watch those stupid reality shows you like so much."

A laugh escapes me as I nod.

I can pretend.

For as long as these feelings last, I can pretend.

The problem is, I'm not sure they'll ever go away.

Twenty One

Melissa

I didn't have the easiest time growing up. My mother left before I even hit puberty, and my dad was struggling to raise me on his own. And on top of that, I was shy, and anxious all the damn time. I could barely form two sentences if I was ever called on by a teacher to answer a question.

I like to think I've grown since then. I'm still shy from time to time, and the anxiety never really left, but I can stand up to myself. I can talk to people – thought I prefer not to – but the one thing I can't do is to talk to guys.

Zaria though has the complete opposite problem. I think that's what drew me to her in the first place. How carefree she is. She was always the funny one, the confident one, the one people love to talk to. And even now, in a packed café, that's still the case, because the barista can't keep his eyes off her.

"What can I get you?" he asks, the corner of his lips lifting in a smirk as he looks at Zaria.

She, however, is completely oblivious to the fact that he's is ogling her, since her eyes are on her wallet. "One large coffee, black and…" She lifts her head, and looks over at me. "What are you having?"

"A hot chocolate is fine," I tell the barista, who's still staring at Zaria.

Zaria and I shift to the side, while we wait for our drinks, and the barista follows her movements. "He's cute," I whisper, nudging her on the arm.

Zaria finally acknowledges the guy, because she lifts her head, and their eyes meet. "Then go ask for his number," she says, smiling at me.

I roll my eyes. "How are you not seeing that he can't keep his eyes off you?"

"He was?" A puzzled expression sweeps across her face.

A chuckle leaves me. "Yes. How did you not notice?"

She shrugs. "I don't know. I mean, I haven't really noticed any guys recently."

My brows lift in surprise. "Because of the doctor you've been seeing?"

"Maybe," she mumbles, her lips twitching.

Nudging her on the arm, I gape. "It's serious?" I ask. "Why didn't you tell me?"

"He's resisting to move forward because he's a few years older than me," she says with a sigh.

"How much older?" I ask, intrigued.

"Eight," she says with a smirk. "I know it's a little older than I usually go for but… I really like him."

"And have you told him you don't mind his age?"

"Multiple times," Zaria says with an eye roll. "He hasn't explicitly referred to me as his girlfriend, but…"

"But?" I probe.

Her face breaks out into a wide smile, her eyes lighting up. "But we've been doing very relationshippy stuff," she admits. "I've even slept over a few times."

"You have?" I frown, wondering how I could have missed it. Zaria often comes home late, and our paths usually cross only on weekends. I can't help but feel a pang of guilt for being so absorbed in thoughts of Gabriel.

Here I am, upset that she didn't tell me about the guy she's seeing when I'm hiding a huge secret from her, too.

"I think I'm ready to settle down, M," she says with a smile. "And I think I want it with him."

"Black coffee and hot chocolate," the barista calls out.

Zaria moves first, grabbing her coffee, finally aware that he's plainly checking her out, but I guess she's not interested.

"Thank you," I tell him, grabbing my drink from the counter.

"God, I needed this," Zaria groans when we sit at our table. "I feel like I haven't seen you in forever. I've been so busy recently," she sighs. "What's been going on with you?"

"Nothing really," I admit, taking a sip of my hot chocolate. "My life's boring."

"It couldn't have been that boring if you went out on a date with Gabriel."

I freeze mid-sip, my eyes widening as the hot liquid threatens to go down the wrong pipe. A coughing fit follows, and I set my cup down, desperately trying to catch my breath.

"What?" I manage to gasp between coughs.

Zaria looks at me with a mix of concern and amusement. "Are you ok there?" she asks. "Do I need to do CPR?"

I shake my head, trying to recover from almost dying. "I'm fine," I breathe out. "What did you say before?"

"Oh, about the date?" she questions. "Gabriel told me."

"He did?"

"Yeah," she replies with a lift of her shoulder. "Was it supposed to be a secret?"

"No," I say, shaking my head. "I just… when did he tell you?"

"A few days ago," she tells me. "He told me how Mason was giving you a hard time, and he helped you out."

Helped me out. Yep. That's exactly what he did. And I spent the whole night having those stupid butterflies that made me believe a little piece of him wasn't acting. But I know that's not true.

"I was… surprised," she says, taking another sip of her coffee. "It was a little weird to hear that my brother basically took you out on a date." Her face screws up, and she shakes her head. "But honestly, I was surprised he was the one who told me instead of you."

I swallow hard, my throat feeling dry and gravelly. "Are you mad?"

"No," she reassures me, reaching out to cover my hand with hers. "I'm struggling to come to terms with it, sure, but I'm not mad."

The tension leaves my shoulders, and I start to wonder if I should tell Zaria about Gabriel. Maybe she'll take it better than I think.

"Of course," she continues, "If you were to actually date him that would be different."

"It would?" I ask, my voice taking on a higher pitch than usual.

"Yeah, I mean…" She shakes her head. "It would be too weird. You're like my sister, M. And he's my brother, it's just… no. Too weird to think about." She takes a sip of her drink, almost wanting to wash away her previous words.

I sink into my seat, feeling a little guilty for even having these feelings. The worst part though, is that I can't talk to Zaria about it.

"Good thing it won't ever happen," she says with a laugh. "Besides, I know Gabriel's not into the whole relationship thing. It's why him and Lucy didn't work."

"Yeah," I agree, my heart shattering into pieces. It's not like anything is ever going to happen with Gabriel, I know that, but hearing your best friend clarify ever reason why it's a bad idea, sucks.

"Hey." We lift our heads, seeing a guy standing beside our table. He looks to be a little order than me, and relatively attractive. And it doesn't hurt that he's tall as hell. Not as tall as Gabriel though. No. Stop thinking about Gabriel.

"I know this is forward," he says, his eyes on me. Wait. Why is he looking at me? "But I just wanted to tell you, you're beautiful."

I blink, staring up at him. "Me?"

A soft laugh escapes him. "Yeah," he affirms, looking at me. "I've been watching you since you walked in, and I knew I had to talk to you, or else I'd regret it."

I gape up at him, unable to form any words.

"Can I take your number?" he asks, pulling out his phone.

From the corner of my eye, I see Zaria smiling at the whole interaction. I, however, am freaking out.

I've been on two dates since I graduated college, and they both bombed. I stopped trying since then, knowing that it would just make my nerves sky rocket.

I don't need a relationship. I've never needed anyone, or craved it.

Except for Gabriel.

The memory of his hand in mine at the staff party brings a comfort, and a warmth that washes over my body.

But I know that he doesn't feel anything for me. Not like I do. Those things to him are out of pity, kindness. He'd do those things for Zaria. It doesn't mean anything, and I need to understand that.

"Sure," I tell him, surprising Zaria, and myself. I don't usually do this, but if I'm ever going to attempt getting over Gabriel, I have to find a way.

"Great," he says with a grin, handing me his phone.

I type my name, and number, and save it on his phone, handing it back to him once I'm done.

"Melissa," he says, smiling as he looks down at my contact on his phone. "Beautiful name for a beautiful woman." My cheeks heat under the compliment. "I'm Shawn."

"Nice to meet you, Shawn."

"Nice to meet you too, Melissa." His grin shows off his perfect, white teeth as he pockets his phone. "I'll call you," he promises, before walking out of the café.

"Did that really just happen?" Zaria asks, gawking at me.

A laugh escapes me as I shake my head, hardly believing it too. I can't help but feel guilty over the fact that I'm going out with another guy while I have these unresolved feelings for Gabriel. They're constant, and overwhelming. I can't stop thinking about him, wanting him, needing him. And I don't know how to make it stop.

"Look at you," Zaria says, grinning from ear to ear as she pokes my cheek. "You're blushing."

My cheeks heat, and I lift my hand to touch my burning face. What would she say if she knew it was about Gabriel?

I need to get over him, and going out with someone else is a good start.

I just hope it's enough.

Twenty Two

Gabriel

The apartment feels empty.

I understand it's my sister's day off, and she wants to hang out with her best friend, but I've been missing Melissa like crazy today.

We usually spend the afternoon together alone since Zaria works late. I cook for her, we watch movies, or those dumb reality shows her and my sister go crazy for, and we spend the whole evening talking, laughing.

I fucking miss it.

Fighting the urge to pull out my phone and stare at the time again, wondering where they are so late, I head into the kitchen and start cooking. Mel gets hungry as hell at night, and I love cooking for her.

I love doing anything for her.

Leaning over the counter, I grab everything I need, and start cooking the first thing my mom ever taught me to make. I happen to know Melissa loves it, too, but that's just an additional factor. I'm not strictly making this dish because I know she likes it.

A sigh builds in my chest. Who am I kidding? If I found out she liked sky diving, I'd get on a plane the next day.

So when I hear laughing from the other side of the door, I stop what I'm doing, and turn to look as she enters the apartment, her eyes crinkled with joy as she laughs along with my sister.

Zaria gasps when she sees me standing in the kitchen, my arms crossed as I look at them. "Oh fuck, I almost forgot you were here," my sister says, placing a hand to her heart dramatically.

I roll my eyes. "It's almost dark out. Where else would I be?"

She shrugs, throwing her purse on the couch. "Looking for apartments maybe. Have you found one yet?"

I lift an eyebrow in amusement. "Is that you politely asking me when I'm leaving?"

"I'd never do that," she says with a glare.

I know she wouldn't. I might be a year older than her, but we grew up pretty close. Our parents always taught us to rely on each other, to be a team instead of arguing.

And for maybe half of the time, we were a team. But of course, we argued too. It's inevitable when you're siblings.

"I'm still trying to look for one close to work." My stomach churned with the idea of leaving. If I was so messed up after spending one day without having Mel there, how would I react when I'd be living alone?

After I move out, the likelihood of Melissa and I talking regularly like we do now is slim. Really fucking slim.

"And the restaurant you wanted to open?" Zaria asks, leaning against the island as she grabs a piece of bread and rips it before stuffing it in her mouth. "Is that still happening?"

"You're opening a restaurant?" Melissa's eyes widen as she joins Zaria, sitting on the stool beside her.

"That's the plan," I admit with a shrug. "There's still some issues though… with the location." I run a hand down my beard, not wanting to divulge any more than that. Melissa doesn't know this is mostly because of her, and I'd rather not tell her.

"Wow," she says with a smile that almost brings me to my knees. "Congrats."

The praise from her makes my chest ache, wanting to kiss her for it, but knowing I can't. "Nothing's set in stone yet, Trevi," I say with a smirk.

She returns my smile, and I just let myself look at her. Want her. Need her.

"Okay, this is weird," Zaria breathes out with a disgusted expression on her face. "You're complimenting each other." Her head shakes. "It's weird."

My smile disappears with Zaria's words. I don't know why I thought I could let myself imagine being happy with her. I can't. Not when it would affect Zaria. And seeing by her reaction from a *smile* between us, it would affect her a hell of a lot.

"You wanted us to get along," Melissa reminds her, furrowing her brows.

"I know," my sister replies, shaking her head. "I did. I thought when you came over to my parent's house you were putting on an act, but I can see you're clearly not. It's just going to take some getting used to, that's all." Zaria straightens off the island and wipes her hands of any crumbs. "I'm going to take a shower. When's dinner ready?" she asks, gesturing to the pots behind me.

"Half an hour," I inform her, turning the stove on. "Will you be done by then?" My eyes narrow at her.

"Yes," she says with an eye roll. "You have no faith in me."

I laugh, shaking my head. "You forget I've lived with you before."

She waves me off, and disappears into the bathroom, leaving Mel and I alone in the hallway.

"Hungry?" I ask her, draining the can of chickpeas.

"Are you making what I think you are?" Her eyes widen, and my heart stops beating.

I love her eyes. I love how big they are. I love the green swimming around in them. I love how beautiful they are. "You're really excited about something so easy to make."

"Easy for you," she says with a frown. "I can barely make grilled cheese without burning it."

I scoff. "How do you survive, woman?"

"Takeout," she says simply, lifting her shoulders. "It's easy, and quick, and I have no dirty dishes when I'm done."

I lift an eyebrow, glancing toward the sink that's piling up with dishes. "You may be on to something."

She laughs, and the sounds shoots straight to my chest. Love that sound. It's shame I don't get to hear it often. Her phone starts to ring, and the laugh settles as she glances at the screen and furrows her brows.

"Hi?" she says, to whoever is calling her. It better not be Mason. If he's calling her after I told him to leave her alone, I don't know what I'll do to him.

I can't hear who it is, but it must not be Mason since Melissa laughs. It's not the laugh she just shared with me, though, this one is controlled, forced even. "Yeah, Shawn right?"

Shawn? Who the fuck is Shawn?

She told me about Mason, but I don't remember anything about a Shawn.

"Tomorrow?" she says, her brows shooting to her hairline.

My pulse starts to race as I try my fucking hardest to concentrate on the chickpeas cooking in the pan, but my attention is solely on Melissa.

"Yeah. Of course. I'm available."

She's available?

For what? An interview? A doctor's appointment?

Please don't let it be what I think it is.

Please.

"Ok," she says with a smile that breaks my heart. "I'll see you then."

She hangs up the phone, and I busy myself with squeezing the tomato puree into the pan, my stomach fucking churning at the possibility of Melissa actually going on a date.

"Who was that?" I ask, trying to keep my voice calm, avoiding looking at her.

"Why?" she asks.

I turn around, my jaw clenched when I see the confused look on her face. "You're going on a date?"

146

She laughs, bitterly. "All of a sudden you care about my life?"

I've always fucking cared.

That's the problem.

"I'm just wondering if you're replacing me," I say with a shrug, smelling the tomatoes burn, and not giving a shit.

"Replacing you as what, exactly?" she asks, confusion flooding her expression.

Crossing my arms over my chest that's beating a million miles a minute, I let out an indifferent sigh. "As your fake boyfriend."

She shrugs. "I'm no longer in need of a fake boyfriend, so no."

My nose stings with the burnt smell, and I turn around, quickly moving it off the stove, and turn back to face Melissa. "So you're looking for a real boyfriend?"

She scoffs. "Something like that."

Fuck.

I hate this feeling.

I fucking hate that I can't do anything about it. I just want to grab her, and tell her I'll be her fucking boyfriend if she wants.

Can't do that though.

All the rules and shit.

"Why now?" I ask, running a hand over my beard, hating myself for ever pushing her away, and getting close to her all at the same time.

"Why do you care?"

Because I fucking want you, and I can't have you.

Because this is breaking my heart.

"Do you even know who this guy is? What he wants?" I ask. What I really want to tell her is that she'll never find anyone who wants her as bad as I do. Who would give her everything she asked for, if I could. "Where did you even meet him?"

She frowns, and I feel like an asshole for putting that frown on her face. "I met him at the café today," she says. "And we didn't get into that. That's why we're going on a first date."

First date.

First fucking date.

Which will probably turn into a second, then a third, and then she'll probably marry the bastard because I can't get some fucking balls and make a move.

Fuck, I hate this.

"That's... surprising."

It's not like I thought she'd be single forever. I mean just look at her. She's drop dead fucking gorgeous. It's expected that someone would want her.

She flinches back, her face tightening with hurt. "Is it really that impossible for you to believe someone wants to take me out on a date?"

What? Did she really think I didn't know with every fiber of my being that anyone would be lucky to be in her presence?

"I know I'm not your type," she says, her lip dropping into a frown. "I hear you loud and clear, but that doesn't mean someone else won't be attracted to me."

Not attracted to her? Not my type? Fuck. I really have made a mess of things when it comes to her.

"Why are you being a dick?" she asks, shaking her head. "I thought we were friends."

Friends. She reduced us to being friends.

Teasing her was easy. She'd say something back, and we'd rally, and I loved seeing the fire in her eyes. We didn't see each other as often because of it, and therefore I wouldn't have to stare at the girl I've always wanted.

But friends?

Being friends with her is fucking torturous. I have to laugh, and smile, and act like everything is fine when every time I look at her, my heart threatens to jump out of my chest.

I can't be her friend. I can't sit and watch her date other guys, and kiss other guys, and make a life with another guy.

I can't fucking do it.

My jaw clenches as I look at her, and I hate myself for ever thinking I could. "Maybe I don't want to be your friend."

Her mouth gapes open, shock taking over her features as she shakes her head. "What?" she asks, her voice slightly cracking. "Why not?"

I look away, the hurt on her face too much to bear and glance at the stove, placing the pan on the heat again. "Dinner will be ready in ten," I tell her, adding the cooked chickpeas to the sauce.

I don't turn around again, but I hear her murmur, "I'm not hungry," before she shuts her bedroom door.

Twenty Three

Melissa

I'm going to be sick.

While this tight, bubbling feeling in my stomach could be interpreted as excitement, I know from past experience, that it's the complete opposite.

I haven't been on a date in over a year, never having felt the urge to. I'd work, come home, go out with Zaria here and there, and that was fine for me.

But that was before I caught feelings for my annoying, irritating roommate.

When we hang out, I find myself reaching for him, even though I know I shouldn't, and while he was a huge asshole yesterday, the feelings are still there, brewing in my chest.

And I hate it.

Being in love fucking sucks. I don't know why people crave it so much.

By the time I get to the bakery that Shawn told me to meet him at, I'm exhausted, and nervous, and half way to crying.

This is why I don't go on dates.

I'm too much of a nervous wreck for this.

What do I say?

What do I do?

Do I kiss him at the end, or is that too forward? And what if we don't get along? What if he's a serial killer?

A groan escapes me when I reach for the door handle. Why did I ever agree to this?

My head lifts at the sound of bells when I walk inside, an older, blonde woman behind the counter flashes me a smile, as I walk toward her.

The place is pretty packed, and while I'd usually find that nerve-wracking, this place is pretty cozy.

"What can I get for you, darling?" she asks, flipping over a page in her notebook.

Should I order before Shawn gets here? What if he doesn't come, and I stand here like an idiot waiting for him?

"I'll have a croissant, please."

"Coming right up," she says, nodding and moves to make my drink.

Rummaging through my bag, I grab hold of my wallet, and pull it out. I'm overthinking this way too much. Just because I agreed to come here today doesn't mean anything. If I don't like the guy, I can always just leave.

"You want a refill, darling?"

I lift my head to correct her when I'm cut off by someone standing behind me.

"I'd love that."

My body tenses, and I draw in a breath, instantly recognizing that voice.

Gabriel.

I spin around, and lock eyes with him, a sly smirk playing on his lips. "Hey, Trevi," he says, nonchalantly.

I shake my head. "What are you doing here?"

His towering figure envelops mine as he reaches around me, grabbing the fresh coffee from the counter. "Just enjoying some coffee," he says with narrowed eyes before he takes a step back and takes a sip.

"Here?" I ask, narrowing my gaze at him. "Where I'm supposed to be on a date?"

He shrugs, taking another sip of his coffee. "Must be a coincidence." My eyes track as he moves past me, and sits down on an empty table.

I lift an eyebrow at him. "You're really not going to leave?"

The asshole just smiles, leaning back into the chair. "Don't worry about me," he says. "Have fun on your date."

The bells of the door ring again, and my head instinctively turns. I catch sight of Shawn walking in, a smile breaking across his face as soon as he spots me.

"Hey, you're here," he says when we approaches me.

I'm painfully aware of Gabriel sitting right beside us, but I try to put it out of my mind and return his smile. "I am."

His eyes drop to the croissant in my hand, and he laughs. "And you ordered?"

"I thought it was safest in case… you know," I trail off, not wanting to let him know how much I was overthinking this whole date.

"In case?" he asks, lifting a brow in question.

I sigh. "In case you didn't show up."

"Ah." He smiles, shaking his head. "I'm sorry I was a little late. I came straight from work," he says gesturing to the expensive looking suit on his body. "I wish you had waited for me to pay for you. I did ask you out on a date after all."

"That's fine. You don't have to pay for me."

"Are you sure?" He gestures toward the display case. "You want anything else? How about a coffee?" He pulls out his card, and calls out to the woman behind the counter. "I'll have two coffee's."

"Really, it's ok." I dip my head, seeing Gabriel watch with a cocky smirk on his face. "I don't want anything."

"C'mon. It's just a coffee."

"She doesn't like coffee, man."

My eyes widen at Gabriel's voice, and Shawn furrows his brows when he looks at Gabriel. "Who are you?"

"No one," I answer before he can. I'm not sure this date will go down well if Shawn finds out Gabriel's decided to become my temporary bodyguard, and came to stalk on my date. "He just overheard me telling Suzy over here that I don't like coffee."

Shawn glances at Suzy, who thankfully remains silent, and then redirects his attention to me. "You're not a fan of coffee?" he questions, as if the idea is preposterous.

"No," I admit, my cheeks growing hotter the more he stares at me.

"Huh. That's… ok. Is there a reason?"

I shrug, wanting to be done with this conversation. "Just not my thing, I guess."

He frowns, but tries to recover by smiling. "Just your croissant, then?" he repeats.

I nod, thankful he's not trying to buy the whole bakery again. "Yeah. I had a late lunch." The lie slips past my lips, but thankfully Shawn buys it.

Reaching over the counter, he grabs his coffee and walks over to an empty table.

"He sounds like a winner."

My gaze narrows at Gabriel, who wears a mix of disgust and amusement. "Stay out of it," I whisper to him. When I face forward again, Shawn has his hand raised, signaling me to join him.

I sit down, opposite him and place my croissant on the table, my appetite completely gone from the nerves swimming in my stomach.

"So, Melissa," he says, taking a sip of his coffee. "I'm glad you came out with me today."

"Me too," I lie, feeling like this day was a huge mistake. One, that Gabriel is witnessing from only a few feet away.

"So, can I ask what you do?" I notice his eyes dipping to my outfit.

"I'm a teacher," I tell him.

His eyes widen with intrigue. "A professor?"

I shake my head. "A middle school teacher," I amend. "I teach the third grade."

The intrigue is wiped clean when he furrows his brows in confusion. "So, you work with… kids?"

Did that sound patronizing? "Yep," I say, ripping off the corner of my croissant, needing something to chew on.

He chuckles, running a hand over his brown, styled hair. "Like a clown?" His attempt at a joke makes me frown.

"Um… not really?" I swallow down the croissant. "I have a masters in English. I just chose to work with kids instead of teenagers."

He shakes his head. "That was a bold choice."

"Why so?" I ask, curious as to why he's acting like this.

He shrugs. "Most people want to do something meaningful with their lives."

My brows furrow. "You don't think teaching is meaningful?"

"It can be," he says with a nod. "But at third grade, what are you really teaching them? Nothing you say or do is going to impact their lives."

I frown, remembering all of the teachers that impacted mine growing up. Especially when my mother had left, and my dad was still trying to figure out how to raise me on his own.

"I, however, am a lawyer," he says, making me blink out of my thoughts. "I work as a criminal defense attorney."

"Wow," I murmur, totally uninterested. "That's interesting. I—" My words are cut off by a ping coming from my phone. "Sorry," I tell him, reaching for my phone. "I forgot to silence it." Hopefully it's Zaria with some kind of fake emergency, and I can get out of here.

But when I open my phone, the name on the screen isn't Zaria.

Gabriel:

That guy sounds like an asshole.

Gabriel? I glance up, seeing him stare down at his phone, his jaw clenched tight. We had each other's numbers – a courtesy of Mr. and Mrs. Anderson in case of an emergency – but we had never used it. Ever.

His message sits at the top of the screen, and I frown, reading over his text, when my phone pings again.

Gabriel:

> Ditch him. This asshole
> isn't the guy for you.

My frown deepens when I read his new message. What the hell is he doing? The whole reason I accepted this date was to get over Gabriel, and now here he is, crashing my date and telling me to ditch him?

"Is everything okay?" Shawn asks. I debate telling him I need to leave, but I know that if I do, then Gabriel wins. And I can't let that happen.

"Yes," I affirm, setting my phone on the table with a smile. "Everything's fine."

"Good. So do you want to hear about it?"

"Huh?"

"About my job, you said it sounded interesting."

"I did?"

"Yes," he says, with a smile. "But we don't have to talk about work if you don't want to." Thank god. "What do you like to do in your free time?"

I shrug, ripping off another piece of my croissant. "I like watching movies, I guess. But my guilty pleasure is watching reality TV," I admit, chuckling before I throw the croissant in my mouth.

He grunts, tugging on his tie. "I'm not really a fan," he says, making me swallow hard at how displeased he looks. "I find them a little trashy and mindless. Do you like to read?" he asks, his brows raising.

I open my mouth to reply, when my phone lights up. Thankfully, I silenced it this time, but the brightness on the table makes it unmistakable. With a groan, I pick it up and open Gabriel's newest message.

Gabriel:

> Seriously? Trashy and mindless?

> C'mon, Trevi. Ditch this guy. I'll watch reality shows with you.

My heart skips reading his words, but I beg myself not to fall for it. I don't know what game he was playing, but I'm not interested in playing. One day we were laughing, and joking around; and the next he tells me he doesn't want to be my friend.

Shawn clears his throat, and I glance up at him. "I'm sorry," I say, with an apologetic look. I hate to admit it, but Gabriel's texts have been more entertaining than the guy sitting in front of me.

"Are you sure there isn't anything wrong?" he asks. "Because you've been getting texts non-stop."

"Yes, I'm—"

My words are cut off with another text flashing on the screen.

I quickly glance down at it, seeing Gabriel's name.

Gabriel:

Emergency.

Emergency.

The texts keep coming, one after the other.

Gabriel:

Tell him you have an emergency.

I'll get you out of here.

"For crying out loud," Shawn exasperates, running a hand through his hair.

"I'm sorry." I press my lips together as I lift myself off the chair. "Can you give me a moment? I need to go to the bathroom."

"Sure," he says, with very little conviction.

I lock eyes with Gabriel and head toward the narrow hallway. I don't have to turn around to know that he's following me.

When we're away from other people, I turn around and shake my head, seeing him stare down at me with that... face. His stupid, attractive face that I hate, and love at the same time. "What the hell is wrong with you?" I whisper-yell. "First you're a complete dick to me, and then you show up here. How did you even know I'd be here." I shake my head, my body growing hot with anger. "*Why* are you here, Gabriel?"

His eyes lock onto mine, and he slightly parts his lips, exhaling a deep sigh. "I'm just trying to look out for you."

I laugh, bitterly. "Are you kidding?" I ask. "After you told me you didn't want to be my friend anymore? Isn't that what you said?"

Closing his eyes, he throws his head back, releasing a low groan. "Fuck. I—" He shakes his head. "I didn't mean that. I was just pissed at you, okay?"

"Why?" I ask, a wave of confusion washing over me. "What did I do to make you pissed at me?"

"You were jumping at the opportunity to go out with a guy that you don't even fucking know," he says, crowding me. "And look how that turned out."

My lips part, and I force myself to breathe as I shake my head. "He's not that bad," I murmur, the conviction in my voice barely there.

"Bullshit," he insists, his voice making my legs weak. "He's not the guy for you, Mel. He has nothing you want."

I lift an eyebrow. "And how do you know what I want?"

Moving in closer, Gabriel closes the distance until he's standing so near that I can feel the warmth of his presence. He slowly lifts his hand, and tucks a stray strand of my hair behind my ear. Our eyes lock, and all I can hear in this narrow, dark hallway is the thudding of my heart beating uncontrollably against my chest, and my heavy breathing.

"Because," he murmurs, his tongue tracing along his bottom lip The intensity in his gaze makes me speechless, and all I can do is stare up at him, as he leans in and whispers, "I know you."

I blink, my breaths coming faster and heavier as his eyes lock on mine. This is too much. Gabriel can't come barging in my life like this and flip it upside down, just to leave again. "If you knew me, then you'd know that I hate being rude. I'm not going to just ditch Shawn because you think you know what's best for me."

His eyelashes flutter as he blinks, and he finally drops his hand, and steps back at the sound of my firm tone. "You never seem to have an issue being rude with me."

Unbelievable. I scoff, shaking my head. "That's because you managed to make my life a living nightmare every chance you got. I wasn't going to sit and take your bullshit."

"But you will with him?" he asks, stepping closer to me. "You'll let him berate you and tear down everything you love?"

"Like you've done for the past ten years?" I ask, pushing at his chest. He flinches, a hurt expression crossing his face. "He's no different than you, Gabriel." A laugh bubbles out of me, but it hurts. "Actually, that's not true. At least Shawn thinks I'm his type." His jaw clenches, and I force myself to continue. "It's not your place to tell me what to do. Especially when you said you didn't want to be friends anymore."

"I told you I didn't mean that."

160

"I don't care what you mean," I say, shaking my head. "I'm sick of looking for meaning in your words when I know there aren't any."

"What the hell does that mean?" he asks, furrowing his brows.

It means I need to find a way to stop loving you. "It means that I'm going to go back there, and finish the date. And maybe we'll hit it off and go on a second date."

"You're not fucking going out with him again."

"Careful," I murmur, narrowing my eyes. "You almost sound jealous."

His jaw clenches, and he stares at me before turning around and leaving the hallway, until I hear the unmistakable sound of the bells signaling he left the café.

Forcing myself to take a deep breath, I slowly leave the hallway, spotting Shawn still in his seat, his eyes widening when I sit back down opposite him.

"You're still here," I say, a little surprised he waited for me.

"Of course," he says. "I actually wanted to ask if you'd be willing for a do-over."

"Like a second date?" I ask, blinking. I was talking absolute crap to Gabriel about going on a second date with Shawn. I didn't even know if the guy was interested in me anymore, but if he's still here...

"Yeah. Exactly like a second date. Maybe somewhere quieter, with no distractions?" he probes, glancing down at my phone in my hand.

"Okay," I agree, releasing a breath.

"Great." Shawn lifts off his seat, with a grin, and I follow, leaning forward as he embraces me in a hug. It's a little awkward considering we only just met, but it's not awful. "I'll call you," he says, shooting me a smile.

He pulls back, and heads toward the exit.

"You ok there, darling?" I turn my head to the woman behind the counter as she gives me a weird look. "I hope you don't mind me saying, but it didn't seem like you were too into him."

I sigh. "Was it that obvious?"

She laughs. "I've been on my fair share of bad dates before. I can tell when it doesn't click."

I didn't feel a connection with him, either, but getting over Gabriel is my priority. Maybe if I get to know Shawn, it'll be different.

I hope.

Twenty Four

Melissa

"Woah, M." Zaria's eyes widen, and she lets out a low whistle, her gaze sliding down to take in my outfit. "I know you hate wearing dresses, but you look amazing."

I smile down at her face glowing on my phone screen, the warmth of her compliment making me feel a little better about tonight. "It's not that I hate them," I explain, adjusting the straps of my red satin dress that has seen very little wear. "I just never really get the chance to wear them." Given that my work involves being around kids, jeans almost always become my default choice.

Other than occasionally going out with Zaria whenever she managed to convince me, there was rarely a reason for me to dress up, and I didn't have a strong desire to do so either. However, tonight is an exception.

Shawn called two days ago and planned a date at Prime Vista, one of the more upscale restaurants in San Francisco. If I didn't already suspect he had money after the suit he wore last week, it's clearly evident now from his choice of venue for our date.

"Are you sure this isn't too much cleavage?" I ask her, warily, gesturing to the low-cut top that, with a slight adjustment, could easily lead to my boobs spilling out.

She laughs, shaking her head. "No such thing."

"There definitely is," I retort, shooting her a glare. "I don't want everyone staring at me when I walk in."

Her lips twitch, and a glint sparkles in her eyes. "Trust me. They'll be staring even if you don't show your boobs. You look drop-dead gorgeous tonight."

I relax, my shoulders easing as I break into a genuine smile at her compliment. "You always know how to make me feel better."

"That's what best friends are for," she says with a nonchalant shrug. "Are you sure you'll be okay? Is he picking you up?"

"No. I'm driving there." I run my fingers through my hair, sensing the disapproving expression on her face. "Don't look at me like that. I offered to drive there."

Zaria lifts her brows, shaking her head. "If a guy didn't pick me up, I'd block his number. That's like Dating 101."

I scoff, a playful grin forming on my face. "Did the doctor pick you up tonight?" I ask, raising an eyebrow.

Her eyes narrow, a sly smile playing on her lips. "His name is Dominic. And as a matter of fact, he did. He opened the car door for me and everything. I made it clear if he doesn't put in the effort then I'm not interested."

"He does sound amazing," I reply with a smile, happy that my best friend has found someone who takes care of her so well. I can't help but feel a little twinge in my chest, reminding me of how I don't have that. Not even close.

"By the way, where is your date?" I ask, arching an eyebrow. "Isn't he concerned about you calling me instead of spending time with him?"

"I told him I needed to use the bathroom," she says with an eye roll, her laughter echoing through the phone. "I wasn't about to hang up when you called me."

A puzzled expression crosses my face, and a comforting warmth washes over me. "You left your date to answer my call?"

"Of course," she says like it's a given. "I'm never too busy for you, you know that."

A smile curves my lips as I shake my head slightly. "You're going to make me cry. It took me so long to do my makeup."

A chuckle leaves her lips. "And you look amazing," she reassures me. "Seriously, he's not going to be able to keep his hands off you."

Her words make me pause, my smile slipping off my face. I hadn't even considered that, and now I'm unsure about how I feel. The idea of anything more with Shawn feels overwhelming. I don't think I'm ready for that.

I shake the thought out of my head, attempting a reassuring smile. "Seriously, you should go back to Dominic. I'll be okay, I promise."

"Call me if you need anything," she insists, concern softening her eyes. "Anything at all."

"You're on a date, Zaria," I remind her with a chuckle.

"And I'd drop everything if my best friend needed me," she says, with a genuine look in her eyes. "Or you can call Gabriel if you really need to. I'm sure he'd help."

The mention of Zaria's brother sours the mood. Since he crashed my date with Shawn last week, we haven't spoken, or seen each other, and I decide not to tell Zaria about it, knowing she'd just be disappointed.

"I will," I lie, managing a strained smile. "Have fun."

After ending the call, I lift my head, meeting my own gaze in the mirror. A heavy sigh escapes me, and my thoughts linger on how I left things with Gabriel. I shake my head, trying to push those thoughts aside.

The idea of calling Gabriel crosses my mind, but I quickly dismiss it. There's no way I'm going to stoop that low after everything that happened between us. "Stop thinking about him," I mutter to my reflection.

Glancing at the time, I realize I need to leave soon. I open my door, stepping into the hallway, determined to put any thoughts of Gabriel behind me.

But that's impossible when his bedroom door snaps open, and he strides out, his gaze locking onto mine. Since the incident last week, I've been consciously avoiding him, especially after promising myself that I would try to move on from him, but in this moment, any attempt at distance disappears.

His eyes darken as he takes in my outfit, his gaze tracing the lines of my dress, down to my legs, and then slowly making his way back up.

"Shawn?" he asks, his jaw clenching, making it clear he's picked up on my plans for a second date from my outfit.

His voice snaps me out of my involuntary ogling of his muscles visible through the thin fabric of his white t-shirt. Blinking up at him, I quickly stuff my phone into my purse. "Yes," I admit, slinging my purse over my shoulder. "I'm running late, actually. I should get going."

My attempt to move toward the door fails as Gabriel steps in front of me, his eyes dropping with a pained expression on his face. "Don't go," he pleads, the vulnerability in his voice making my pulse race out of control.

"What?" I ask, disbelief lacing my tone.

"Don't go tonight, Melissa," he repeats, his throat moving visibly as he swallows hard. "Please don't fucking go on a date with that asshole."

"Why not?" I ask, confusion painting my expression. "You don't even know him."

"And you do?" His eyes narrow, a flicker of anger shining in his eyes. "What the hell do you know about him?"

I blink at his tone, shaking my head. "Give me one good reason why I should stay, Gabriel."

His eyes lock onto mine, frustration brewing in them. I notice his jaw clenching, almost keeping himself from speaking. His lips part, and I think he's going to give me a reason as to why he's acting like this, but he releases a resigned sigh instead. "Just… don't go," he pleads.

A scoff escapes me. "I don't have time for this. You can't just ask me to just stand him up."

"I'm not asking," he insists, leaning closer, making my breath hitch. "I'm telling you. Don't go tonight."

"You're telling me?" I repeat, shaking my head in disbelief. "You have no right to tell me to do anything. The things I do don't concern you."

"Everything you do concerns me." His voice lowers, and I can almost feel the intensity rumbling through his chest and vibrating through my own.

"Let me go," I tell him, staring up into his dark eyes. "You're not my father, you're not my brother, and you're definitely not my fucking boyfriend, so why do you care?"

A rough groan escapes from the back of his throat. "Don't push it, Melissa," he warns, the warning in his voice hanging heavy in the air.

"Or what?" I push, defiance sparking within me. The intensity in his eyes is undeniable as his gaze burns into mine, lingering on my mouth. My lips part on impulse, and the anticipation makes my breath thick and heavy. I've never seen him look at me like this, and a curiosity ignites within me, demanding to know what it means.

"You better shut that pretty mouth, or I'll do it for you," he threatens, a heat simmering in my core from his proximity. He's so close, I can smell the rich, deep scent of his cologne and it invades my senses, making me feel dizzy under his presence.

"Make me."

Two words.

Two words, and Gabriel loses control, groaning as he slides a hand to grab my face. "Fuck it." That's his only warning before his lips crash into mine, eliciting a gasp out of me as he devours my mouth.

Gabriel is *kissing* me.

Gabriel is kissing *me*.

His hand slides in my hair, tugging it back and my lips part, allowing his tongue to enter my mouth, sliding across my own. A moan rumbles out of me, but unfortunately it breaks the moment because he pulls back suddenly.

"Fuck," he curses, his chest rising and falling as he breathes hard. His eyes widen with regret as he runs a hand over his face. "Fuck. I shouldn't have done that," he says, making my heart crash and burn to the pit of my stomach.

I lift my fingers to my mouth, still feeling his kiss against my lips. I haven't been kissed in a long time, but I don't ever remember it being that intense before. "Do you regret it?" I ask him, anticipating his response.

He drops his hand, fixing his gaze on me. His tongue darts over his lips as he breathes hard, his eyes locked onto mine. "Do you?" he questions, his brows knitting together.

I shake my head, and take a step toward him. His eyes swim with uncertainty as I press my hands against his chest, and feel the strong, erratic beat of his heart beneath my fingertips. "Kiss me again," I whisper in a breathy murmur as I slide my arms around his neck.

His eyes widen, surprise etching across his features. "You're serious?"

I nod, leaning on my tip toes to press my lips to the corner of his mouth. "Kiss me, Gabriel," I plead, a whimper leaving my lips.

"Fuck, Mel," he groans, brushing his lips against mine and pulls me against him, kissing me deeply. His tongue swipes across my bottom lip and I sigh against him, our lips molding together as he tugs at my hair, tilting my head back. When his teeth tug at my bottom lip, my mouth opens on a gasp, and he takes that as his advantage to slide his tongue against mine, groaning the minute he does.

His big hands cup my face, his thumb rubbing against my cheek as he devours my mouth. My need for him grows the more he kisses me, and I grab the back of his neck, pulling him into me.

His groan travels straight to my core as his hand grips my chin, and pulls back, pressing his lips along my cheek, my jaw, dipping down to my neck. My skin tingles when his soft tongue swipes across my skin and he nibbles on the sensitive flesh. A whimper leaves my lips at the sensation, and I tug at his shirt, needing his mouth back on mine.

His breath hits my skin as he chuckles, tugging with his teeth again. "So fucking needy," he murmurs before his lips fine mine again.

Another moan builds in the back of my throat and Gabriel eats it up, groaning back into my mouth. "You're killing me with those noises, Mel," he murmurs against my lips.

Twenty Five

Gabriel

Holy fuck.

Those are the only words I can use to describe what kissing Melissa feels like. There's nothing in the world that compares.

She tastes so fucking sweet. I don't think I've ever tasted anything so sweet before. And the moans she lets out when I kiss her are my favorite noises I have ever heard. They're soft and needy and I fucking eat it up with every kiss.

I've wanted her for so long, I can't comprehend that this is really happening. And to think it wouldn't have if she left tonight kills me. The thought of Melissa going on a date with that asshole, made me fucking lose it, and I didn't even know what I was doing or saying until I realized I had kissed her.

I realized a little too late that I had fucked up. It was the best, and the worst thing I could have done.

Ten years I've spent trying not to go there with her, trying to push her away and make myself forget about her. But forgetting Melissa isn't fucking possible, no matter how hard I tried.

Every single promise I made to stay away shattered the moment my lips landed on hers. And I'm never going back.

"I want…" The words come out ragged and breathy as she mumbles against my lips.

"What do you want, sweetheart?" I ask, pressing my lips to her sweet, smooth mouth. "Use your words."

Another whimper that shoots straight to my cock leaves her lips and she shakes her head. "I…"

"Say it," I whisper, tracing my tongue over her neck. "I want to hear you say it."

She exhales a sharp breath. "I want you…" I nibble on her skin, loving her breathless moans. "I want you inside of me."

I groan, diving back in to kiss her full mouth like my life depends on it. She's so fucking sexy, and doesn't even know how much. Her hands roam over the short strands of hair, pulling me into her.

I want her so bad.

Playing with the straps of her little, red dress, I drop them down, wanting it off her body. My cock twitches at the thought of finally seeing her. I pull back from her lips, and tug her dress over her head, throwing it across the room. My eyes zone in on her bare breasts, and the tiny scrap of her black, lacy underwear.

Jesus fuck.

She's the most beautiful thing I've ever seen.

Her cheeks redden under my ogling, and she attempts to hide her bare chest with her arms, but before she can hide from me, I dive in and wrap my lips around her sensitive nipple.

"Gabriel," she moans making me groan around her. Those noises are going to be the death of me. Swirling my tongue around her hard bud, I suck it in my mouth, feeling her melt in my arms.

"Did you wear this for him?" I whisper, moving to her other, neglected nipple and tug with my teeth.

She moans, tilting her head back. "Please," she begs, squeezing her eyes closed.

"Eyes on me," I snap, pulling back completely. Her eyes open and she breathes hard, looking down at me. "Tell me. Were you going to show him this?" I ask her again, grazing my fingers along the hem of her underwear.

She shakes her head, her lips parting in desperation.

"Good." My hand slips inside, and I spread her open, letting my fingers get coated in her arousal. "Fuck, Mel," I groan, feeling her drip all over my hand. "You're soaked." She moans again, and I dip down, plunging a finger inside her. She hisses at the tight fit, and I curse, feeling my cock leak in my pants. "And so fucking tight."

Jesus. The feel of her clenching around my finger makes me lightheaded. Her hips buck against my hand, wanting me deeper, and I give her what she wants. I take her nipple in my mouth as I thrust my finger deeper inside her, feeling her tight pussy contract around me.

"I've wanted you for so long," I pant, lifting my head to look into her eyes. "You have no idea how many times I fisted my cock thinking about you, thinking about this."

"Please," she begs, grinding her clit against my hand. "I want you."

"Want me to take care of you, baby?" I ask, leaning down kiss her full lips. "You want me to fuck you?" My finger curls inside her, and I use my thumb to rub slow circles over her swollen clit.

She nods, her lips parting as the orgasm courses through her, making her clench hard around me, beautiful moans leaving her lips. "Oh god," she whimpers. "I'm…"

"Come baby," I murmur, kissing her. "Come all over my hand."

Her body twitches as she settles from her orgasm, moaning into my mouth. The cold air hits my skin as she lifts my shirt up, and runs her hands all over my skin. "I need to see you," she murmurs, attempting to lift my shirt higher.

I help her out, pulling off my shirt until my skin is exposed. Her eyes widen, need glimmering in her gaze as she drinks me in. It doesn't take long until she reaches for me again, pulling off my belt until my pants come flying off too. I can't fucking wait to feel her.

I clutch her ass in my hands, pulling her into me as I lean down and kiss her again, addicted to the taste of her lips. "Hold on, baby," I whisper between kisses before hoisting her up so her legs wrap around my waist.

My lips meet hers again as I walk her over to the kitchen island, propping her down on it. She shivers from the cold porcelain against her back, and I chuckle, breaking the kiss to trail my lips down her neck, her breasts, until I reach her stomach. "I want to taste you," I mumble against her stomach, pressing kisses all over her skin.

When I glance up, waiting for her answer, she nods, a harsh breath leaving her lips.

Fuck yes.

Her lacy underwear taunts me as I grip the hem, pulling it down her legs. My nostrils flare when I fling them across the room, and stare down at her bare skin, her thighs coated in her arousal. "You're so fucking beautiful." Without hesitation, my hands grab her thighs and I spread her out for me, looking at her pretty little cunt dripping wet for me. "I can't wait to feel you come on my tongue."

A soft, little whimper escapes her when I dip down and flick my tongue over her clit, teasing her, playing with her. It isn't long until she's writhing against my mouth, letting out frustrated groans as I continue to torture her with soft flicks of my tongue.

Her taste surrounds me and I groan against her when she whimpers, frustrated as hell, and finally suck her clit into my mouth. Her breathless screams make me way too close to embarrassing myself and coming in my jeans.

"Gabriel," she pants, grinding against my face.

"I know, baby," I murmur, spreading out her pussy before flicking her with my tongue. "You taste so fucking good."

"Oh god. I'm gonna…"

"Come, Melissa," I urge, sliding a finger back inside her soaked entrance. "Come on my tongue, baby. I want to feel you."

"Ughh. Fuck," she moans, throwing her head back as she comes, her body twitching as she does.

Kissing her was fucking amazing, but giving Melissa pleasure is the best thing in the world. I love hearing her sweet moans, seeing her flushed face, having her body shake against mine. I could do this all fucking day, and night.

"Fuck, Mel." I lift my head, leaning over her on the kitchen island. That was the hottest thing I have ever experienced.

Our lips meet, and I grab the back of her thighs, lifting her up once again. She buries her flushed face in the crook of my neck.

"My bed or yours?" I ask her, dying to feel her on my cock.

"Yours." Her voice comes out muffled and I chuckle, kicking open my bedroom door. I don't want her out of my arms, but I also want my time with her, so I drop her onto my bed, and kiss her again, devouring her mouth like I've been wanting to for the past ten years.

Fantasizing about her all those years was nothing close to reality. She beat every one of my fantasies by a mile.

Her naked body grinds against my cock, and I pull back, lifting an eyebrow at her eagerness. "Patience, baby. We've got all night."

"I want you," she says, her lips dropping into a frown.

"I want you too," I reassure her. "So fucking bad, but I don't want to rush this. Let me take care of you."

She moans when I bring my lips to her neck. "You have," she breathes out. "I want to see you. Please."

Her eyes burn into mine when I move back, and I nod, wanting her to have anything she wants.

The little tease licks her lips making my cock twitch and her eyes drop to my boxers, her soft fingers running a path over my erection before she grabs the hem and pulls them down and off.

Her eyes widen as my cock flings straight up, leaking at the tip at the sight of her. She swallows visibly, and I can almost hear every thought in her head.

"It'll fit," I assure her, an amused smirk on my lips.

"How do you know?"

"It might be tight at first," I say, remembering how tight she was around my finger. "But we'll go slow until you stretch for me."

Her eyes widen with a spark of intrigue and she breathes heavy. "What if—"

"Mel," I whisper, pressing my lips to her forehead. "Don't overthink this. If you don't want to do anything, we won't. If you want to stop, then we will. I'll take care of you, sweetheart. I promise."

She pulls her bottom lip between her teeth, watching me as I walk toward my nightstand, and pull out a condom from the drawer. Was I planning on sleeping with anyone while living here? Fuck no. I never thought this would ever happen, and I definitely wasn't interested in sleeping with anyone else, but thank fuck I remembered to bring some.

Melissa watches, intrigued, as I tear off the wrapper, and roll the condom over my slick cock, stroking my hard length as I try not to blow at the sight of Melissa, naked and wet in my bed.

She buries her head in her hands, groaning. I chuckle, pulling her hands away. This girl thinks too much. I have no doubt there are about a million thoughts running through her head at this moment. But I need her to know she has nothing to worry about. "You still want me to fuck you?" I whisper, staring into her eyes I love so much.

She nods, chewing on the inside of her mouth. My gaze narrows down at her, noting her nervous tick. "I'm going to need to hear you say it, Mel. Tell me what you want."

She releases a shaky exhale, her lips parting, and her gaze meeting mine. "I want you to fuck me," she whispers, her soft voice turning me on.

"Good girl, baby." Leaning in to press my lips against hers, I lie her flat on the bed, crowding over her as she opens up for me, spreading her legs to accommodate for my size.

My body tenses, hissing a breath when I feel her pussy against my cock, dying to be inside her. "Open up." Grabbing my cock in my hand, I bring it to her entrance, resting it there. Mel's breath quickens when I slip the tip inside of her. "You still with me?" I ask her, shaking as I beg myself to have some control.

She nods again, and I push deeper inside of her until she winces, biting her lip. "Fuck," I groan, feeling her tighten around me. "You feel fucking amazing."

"Gabriel," she gasps, clutching my face in her hands. "Fuck me. Please."

Forcing myself to go slow, I push deeper, and deeper until she's completely full of me. I mumble words under my breath, waiting for her to accommodate for my size.

"Are you going to move?" she asks, breathlessly.

Stars fill my vision when I blink down at her. "I need a minute," I tell her, attempting to pull out an inch. "If I move, I'm going to bust." Her laugh makes her move against me, and I groan when pleasure curls up my spin. "You think that's funny?" I ask her, narrowing my eyes at her.

"Maybe," she teases, a smirk playing on her lips.

A dark laugh leaves my lips. "I'm going to make you regret that." Before she can process my words, I pull back and thrust in to the hilt, making Mel gasp, and grip the sheets above her head.

"Holy fuck," she breathes out.

"Still think it's funny, sweetheart?" She shakes her head, a desperate moan spilling out when I start to move inside of her, shifting on my knees to get closer, needing deeper inside of her.

"You're so deep," she cries out, throwing her head back in pleasure.

I thrust again, feeling her contract around me and sounds of pleasure spill from my lips involuntarily. The pleasure coating my body is unlike any other. I've never felt this with anyone. "Look at me, Mel," I pant, my voice ragged. "I want you to look at me when you come on my cock." Leaning forward, I let my pelvis grind against her clit, and she moans loud enough for the neighbors to hear, and grips the back of my neck.

"I'm… fuck. I'm going to come again," she cries out, squeezing her eyes closed.

"Open." Her eyes snap open, locked on mine. "Focus on me. Come for me, baby."

Her lips part as the orgasm takes over, and her pussy clamps around my cock, riding it out. Fuck, I'm going to come.

She shakes, her pussy pulsing around me. "Fuck me," I groan, slowing down my movements before I blow.

"That's what I'm doing."

She yelps when I smack her ass, lightly. "Don't test me, woman." Pulling out of her, I grab her hips, and flip her onto her stomach. She glances at me over her shoulder, and the look in her eyes, makes me groan. She's so fucking hot when she's drunk from orgasms. "I want another one," I pant, slowly sliding back inside of her. Making Melissa come is my new favorite hobby, and I want to feel her come on my cock again.

"I can't." Her gasp turns into a moan when I lean over her, and nibble on her jaw, playing with her swollen clit.

"You can," I whisper, rubbing circles over her clit. "And you will." I thrust hard into her, feeling her clamp around me. Fuck, I need her to come before this ends. I don't want this to end. Ever.

"Gabriel," she cries out, her forehead covered in sweat. "Fuck. Fuck. Fuck."

"You feel so fucking good," I murmur against her skin, wanting to live inside of her. "You were made for me, baby."

Pulling her hips against me, I thrust hard, hitting a spot inside of her that makes her back arch, and moan even louder.

"Yes," I grunt, feeling her pulse around me again. "Fuck, I'm gonna come." The feel of her clenching around me is too much to bear, and I spill inside the condom, coming on a groan.

Mel falls onto the bed, and I follow, crashing beside her, sweaty and panting, and a fucking wreck. Holy shit. That was better than I ever thought possible.

"Did that really just happen?" Melissa mumbles, her voice barely audible as my ears ring from the immense pleasure.

I turn my head, gently grabbing her face in my hands, and lean forward to press a light kiss against her forehead, damp with sweat. "I'm right here with you, Mel. Please don't overthink this." I don't want her thinking too much, and coming to the conclusion that this was a mistake. Being with her could never be a mistake. I was just too dumb to realize that.

Those bright green eyes swim with uncertainty, and I press my lips to them, kissing her shut eyelids one by one. "I'll be right back," I whisper, lifting off the bed to go to the bathroom.

I tug the condom off my cock, and tie it up, disposing of it. I need to remember to take the trash out tomorrow, before Zaria finds a condom in the trash, and starts asking questions.

The high fades at the reminder of Zaria. My sister was the reason I decided to not make a move on Melissa before, even if I've practically loved her for years, even if I never thought I'd find someone else I wanted as much as her. And now, I've gone and fucked my sister's best friend.

I want to feel guilty, and know that I was right in not getting involved with Mel. But after what just happened, there isn't an inch in my body that feels guilty. I've wanted that girl since before I even knew what love was, and now she wants me too.

I don't know what I'm going to do about Zaria, but my priority is making sure Melissa knows where this is heading. I want her to know I'm all in. For as long as she'll have me.

I grab a warm washcloth, ready to take care of my girl, knowing she might be a bit sore for the next few days.

A smile creeps onto my face as I remember everything we did, excited about doing it all over again. I head out of the bathroom, eager to see her, to kiss her, to touch her, wanting to do everything I denied myself for so long.

But when I walk back inside, Melissa's crying.

Twenty Six

Melissa

"Hey, hey." I lift my head to see Gabriel stand above me, gently brushing the hair out of my face. "What's wrong, baby?" he asks, searching my face for answers. "Did I hurt you? I know I went a little hard before, but—"

"No," I say, shaking my head. "You didn't hurt me." It was perfect with Gabriel. It was everything I've ever wanted, and didn't think would ever happen. And now I'm crying like an idiot.

"Then what happened?" Gabriel's voice softens, concern etched across his face. "Why are you crying, Mel?"

"I thought you left me," I admit, tears slipping down my face, feeling the gentle brush of his thumbs on my cheeks. The sweetness and tenderness of the gesture only makes me cry even more.

"Sweetheart." The gentle tone of his voice soothes me as I look up at him. "I went to grab you a warm towel." My eyes drop to the towel in his hands, and he leans in, planting a soft kiss on my forehead. "Lie back, Mel."

I ease back on the bed, and I feel the comforting touch of Gabriel's hands as he runs the warm cloth over my thighs, making his way up to my over sensitive clit. My body involuntarily winces as he makes contact with it, and he moves the cloth back to my inner thighs. "Are you sore?" he asks.

"A little," I admit, biting my lip when he runs the warm cloth over my pussy, wiping up the mess we made.

"Want to go shower together?" he asks, pressing his warm lips to my inner thigh.

"Maybe later," I mumble, a moan building in my throat as he continues his kisses. "Can you just... hold me for a bit?"

He lifts off the ground, gracefully settling onto the bed beside me. His arms wrap around my body, cradling my face as he whispers, "I'll always hold you, sweetheart." The warmth of his embrace and the softness of his words make my worries dissolve as his lips find mine, and I sigh into the kiss.

"Can you tell me why you were crying?" Gabriel asks, his voice gentle. "If you want to tell me, you can. I want you to be able to trust me."

I hesitate, wanting to tell him, but hating the thought of having to repeat the story. "I do trust you." With my eyes tightly closed, I blurt out, "My first time was in college."

His lips turn into a frown, and I force myself to continue. "I had this roommate, Stella, who loved going to parties. She used to try to get me to come along, and I never took her up on it. It was never my thing," I admit. "But it got to a point where she'd stop inviting me, and I just felt... alone. Stella didn't really talk to me much once she realized I'd turn her down, so one day I told her I'd go."

Gabriel's gaze focuses on me, and he rubs his hand up and down my back. "I've never dated anyone. The only guy I had kissed was my prom date in high school, and… it didn't end well. When he came up to talk to me, I didn't know what to do," I tell him, sensing him tense up. "No guys had been interested in me before, so when he couldn't keep his eyes off me, I let him flirt with me, kiss me, and I let him take me upstairs to his room."

I squeeze my eyes closed, my body growing hot at the reminder. "I should have waited for someone else. I should have tried to date, but… I just felt so behind everyone else. I just wanted to get it over with, but I didn't expect it to go like that." With a deep breath, I blurt out the worst mistake I had ever made. "It lasted all of three minutes. He didn't ask if I was ok, didn't ask if I liked it. He didn't even know my name," I admit with a bitter laugh. "He just zipped up his pants, and left me there, naked and alone. I had never felt so used, and disgusting."

"You're not disgusting, Mel," Gabriel says, his warm breath brushing against my skin as he presses his lips to my forehead. "That guy was a fucking asshole. If you don't want him to count, then he doesn't fucking count."

"What do you mean?" I ask, my voice slightly shaky as I sniffle.

He lightly brushes his lips against mine. "I can be your first."

"But… you're not."

"I might as well be," he says, kissing me again. "I'm the first guy to make you come, sweetheart. I'm the first guy to feel you clench around me. He doesn't deserve to be your first."

A smile curves on my lips, and I nod in agreement, loving the idea. "Okay," I murmur. "You're my first." I could forget all about that night, knowing that guy didn't mean anything. He was my almost, Gabriel was my definitely.

"And last," he declares, sealing his words with a deep, lingering kiss that leaves my head spinning. I'm so in love with him, and now, finally, I can express it. But when our lips part, I can't help but think about what this means for us.

"I can hear you thinking in there," he says, playfully tapping his finger against my forehead. "What's wrong, Mel?"

"I'm sorry," I sigh, my, my eyes drifting to the ground as I try to sort through my thoughts. "I'm just thinking."

"About what?" Gabriel's eyes narrow, and he eases back a bit, studying my face with a touch of concern.

"About us," I admit, chewing on the inside of my mouth.

His hands cup my face, gently lifting my head to meet his gaze. "Don't do that," he says, gesturing to my cheek. "There's no need to be nervous. Just ask me what you want to know."

"What happens now?" I ask, confusion etching my face. "Are we dating, or is this just a one-time thing, or—"

"Fuck no," he interrupts. "One-time thing, are you kidding? I wasn't playing around when I said you were made for me. I mean it. You're mine, in every sense of the word." He moistens his bottom lip, releasing a sigh. "What happened between us meant something to me, Mel," he says, his throat bobbing as he swallows. "I need you to know that it wasn't just fun for me, it was *everything*."

"It meant something to me too," I admit, feeling my heart beat in my chest. "But... what about Zaria?"

Gabriel releases a sigh, running a hand down his face. "I don't really want to talk about my sister when you're naked in my bed, and your tits are in my face," he murmurs, pressing his lips to my jaw.

"I'm serious, Gabriel," I chuckle when his hand cups my breast, kneading the skin. "What do we do? Do we tell her?"

"Do you tell Zaria everything?" he asks, lifting a brow.

"Yes," I admit. "She's my best friend,"

"Really?" His lips brush over the shell of my ear, making me break out into shivers. "Even about how you've got the hots for her brother?" he whispers, making my hips buck off the bed. "Did you tell her you touched your pretty little pussy thinking about me?"

"No," I breathe out, a moan threatening to slip. Even after all those orgasms, my body still reacts to his touch, wanting him closer.

"Then you don't tell her everything," he says, in an amused tone. "Do you, sweetheart?"

"No," I concede, knowing he's right. I didn't tell her I had a crush on her brother all those years ago, or that I'm in love with him now, so I should be able to keep this to myself, too. "I don't want to lie to her, though," I sigh, thinking about having to lie to Zaria.

"Neither do I," he admits with a groan, his fingers gently grazing my cheek as he pulls back, his eyes intense. "But I want you, Mel. There's no going back from this. I tried to stay away from you for way too long, I'm not doing that anymore."

"I want you too." I shake my head, hating myself for going along with this. "We'll keep it a secret," I suggest, nibbling on my bottom lip "Just until we can figure out how to tell her."

"We'll do it together," he promises, curling his hand around my neck.

My smile widens, savoring the promise in his words, and Gabriel leans in, pressing our lips together until every thought but his touch flees from my mind.

"Gabriel. Open the door. I can't find my keys."

Our eyes widen at the sound of Zaria's voice, and we break apart, lifting off the bed. "Shit," I whisper, frantically looking around. "What are we going to do?"

Gabriel's hands gently curl around my arms, holding me in place. "Stay here," he urges, his eyes concern. "I'll handle this."

He quickly grabs his sweatpants, and pulls them on before he rushes out of his bedroom. I lift my arms, covering my bare chest, hearing Zaria knock on the door.

"Where the hell are my keys," I hear her mutter, slurring her words.

"You can't come in," her brother tells her.

"Why not?"

"Uh..." I squeeze my eyes closed, begging him to think faster. If Zaria walks in, and sees us in this compromising position it will haunt her forever. While I want to tell her someday, I don't want her to find out like this. "Mel's upset. She uh... vomited all over the place."

"Since when do you call her Mel?" she asks. "And if she's upset, I should see her. She doesn't even like you." My stomach drops, guilt racking through me knowing I'm lying to her.

"Just…give me one second," he calls out to her. The sound of the door opening makes my head lift, and I see Gabriel's head pops inside, ushering me out of his room. "C'mon," he whispers, rushing us across the apartment until I step into my bedroom.

I step ahead, but his hand curls around my wrist, gently tugging me back. He plants a firm kiss on my lips. "What was that for?" I whisper with a smile when he pulls away.

"Making up for lost time," he says with a wink before closing my bedroom door.

My smile widens, but as soon as I hear Zaria's voice when Gabriel opens the door, I panic, reaching for my robe to wrap it around myself.

"She's really sick, Zaria. Just let her rest," I hear Gabriel say.

"You're acting weird. Just let me see if she's ok," Zaria replies, knocking on my bedroom door.

My shoulders tense when Zaria walks inside. "Hey." Her words are slightly slurred, as she glances at me, her eyes not fully registering my presence.

"You're drunk," I point out, worry filling my chest.

"What?" she practically yells, waving a hand. "I'm fine. See?" She touches the tip of her nose with her finger, attempting to walk in a straight line, only to almost trip over her own feet.

"Z, you need sleep," I say, chuckling at her inebriated self

"Don't worry about me, what happened with you?" she asks, poking me on the arm. "Gabriel said you threw up?"

Crap. "Uh… yeah," I lie, avoiding eye contact with her. "I… ate some bad fish."

She nods. "So the date was a bust?" she asks. "Or did it go well?"

"It was a bust," I confirm, only now thinking of Shawn. I didn't even call to cancel, but if I'm honest, I didn't want Shawn. I just wanted to move on from Gabriel.

"Let's get you into bed," I say, helping her up when she starts to drift off. Her arm links around mine, and I open the door, seeing Gabriel out in the hallway. Our eyes lock, but we don't say anything as I open Zaria's door, and get her into bed, propping her on her side in case she throws up.

Once Zaria starts snoring, I quietly leave her bedroom, seeing Gabriel sat on the couch, his arms crossed. "Hey," I whisper.

"Is she asleep?"

I nod, walking over to him. He pulls me in, and softly cups my face. "This is going to be so fucking hard," he says with a groan. "How the hell am I supposed to stay away from you?"

"You managed before," I point out. "I'm sure you'll manage now."

His eyes narrow. "It was fucking agony for me, Mel. And that was before I had tasted these lips." His thumb brushes over my bottom lip, tugging on it. "And now that I have?" He shakes his head. "It's going to be fucking torture."

"I'll make it worth it," I whisper, my lips curling in a smirk.

"Yeah?" he asks, raising his eyebrow. "How so?"

My arms wrap around his neck, and I lean in, pressing my lips to his. "When Zaria's asleep, I'm all yours."

He breathes hard. "You're mine when she's awake too, sweetheart, don't forget that." His lips meet mine in a soft kiss. "We'll just have to hide it a little longer."

"As long as I have you, it'll be fine."

He smiles, kissing me deeper, sliding his tongue inside of my mouth until I moan. "You'll always have me, baby."

This was what had been missing from my life. This feels like home.

He feels like home.

Twenty Seven

Melissa

This is agony.

It's been two days since Gabriel and I officially got together, and it was also the last time we had kissed.

Somehow, my lie became Zaria's reality, and she ended up getting food poisoning from the fish tacos she ordered for her hangover cure.

I've always taken care of Zaria, especially when she gets drunk, or hungover, so it's not a rare occurrence for me. But I haven't been able to be alone with Gabriel because of it.

I turn my head, and our eyes lock, already finding him looking at me. Attempting to hide my smile, I pull my bottom lip between my teeth, but he catches on, shooting me a grin.

But when Zaria groans for the umpteenth time, and rests her head on my shoulders, my smile drops, snapping out of it before she notices.

"I feel horrible."

"You've said that ten times today, Zaria," Gabriel replies with a chuckle.

"If you're not sick, you don't get to complain. I feel like my stomach is eating me alive," she groans again.

"I can get you another glass of water," I suggest.

She shakes her head. "Nope. If I eat or drink anything else, I'll puke."

"Warn me before that happens," her brother says.

Zaria narrows her gaze on him. "I'd lift my middle finger if I had the energy."

Gabriel chuckles. "This wouldn't have happened if you ate my cooking," he says with a shrug.

"I needed hangover food, not gourmet restaurant health nut food." Her head tips back on the couch. "Why do those fish tacos have to be so good?"

"Because they're covered in grease," her brother supplies.

"M. Do me a favor and smack my brother, will you?"

"Zaria," I chuckle. "I'm not going to do that."

Gabriel raises an eyebrow at me, his lips curling into a smirk. "Any particular reason why?" he asks. "Have you had a change of heart?"

My eyes narrow at the nickname, and I face the TV, ignoring the asshole who knows he's playing a dangerous game. Zaria might be a little out of it, but she'll still be able to figure out something's going on if he continues.

"I'm just not interested in looking at your face."

Gabriel chuckles, but he doesn't reply, and I start to get suspicious until my phone buzzes in my lap, and I see his name on the screen. I quickly move it out of Zaria's sight, and open up his text.

Gabriel:

> Liar.

> You love my face. And my mouth. And my hands.

My cheeks start to heat, and I flip my phone over, trying to pay attention to the movie that Zaria suggested we watch.

"Can we please watch something else?" Gabriel asks with a groan. "I'm sick of these chick flicks."

"Tough shit," Zaria says. "I get to pick."

I flip over my phone, and type out a message.

Melissa:

> You didn't mind watching them with me.

From the corner of my eye, I see Gabriel turn over his phone, and a minute later, my phone buzzes in my hand.

Gabriel:

> I didn't care about the movie, sweetheart. Only that you were there with me.

My body grows warm, and before I can even think, I get another text.

Gabriel:

I miss your mouth.

Melissa:

On where?

A choking sound comes from Gabriel and I fight the urge to smile, knowing I'm affecting him.

Zaria's head snaps to her right, and she looks confused, but luckily, she doesn't say anything.

My phone lights up with another text.

Gabriel:

You trying to kill me?

Melissa:

Just teasing like you've been doing. It's not nice is it?

Gabriel:

When I'm hard as fuck and I can't do anything about it, no it fucking isn't.

Melissa:

You are?

Gabriel:

I'm what? Say it, sweetheart.
Ask what you want to know.

I lift my head, taking a quick glance at Zaria who's eyes are fighting sleep, and type out the text that makes my core grow hot.

Melissa:

You're hard?

Gabriel:

Baby, you made think about your lips around my cock. Of course I am.

A groan slips past my lips, and my eyes widen when Zaria's head turns to face me.

"Are you okay?" she asks, her brows furrowing with concern.

"Yep," I squeak, my voice barely audible, as I shift in my seat, crossing, and uncrossing my legs.

Gabriel:

> You need to be less obvious than that.
> Are you trying to get us caught?

Melissa:

> Of course not.

Gabriel:

> Then be a good girl and stay still. If
> you behave, I'll give you a reward.

I stop moving, trying to remain still as my core clenches around nothing, desperately getting wetter by the second, until I get another text.

Gabriel:

> Is your pussy wet right
> now, sweetheart?

I don't even hesitate, gulping as I press send.

Melissa:

> Yes.

Gabriel chuckles, causing myself and Zaria to turn to him.

"For someone who claims he hates this movie, you're laughing a lot," she says, accusingly.

He shrugs, his eyes locking on mine for a second. "I'm starting to see the appeal."

My phone buzzes again, and I glance down at the screen.

Gabriel:

> Don't worry. I'll take care of that sweet pussy later.

Turning my phone over, I try to put his texts out of my mind, and focus on the movie, attempting not to look over at Gabriel.

Messaging each other while his sister is sitting between us, is too risky, and I don't trust myself enough to act like nothing is happening.

When I feel my phone vibrate on my leg, I try my hardest to ignore it. I last all of ten seconds before I give in and turn my phone over, reading Gabriel's newest text.

Gabriel:

> I think she's asleep.

Turning my head, I see Zaria's head tipped back against the couch, her mouth open, and her eyes closed, and when a soft snore leaves her, I know she's fallen asleep. My gaze shifts to Gabriel as he gestures toward my bedroom. I lift off the couch, covering her with a blanket before I follow Gabriel into my room.

As soon as we're alone, and he closes the door, he spins me around, and crashes his mouth to mine, sliding his tongue in my mouth tasting me for the first time in two days.

"I fucking missed you," he grunts, breaking the kiss to lift me up, skillfully wrapping my legs around his waist. I love how big and strong he is, and how he takes control.

His hands roam up my stomach, lifting my tank top as he goes until he pulls it off me and throws it across the room. A gasp leaves my lips when my back hits the bed, and his lips press along my jaw, sucking the hollow skin of my neck. "It's fucking torture," he whispers, moving his lips down my body before taking a nipple into his mouth, "being around you and not being able to kiss you."

My sweats are next to go, but Gabriel halts, teasing the hem of my panties as his eyes lock on mine. When I nod, his face lights up into a grin and he pulls them off, groaning at the sight of my bare pussy.

"You've been completely drenched this whole time?" he asks, his fingers lightly grazing my pussy.

I nod, a whimper leaving my lips when he leans in and kisses my clit so gently I almost scream. I want his mouth on me so badly.

"Don't worry baby," he murmurs, his hot breath teasing me. "You were so good, and I promised you a reward." He parts my pussy, shifting on his knees to come closer. "Now let's see how hard you can come." A hot breath escapes me, waiting for it, needing it. "Can you keep quiet?"

Quiet? I shake my head in agony, knowing I'll be a whimpering mess by the time he's done with me.

Gabriel chuckles, lifting off his knees. I turn my head in confusion wondering where the hell he's going, when I see him open my nightstand, and pull out a pair of my red, lacy underwear. His eyes shine with lust as he bunches it up and holds it out to me. "Open," he says, shoving them in my mouth when I open my mouth as wide as it can go. "Be a good girl and scream into those."

My eyes snap closed, waiting for him to do whatever he wants. My legs start to shake when I feel his hands on me again, parting me wide open. When his tongue flicks over my swollen clit, and he slides two of his thick fingers deep inside of me, I moan loudly into the underwear, intense pleasure washing over me.

I open my eyes when I don't feel his tongue on me, to find him smirking. "You need to be quiet, sweetheart," he says, curling his fingers inside of me. "If you make too much noise, I'll spank you. Got it?"

I nod, eagerly wanting him to touch me again, and he does just that, lapping up my pussy, drinking my wetness before he sucks my clit into his mouth, french kissing my pussy like a man starved.

Another moan escapes me when his fingers curl inside me, hitting a spot that makes me see stars. I bury my face in my hands, attempting to stifle my moan, but when my ass stings from a light smack, I moan even more, knowing I didn't do a good job.

My pussy clenches around his fingers as his hand rubs the smooth skin of my ass. "You like when I spank this ass, sweetheart?"

I nod, whimpering into my panties when his tongue finds me again. He keeps his focus on my clit until I'm shaking so hard, and the orgasm ripples out of me. "Fuck," he grunts, keeping his mouth on me as I let go, riding his fingers.

Leaning up onto my elbows, I look down at his between my legs as he pulls out his fingers and wraps his lips around them, cleaning up my wetness. His eyes roll to the back of his head, and a deep groan escapes him as if it's the best thing he's ever tasted before.

When he lifts off his knees, my eyes drop to the bulge in the front of his pants, and I lick my lips, wanting to taste him.

"My turn," I breathe out, reaching for his belt.

He chuckles, lifting my chin with his thumb. "You want my cock in your mouth?" he asks, a smirk on his lips.

I nod, unbuttoning his pants, and pulling them off. It's been two days, but I still remember how big and thick he is, so when he slides his boxers off, and his cock springs free, I start to panic a little. I know he's been with other girls, whereas I've never done this before.

I gulp, looking up at him, and he senses my apprehensions because his fist curls around his cock, and he strokes it for me, showing he exactly how he likes it.

"Give me your hand," he grunts.

I slowly wrap my hand around his cock, admiring how thick it looks compared to when he was stroking it. My eyes lock on Gabriel's, and I start to move my hand up and down, copying his previous movement.

"Fuck, that's it," he groans, tipping his head back, when I stroke him harder, and faster. My mouth waters at the sight of his cock in my hand, and I deicide to be bold, scooting closer to him until I can wrap my lips around it.

"Mel," he groans. "Fuck, yes, baby. That feels so good." His hips thrust, and I move down, working him inside my mouth. The tip of his cock stabs the back of my throat when I move too far, and I gag, pulling back as tears stream down my face.

"Slowly," he says. "You don't need to take me all the way. What you're doing feels amazing, baby." His thumb caresses my cheek as he brushes away the tears falling down my face from choking on him. "Relax your throat."

Leaning my head back, I open my mouth wider, and attempt to relax my throat as he slides inside my mouth again. "Take what you can," he says. "I love your mouth on me."

Moaning around his cock, I move him up and down, sliding my tongue over his thick shaft. His groans fill my ear as I suck his cock faster, managing to keep him from going too deep.

"Fuck yes, Mel," he grunts. It's the only warning I get before his cum hits the back of my throat, coating my mouth with it. Gabriel pulls out on a groan, staring down at my mouth, filled with him. "Swallow it," he tells me, his eyes darkening with lust. "Swallow me down, baby."

I gulp, swallowing his cum before licking my lips. The salty taste isn't unpleasant like I thought it would be, and I lick my lips, cleaning every last drop.

"You're so fucking perfect." He tilts my chin up, and smashes his lips against mine, kissing me deeply.

Not wanting to be done, I wrap my hands around his cock again, stroking him.

"Mel," he groans, pulling back. "I want to be inside you again, so badly, but…" He shakes his head. "I want my time with you. I want to kiss you slowly, and fuck you for hours until you can't breathe."

"I'm pretty breathless right now," I say with a smirk.

He tilts his head, chuckling at my eagerness. "Smart ass," he murmurs. "I'm serious. Zaria could wake up at any minute and find us."

The mood sours, and I drop my hand. "Fine," I sigh, knowing he's right.

"I'm going to take a shower," he murmurs, leaning down to kiss me. I smile against his mouth, wondering if we could take one together, but his eyes narrow when he pulls away, knowing what I'm thinking. "Separately," he warns, a smile tugging at his lips.

He grins, effortlessly slipping back into his clothes. A laugh escapes him as he makes his way toward the door.

"You're fucking trouble," he murmurs, stealing a quick glance back at me. "But you're the best kind of trouble I could ever want."

Twenty Eight

Gabriel

Two weeks ago, the mere idea of me taking Melissa on a date seemed impossible. We were just roommates who were forced into a living arrangement, trying to make the best out of it. I, however, had been head over heels for that girl since before I even know what love was, but of course I couldn't let her know that.

Now, as I knock on her bedroom door, and hear her soft voice inviting me in, a grin spreads across my face. She's become so much more than just a crush. She's my whole entire world, and I'm prepared to show her just how significant she is to me.

"Hey, baby," I murmur, softly closing her door behind me until I hear a click. Her beautiful face lights up, letting me know she loves the nickname, or maybe it's just my presence. Either way, I savor the sight.

"Hey," she whispers back, a hint of a smile on her lips as she leans forward, pressing her lips against mine.

The feel of her lips is intoxicating. I could kiss Melissa for hours, and hours, and never get enough. "Get dressed," I mumble against her mouth.

"Why?" she asks, her eyes still closed as our lips brush together.

"Because," I say, leaning in for a fleeting kiss. I want to relish this moment, maybe get into bed with her and press her body against mine. The thought of being able to kiss Mel without hiding away is enough of an incentive to pull back, breaking the kiss off. "I'm stealing you away," I finish, tugging her covers off.

"Where are we going?"

"Patience, sweetheart," I chuckle, loving how eager she is. "You'll know when we get there."

She breathes out a sigh, climbing out of bed to grab an oversized sweatshirt from her closed. As she slips it over her head, my eyes remain locked on her, unable to look away. She replaces her sleep shorts with denim shorts, offering me a view of her tight, little ass in a teasing pink, lacy underwear that makes my mouth water.

She catches me checking her out in the mirror, and smirks at the sight. I mentally scold myself, questioning why the hell it took me so long to act on my feelings for her. A gasp escapes her lips when she senses me pressing against her back. Without hesitation, I wrap my arms around her waist, and draw her back into me.

"Hey, girlfriend," I murmur with a grin.

Her eyebrows shoot up, and she turns her head to look up at me. "Girlfriend?" she asks, a mix of hope and surprise in her tone.

"Yes," I affirm, kissing her jaw. "Girlfriend, baby, my girl. Take your pick."

"I like all of them," she admits, her face breaking out into a cute ass smile that makes my body warm.

My heart swells with love for this girl, and I draw her into my chest, planting a soft kiss on the top of her hair. "I fucking missed you, Mel," I sigh.

"You saw me this morning," she reminds me, her voice slightly muffled against my chest.

A laugh escapes me. "Yeah, and I fucking missed you then, too." Zaria's constant presence around us makes it hard to see each other, so even though we live in the same apartment, it still feels like we're miles apart, until we can have little stolen moments when I sneak into her bedroom late at night.

Every time I look at Zaria, I'm reminded of how much I betrayed her by getting involved with her best friend. Mel and Zaria have been inseparable since they were fourteen, and I'd be a dick if I was to cause any damage between their friendship. While Zaria isn't exactly one for the dramatics, I'm not naïve enough to believe she'll be instantly okay with our relationship.

Melissa's laughter ripples against my chest, pulling me out of my thoughts. I savor the joy of being close to her and tighten my hold around her. My hardening erection from her presence prods her stomach and she shifts against it. "Someone's trying to get my attention," she jokes.

I lean down, capturing her lips with mine. "You've always had my attention," I whisper against her mouth. Little does she know just how true that statement is. While she's aware of my feelings for her, she doesn't realize just how long I've been burying my emotions for her.

"Stop distracting me," I whisper, narrowing my gaze on her. "I want to be able to get you out of the house before Zaria wakes up."

Interlocking her fingers with mine, I slowly open her bedroom door, and peek out into the hallway, making sure it's empty and Zaria is in bed. "All clear," I whisper, pulling her through the door.

Getting Melissa out of the door is an impossible mission, especially when we're trying to be stealthy, and her shoes are the squeakiest things I've heard. Thankfully, we make it out of the apartment, and inside my car.

"Can I guess where you're taking me?" she asks when I shut the car door.

"No," I chuckle at her impatience, shifting the car into drive as we merge onto the road.

"Fine," she concedes with a sigh as she makes herself busy with turning on the radio, tapping her foot along to the beat.

I'm unable to take my eyes off her, constantly shifting my gaze to look at her sing along, or smile. I've been hooked on her, even when I couldn't have her, and now that I can, it's ten times worse.

"Focus on the road," she tells me, the corner of her eyes crinkling when she laughs at my ogling her. "You'll get us killed."

"I can't help it. You're distracting," I tease, stealing a glance at the road before turning my gaze back to her.

She rolls her eyes, a smile playing on her lips. "Stop flirting with me and drive."

"Never," I whisper, lifting her hand to press a kiss against her skin. The urge to kiss her everywhere is overwhelming. I want to explore every inch of her, from the top of her head to the tips of her toes. I want to shower her with affection, and kiss, lick, and love every part of her.

She leans her head against the headrest, staring out of the window. The soft music fills the silence in the car, as we drive through the dark city, lit by the buildings surrounding us.

As I pull up to the beach, her head snaps toward me, realization dawning when she notices the car slowing down. "Are we here?" she asks, the excitement clear on her gorgeous features.

"I told you to be patient, Trevi," I chuckle, opening my car door. She reaches for the door handle, but I intercept her, opening it for her.

Her cheeks turn the cutest shade of pink as she places her hand in mine, stepping onto the ground and glancing down at the soft texture beneath her feet. "The beach?" she asks, digging her shoes into the sand.

"Yeah." I extend my hand, intertwining our fingers before grabbing the supplies I stashed in the back seat. "Do you like it?" I admit I haven't seen her here often, always searching for her whenever my friends and I hang out at the beach.

"I don't know," she says with a shrug. "I've been a couple of times. It was always too busy for me to enjoy, but I've never been at night."

I grin, pressing a kiss to the side of her cheek as I lock the car and grab the supplies in my other hand. "Then let's go, sweetheart."

Twenty Nine

Melissa

I never really liked the beach.

My dad always tried his hardest to get me out of the house during Summer, but I always turned him down. I hated dealing with the huge crowds of people, strutting around in a tiny scrap of a swimsuit that was uncomfortable, and itchy, and the fact that sand managed to infiltrate every nook and cranny.

Yet, as Gabriel and I walk deeper into the beach, my feet digging into the soft sand, I can't help but feel like I've been missing out this whole time. The beach at night is completely different than it was the few times I went as a teenager. I lean into Gabriel, pressing my head against his chest as we look out into the dark ocean, the moon shining above it as the soft waves crash into shore.

"It's beautiful," I murmur, turning my head to look at him.

"Yeah. I used to love coming here."

A scoff escapes me. "With girls most likely," I murmur, trying to forget the fact that Gabriel has been with other girls.

His hand curls under my chin, lifting my head to look up at him. "While I love seeing you jealous, there's no reason to be, sweetheart," he says with a smirk. "You're the only girl I've ever wanted."

The crisp air hits my skin, making my skin rosy, and flushed, hiding the blush creeping on my face from his words. "How long have you wanted me?"

He chuckles, dipping his head to brush his lips against mine. "A long fucking time."

My eyes drift closed when his lips land on mine, enveloping them in a deep kiss that makes my belly swarm with heat. His eyes search mine, as his thumb gently caresses my cheek. "I wish I could have brought you here in high school," he says with a warm smile. "I have a feeling you'd enjoy it a lot more if you were with me."

"Not even you could get me to enjoy the beach."

His smile widens, his hands cupping my face. "You're enjoying it right now," he points out.

I roll my eyes, unable to stop smiling. "That's because it's just me and you here. If we were in a crowded place, I'd be begging you to go home."

He chuckles, unravelling the towel he brought, and lowers it to the sand, pulling me down to sit beside him. "I'd never do that to you," he says. "I wouldn't bring you somewhere you'd be uncomfortable."

"I know you wouldn't," I say with a smile, remembering how considerate he was at the staff party, always checking in with me to see if I wanted to leave. "You know me better than anyone else."

"I told you I did," he says, nudging my arm before opening the pizza box.

I want to call him out on being arrogant, but he's right. "So… is this a date?" I ask him, tucking my knees into my chin. We haven't had the chance to go out yet without Zaria being around, so the prospect of this being our first date excites me a lot.

"Yes, sweetheart," he says, leaving soft kisses on my cheeks before finally finding my lips. "The first of many."

His kiss makes me dizzy, and I breathlessly pull away from him. "Wasn't the diner our first date?" I ask. "Technically speaking, of course."

"I counted it," he says with a shrug. "But this is the first date where you're officially mine."

My cheeks ache from constantly smiling, but honestly, I'll take it if it means I get to be this happy. A memory floods back of the last time I felt this genuinely content, and I look out into the water reminiscing on it.

"The last time I was here, it was with my dad," I murmur, taking a bite of the pizza. I remember him hoisting me over his shoulder, hauling me into the water with him, and I let out a laugh. "It was my thirteenth birthday, and… I didn't exactly have too many friends to celebrate with," I admit, my face heating with embarrassment. "He took me all over the city that day, but the beach is what I remember most."

I quickly blink back the tears, wishing I had known it would be the last time I went to the beach with him. I would have appreciated it more, I would have gone every summer like he asked me to, instead of saying no.

"You must miss him a lot," Gabriel says, wiping away a tear that slips down my cheek.

I nod, attempting to hold back the tears. "He was the best father I could have ever asked for. He tried his best to be everything I could have ever needed when my mother left us." Gabriel reaches out, squeezing my hand. "She didn't even fight for me. I don't even remember her saying goodbye to me. One day she was here, the next she had left, and my dad was telling my she had moved halfway across the world."

"You don't need her, Mel," he says, pressing his lips to my forehead. "You're strong, and beautiful, and kind, and she has nothing to do with that. It's her fucking loss."

"My dad was still in love with her," I murmur. "He admitted it to me a few times. He never remarried, and I don't think he ever dated anyone after her either." My eyes close, tears spilling out down my cheeks. "He could have gone with her, but he stayed for me."

"You're worth it," he whispers, wrapping his arms around me.

"I don't know," I say with a shake of my head. "When he got sick, I was all he had. I always wondered whether he wished he'd gone to Spain with her. He could have spent those last few years with her."

"It's not your fault," Gabriel says. "Your mother made the choices she made because she was selfish. She gave up on you, and your dad. Don't blame yourself, Melissa."

I try. Believe me, I try not to, but there are times that I think I'm the reason my mother left in the first place. "Your family is so important to me, Gabriel. They're all I have left."

"They're your family too, sweetheart," he says, concern filling his eyes. "You know we'll always be here for you."

"What about Zaria?" I ask him, swallowing harshly. "What will happen when she finds out about us?"

His eyes close, a sigh leaving his lips. "Come here," he murmurs, pulling me into his lap, sitting me down on his thighs, my legs on either side of his. His cold hands cup my face, gently stroking his thumb across my cheek. "Are you happy?" he asks, staring into my eyes. "With me?"

"You know I am," I reply, my eyebrows tugging together. Although Gabriel drove me crazy in the past, there's always been a part of me that just wanted him to see me. And now he is, and it's the best feeling in the world.

"Then whatever happens, just know we'll go through it together," he says, tucking a strand of hair behind my ear. "My parents love you, Mel. They'll be happy for us. I know they will."

My cheeks turn pink and I smile. "Your mom might already know how I feel for you," I admit.

Gabriel laughs. "She knows I'm crazy about you too," he says. "That woman knows everything."

"And Zaria?" I ask.

He shakes his head. "I don't know how she'll react," he admits. "It was the biggest reason why I pushed you away, but she's your best friend, and my sister. She'll have to be happy for us. Maybe she just thinks I'm too good for you or something. She's always known me as the guy who doesn't do relationships."

"Until Lucy," I blurt out, mentally scolding myself for bringing up his ex-girlfriend. "Why did you guys break up?"

He sighs. "I don't want to talk about that whole mess," he says. "I promise I'll tell you another time. I just… let's spend tonight together before we have to spend the whole day ten feet away from each other," he whispers against my lips, catching my bottom lip between his teeth before he slides his tongue in my mouth.

I moan into his mouth, wrapping my arms around his neck as his hands drift to my ass. He pushes me into him, grinding me over his thick erection. I swallow his groan down while he grinds me down into him. "I want you," I murmur into his mouth. "Now." I make my words clear when I reach down, and palm his cock through his pants.

"Fuck," he groans at my touch. "I didn't bring any condoms."

"I'm on birth control," I whisper, gently biting his jaw.

His body visibly shivers as he clutches my ass tighter. "I haven't been with anyone in a really long time, Mel," he says. "My last test was negative."

I'm reminded of Lucy, wondering what 'a really long time' means to Gabriel. He just broke up with her a few weeks ago. I don't want to ruin the mood by bringing up his ex, again, so I shake it out of my mind. "I trust you," I whisper, looking into his eyes.

"Let's go to the car," he says, lifting me up. "I don't want to get sand in my ass crack."

"Good point," I chuckle, rushing toward the car.

Gabriel wastes no time unlocking the car, and pulling me into the back seat until I'm straddling him again. His hands curl around the hem of my shorts, and tugs them down, pulling them off completely. His eyes lock on the triangle of lace covering my pussy and he groans, tracing the material. "I'm starting to see why you like pink so much."

A laugh bubbles out of me as I reach for his pants, and pull them off, until his cock bobs free, leaking at the tip. My mouth waters, wanting to taste him, but when he curls his fist around his cock and strokes it, I decide I want him inside of me instead.

Wrapping my arms around his neck, I lift my ass, waiting for him to fuck me, but Gabriel just smirks, tracing my underwear again.

"You're so greedy for my cock, baby," he whispers. "You didn't even take your panties off."

I groan, not wanting to waste time. "Get rid of them," I plead, grinding my hips over his erection. "Hurry up."

He chuckles at my impatience, his fingers moving the cloth to the side, before I hear the distinct sound of cloth ripping. I gasp, looking down as he rips them clean off my skin, and throws them onto the dashboard.

"That was my favorite pair," I say, narrowing my eyes at him.

"You told me to hurry up," he says with a shrug. "Now get that needy pussy over here and ride me, sweetheart."

My body shivers as he strokes his length, holding onto my hips before he positions his cock at my entrance. I slowly slide onto him, groaning when his tip slips inside. We've only had sex once, and he's huge, like really fucking big. It takes a while until I've adjusted, and I can lower myself again, letting out a whimper when I do.

"That's it," he coaxes, gently lowering me onto his cock. "Fuck. Look at you, swallowing me whole." My pussy clenches around him at his words, and he groans, gripping my hips. "If you keep doing that, I'm not going to last very long."

"How promising," I tease.

His chest shakes with a laugh. "You do great things to a man's ego."

"Your ego's big enough."

"Not as big as my dick," he says, lowering me another inch, pulling a moan from my lips, when I drop down to the hilt. "Fuck, you feel good," he breathes out, thrusting into me.

I lift my ass, and drop back down, groaning at the friction, and fullness. Having him inside of me without any barriers between us is incredible. And when Gabriel thrusts into me from below, I'm certain I won't last much longer.

"You're so fucking beautiful," he grunts, speeding his thrusts as he grips my sweatshirt, and lifts it off my head, baring my chest. "God, Mel. I was a fucking idiot for thinking I could live without you." Pressing a hand to my back, he leans me into him and tugs a nipple between his teeth, before soothing it with the lick of his tongue. "So beautiful," he murmurs again, lifting his head to lock eyes with me.

"Gabriel," I gasp, slamming down on him again, and again. The windows fog up as sweat coats my skin, and I grind down on him, needing him deeper, harder, faster.

His eyes darken with lust. "Say that again," he demands, cupping the back of my neck.

"Gabriel," I moan. "Gabriel."

"Fuck." A groan rumbles out of him as he leans in and devours my lips, kissing my mouth while he fucks me hard, his hand gripping my hips so hard I don't doubt it will leave a mark. "I'm too fucking close," he says, moving his thumb to my clit. "Come for me, sweetheart. I need you to come before I do."

His thumb continues rubbing over my swollen clit as he thrusts, his groans making me wetter by the second. "Yes," I cry out, feeling my orgasm crash into me.

Gabriel's groans fill my ear as he grabs my ass, and lifts me off his cock, slamming me back down until he fills me with his cum. Gabriel holds me against him until our breathing slows, and we come down from the high.

His head drops onto my chest, and he presses his lips over the skin where my heart is. "There's no one like you," he whispers.

Thirty

Melissa

My face hurts from smiling so much the last couple of days. Our date a few days ago was perfect, and I can't wait until we have a chance to repeat it.

Zaria is constantly in the back of my mind, though. I have to be careful when I'm around her, and Gabriel is there. We sneak around as much as possible, but I'd love to just hang out with him during the day. Every time I see him, I have to fight the urge to kiss him, and honestly, it sucks.

The idea of telling Zaria scares me. I don't want to lose her, or make her feel betrayed by the fact that we're dating behind her back, but I'm also scared to tell her in case she doesn't approve.

Knowing Gabriel is home right now, waiting for me eases me a little. Zaria will be working late tonight, so Gabriel and I can spend some time together without having to act like strangers.

My smile widens when I see my apartment block, but it disappears when I see the last person I ever expected to see. My heartbeat quickens, banging against my chest at the sight of her, and I blink, trying to make sure I'm not imagining it.

It's her. I blink again, my brows tugging together. She's really here. In front of my apartment. I spent so much time trying to convince myself I didn't need her, and I didn't miss her. I even convinced myself that I didn't remember what she looked like, but seeing her here, now, I could never forget.

Her skin is a little darker than I remember, probably because she spent the last thirteen years in Spain. My eyes glance over her light brown hair, lighter than mine, cut just below her shoulders.

I always wondered if any part of me resembled her, especially now that I'm an adult. I have the same pouty lips as her, and the same short nose. I had my dad's eyes, and his dark hair, but I have my mother's face. My lips run dry as I look at her for the first time since I was eleven. She looks just like me, and I don't even know who she is.

Her head snaps to the side, and her eyes find mine. I hold my breath, wondering what she's going to say. But her eyes leave mine as she continues looking around, looking right past me as if I'm a ghost.

My eyes drift closed, feeling the tears brew. She doesn't even recognize me.

Shaking my head, I take a deep breath and walk toward her. I need to know what she wants. I need to know why she's here.

"Mom?" I say, the words feeling funny, and foreign on my tongue. I haven't used that word in a long time.

Her eyes meet mine once again, and this time, her mouth drops in recognition. Her eyes widen as she looks me up and down, shaking her head. "Melissa?" she asks, warily. The one thing I could never remember was her voice. I'd forgotten what her voice sounded like, and now I wish I had never heard it. Her voice is like honey, sweet and thick with a Spanish accent. How am I supposed to go the rest of my life without hearing it again?

"Is this really happening?" I mutter to myself.

"Is this a bad time?" she asks, tugging her brows together.

A scoff escapes me as I glance up at my mother. "As good as any considering you're thirteen years too late."

She drops her eyes, guilt racking through her. "Can we talk?" she asks, her lip wobbling. "Please?"

I probably should say no, and go on with my life, but a small part of me still calls out for her after all these years, and even if it's the last time, I want to be around her, to see her, to talk to her.

The walk from the entrance to my apartment feels like the longest two minutes of my life. We don't talk when we enter the empty elevator, or when the doors open, and I step out into the hallway, or even when my hands shake when I pull out my keys and open the door.

"This is a beautiful apartment," my mother says, running her hands over the kitchen island. "Do you live here alone?"

"No," I mutter as I hang up my coat, and take off my shoes. "I live with my roommate, and—" I bite my tongue when I think better about telling her about Gabriel. She doesn't have a right to know. "And my other roommate," I finish, glancing toward her.

She nods, a faint smile on her lips. "I don't know if you remember," she says, looking everywhere but at me. "I was a real estate agent, just like your dad."

"I know," I reply, flatly.

Her eyes meet mine, and she swallows harshly, the slender lines of her throat moving when she does. "How is he?" she asks.

My eyebrows tug together, and my heart breaks. Did she really never check up on us? Ask around about us?

"Dead," I reply, turning around to grab the coffee pot. "You want some coffee?"

"What?"

"Do you want some coffee?" I repeat, holding up the coffee pot, unable to look at her right now. "Or do you prefer tea?"

"Your dad... he's dead?" Her distressed voice cracks, tugging at my heart.

"Yes." Opening up the cabinet door, I pull out the different coffee beans, trying to read some kind of instructions on how the hell you do this.

"How?" she asks.

I try to rip open one of the bags, but the coffee beans spill all over the counter, and I drop the package, tears stinging my eyes. "Cancer."

I hear her suck in a breath, and I squeeze my eyes closed, begging myself not to lose it in front of her. I have no right to feel bad for her. She's the one who left.

"Can I ask when?"

A heavy sigh leaves my lips, and I turn around, crossing my arms. "He started getting sick when I was around seventeen," I confess, the memory invading my brain. He was eating less, moving less, until he was no longer the strong, brave man I knew. "He died in my freshman year of college."

Her lip trembles as she shakes her head. "You graduated alone?"

"I had my family there. They were there for me when my own mother didn't want to stick around."

Her face drops, making my heart fall to the pit of my stomach. This woman is a stranger to me, but I can't help but feel guilty for hurting her.

"I deserve that," she says, her eyes dropping to the ground.

"Why are you here?" I ask her. "How did you even know where to find me?"

She lifts her head, and nibbles on her bottom lip. "I went to your dad's house. I still remember where it is, but when I didn't see anyone there, I asked around." She takes a step closer to me, reaching out her hand, but then retreats it, realizing I'm practically a stranger. "I wanted to come see you."

"Why now?" I ask, the sound of my heart deafening me. It's beating so loud, I can feel it in my throat. "It's been thirteen years since you decided to leave me, so why now?"

"I didn't leave you," she says, shaking her head. "I wanted to go back home, Melissa. I missed my family."

"I was your family," I say, my voice cracking. "Dad was your family. You missed them, but you didn't miss us?"

"Of course I did." She takes a step closer to me again. "I've thought about you every day."

"Really?" I say with a laugh. "Because for the past thirteen years I haven't heard so much as a peep from you."

"It's complicated," she says.

"Then uncomplicate it," I tell her, wanting to know why she came all the way to America to come find me. "Why are you here?"

She lets out a sigh, pressing her fingers to her chest. My eyes drop down to the ring on her finger. "I'm getting married," she says, dropping her hand. "And I really want you there."

I can't tear my eyes off the ring. "Why?"

"Because your my daughter, Melissa." I lift my eyes to hers seeing them red, and filled with tears. "I want my family at my wedding."

"You're not my family."

"I know you're angry," she says, approaching me. "I understand you must hate me." A laugh escapes me. That's the problem. I don't hate her. I still love her. I still want her. I still need her, and she's not fucking here. "But please don't say that." She shakes her head. "I'm your family."

"Where were you?" I ask her, my eyes brimming with tears. "You say you're family but where were you when I needed you? Where were you when dad died, and I got my first period, and I graduated college? You weren't there, Sofia."

She winces at the use of her name, tears spilling down her cheeks. "Please," she begs. "Please. I know what I did was wrong but—"

"What you did was more than just wrong. It was plain cruel." The pain in my chest intensifies by the second, and I press down on it, feeling my heart break all over again. "Dad still loved you until the day he died," I admit, seeing her eyes widen, glassy with her tears. "And I needed you when he wasn't there anymore."

Gabriel is right. It's not my fault she decided to quit being my mother. She's had years to make it right, and now it's too late. Moving past her, I reach for the door handle, and fling it open. "I have nothing else to say to you." I wipe the tears dripping down my face and wait for her to leave.

"Melissa," she says, approaching me.

"You had your chance to make amends," I say. "There's nothing you can do to fix what you did." I look at my mother one last time as she pleads me with her eyes. She must see I've made my mind up, because she drops her head, and walks out of the door, and out of my life.

As soon as I close the door, I drop to the ground, the pain in my chest too much to bear. Sucking in huge breaths, I try to calm my heart rate down, but nothing is helping. That's the last time I'll ever see my mother.

The thought escalates the pain, my vision blurry as I press my hand to my chest, feeling the air being sucked out of my lungs.

"Hey, hey. I'm here. Breathe slowly." Gabriel's hands cup my face, brushing the hair out of my face as he cradles my head in his hands. "Fuck, Mel. Just breathe for me. Come on."

My eyes open, seeing his face filled with anguish as he caresses my skin with his thumbs. "Gabriel?" I say, sucking in a breath as I try to calm my heart rate.

"I'm right here, baby," he says, brushing his lips against mine. "Just focus on me." My chest rises as I breathe in, staring into his eyes. "That's it." His hand curls around my neck as he pulls me against him, letting my arms wrap around his waist. "Fuck. You're ok, Mel. You're going to be ok." His lips find my forehead as he presses a deep kiss against my skin.

I love you. The words are right on the tip of my tongue as I bury my head into his chest, feeling his big hands rub up and down my back.

"Who was the woman that just left?" he asks, tensing a little.

"My mother," I affirm. While Gabriel had never met her, she looks just like me.

He tightens his hold around me, cradling my head. "Are you feeling better?" he asks, his voice wary.

I nod against him. "Don't let me go yet," I whisper, wanting to stay in his arms forever.

"Never," he confirms. "I'll never let you go."

My stomach flutters, and I lift my head to press my lips to his, melting into his touch, when he kisses me softly.

"Mel," he murmurs against my lips.

"Hmm?"

"Why is there coffee beans all over the counters?"

Thirty One

Melissa

I never thought I'd see my mother again.

he hope and prayers that she'd change her mind and come back home had faded away a long time ago, right around the time my dad got sick.

Seeing my dad like that was hard when I had no one else there. It was just me and him living in that house, and I was the only person he had to take care of him, until I had to leave for college.

I didn't want to leave him alone. He was getting weaker by the day, and the thought of living somewhere else away from him was my worst nightmare. I promised him I'd stay at home and take care of him. I could still drive to college seeing as I was attending Berkely, it wasn't that far away. But my dad didn't want that for me. He made me promise I'd go to college and live my life. I think he just wanted to see me socialize more, but that didn't end up happening either.

I came back to visit him as much as I could. I'd come home every weekend, take him to his appointments, and I'd take care of him as best as I could. Until it was too late.

It was a little over four months after I had left for college, and I was in the middle of class, when I got the phone call that broke my heart. I lost the only person that cared about me that day.

I remember being so angry at my mother, wondering where she was, what she was thinking, if she knew what happened to my dad, why she didn't call. But after she didn't show up at my dad's funeral, I knew she hadn't heard about it, or she didn't care. I forced myself not to think of her ever again.

I'd slipped up here and there, wondering about her, thinking about her, but for the most part I was doing good, until she showed up here for the first time in thirteen years.

"Mmm," Gabriel mumbles, stirring awake. I blink up at him, his eyes fluttering as he tries to open them. His arms tighten around me when he sees I'm awake. "Morning, baby," he rasps, his morning voice causing a smile to spread across my face.

"Morning," I whisper, my breasts pressed against his chest.

He leans down, kissing my forehead, snuggling against me. "I love waking up with you," he mumbles, kissing my cheek, my jaw, my lips.

I chuckle, loving the affection he's showing me. "Me too." Luckily Zaria sent me a text last night letting me know she was sleeping over at Dominic's. While Gabriel wasn't too happy to learn that his sister was sleeping over at some guy's house, his mood lifted when I mentioned that it meant we could sleep in the same bed.

I love waking up pressed against him, kissing him, cuddling with him. It was something I never thought would happen, especially with Gabriel.

"How are you feeling?" he asks, searching my eyes.

A heavy sigh escapes me. "I feel much better." After my mother left, I broke down and talked to Gabriel about her for hours. He held me, and comforted me while I told him every thought I've had about her, and how I felt when she left.

He suggested I look into getting a therapist to help me with all these emotions, and even the occasional panic attacks I deal with. I've thought about reaching out to a therapist before, back when my father passed away, but I always told myself they wouldn't really care about my problems, and I'd just end up being a burden to them.

Gabriel made me realize that it wasn't true, and therapists could actually help me cope with thoughts and feelings I couldn't navigate on my own. "I'm proud of you," he says, pressing his lips to my forehead. "For opening up and letting all those emotions out."

A smile curls my lips, and I fight the urge to tell him I love him. It's way too early, but I know I do. My heart hurts with how much love I have for him. "Thank you for listening," I say, caressing my thumb over his cheek.

"You don't have to thank me. I'll always listen to you." His eyes lock on mine, and he shakes his head, dropping to my chest. "You're so beautiful in the morning," he mumbles against my skin, kissing me neck.

"Gabriel," I moan, unashamed when his lips find my nipple, swirling his tongue around the hard bud. "We don't have time for this. I need to be at work in twenty minutes."

He chuckles against my skin. "I can do a lot in twenty minutes, sweetheart."

"I'm serious," I say, leaning away from his touch before I do something crazy and call in sick.

"Fine," he sighs, pulling the sheets off. "I have a meeting in half an hour, too." With a groan, he gets out of bed, and reaches for a pair of black boxers, pulling them on. "Want me to make you some breakfast?"

"There's no time," I say, sadly, loving when he cooks for me.

He groans, reaching for me, cradling my face in his hands. "One of these days, Mel," he whispers, staring into my eyes. "I'm going to be able to have you all to myself. A whole day where we do nothing but kiss, and fuck, and I cook for you." His lips find mine, teasing me with a soft, gentle kiss. "You want that, baby?"

My body shivers at his words, thinking about what a perfect day that would be. "Yeah," I breathe out, running my hands up his chest. "I want that."

"I'll make it happen," he says. "I promise. Now get in the shower before I take you back to bed and make you scream."

Gabriel laughs when a whimper lets loose, and I turn around, heading toward the door. He's too dangerous. One kiss, and I want to throw away all my plans.

Ten minutes later, I climb out of the shower, and get myself dressed as quickly as possible. I could have gotten out of bed earlier, but that extra time with Gabriel this morning was worth it.

Steam follows as I open the bathroom door, and I walk toward the front door, leaning down to put on my shoes.

A light smack on my ass makes me gasp as I look back, and see Gabriel standing behind me with a grin as he stares at my ass. His gorgeous body in nothing but a pair of black boxers is tempting me to continue what we didn't finish in the bedroom this morning. "Are you done staring at my ass?" I ask, turning around to grab my purse off the counter.

"I spent ten years trying not to look," he says, grabbing my wrist to pull me into him. "I'm nowhere near done, sweetheart." His lips land on mine and I get lost in him, wrapping my arms around his waist.

God, I love when he kisses me. It makes me feel light, and airy, and dizzy. "You're too distracting," I say, pulling back. "You need to get in the shower or you'll be late, too."

Pressing my hands against his chest, I push him back and he grins, allowing me to push him. "I'll be thinking of you," he says with a wink when I push him into the bathroom.

I groan when the door closes, thinking of him under the water, stroking himself to the thought of me. Maybe one day off won't hurt. No. Fuck. I shake my head, snapping out of it. He *is* distracting.

My head jerks when I hear a knock on the door. I frown in confusion wondering who it could be. Zaria's probably at work by now, and Gabriel's in the shower. Who else would come here?

"Just a minute," I call out, walking toward the door. When I open it, and the door flings open, my breath gets stuck in my throat at the sight of her.

Fuck. I forgot how beautiful she is. I haven't seen Lucy since a few months ago when Zaria and I ran into her at a mall. I remember thinking that she's the type of girl Gabriel likes, and I'm nothing like her. My eyes drift down to the dress hugging her figure, the blue fabric a contrast to her pale skin, complementing the blonde hair draping down her back, long and straight.

"I'm looking for Gabriel," she says with a smile, her glossy pink lips making me blink. "Is this where he lives?"

My eyebrows drop slightly, realizing she doesn't remember who I am. Why would she? We only met once, and she was oblivious to me. I was the one obsessing over Gabriel's new girlfriend. How beautiful she was, how I would never be as confident or outgoing or fun as her.

"Hi Lucy," I say. "I'm Melissa, Zaria's best friend. We actually met once."

She blinks, her eyes dropping to my usual work attire of a t-shirt and jeans. "Right. Of course." She shoots me a smile that makes me feel uneasy, and then her eyes flash to the apartment behind me. "Is Gabriel here?" she asks again.

"Uh… yeah, he is," I say, furrowing my brows. Why the hell does she want to know where Gabriel is? "He's in the shower. He should be out any minute."

But Lucy's eyes drift behind me, and she smiles. "I didn't expect to see this so soon," she says, her tone flirtatious.

I turn around to find Gabriel standing behind me, in nothing but a white towel wrapped around his waist. His eyes shift from me to Lucy. "What are you doing here?" he asks her.

"You asked me to meet you, remember?"

My lips drop into a frown. Gabriel's meeting was with Lucy?

"Not here," he says with a narrowed gaze. "I asked you to meet me at the restaurant."

Lucy shrugs. "Guess I got it mixed up."

He's meeting with her? Behind my back? Of course he is. Why did I think he was done with her? He didn't even want to talk about her back at the beach. Was I just someone who was convenient for him while he was living with us?

I shake my head, a laugh bubbling out of my mouth. "I'm such an idiot," I mumble, looking back at Gabriel. "I'll leave you and your girlfriend alone." Turning around, I move past Lucy and rush toward the elevator.

"Mel, wait," Gabriel calls out behind me.

"I need to go to work. Go back to your girlfriend." The word lands on my heart like a heavy blow.

"What are you talking about? Just… fuck. Just come here, please."

I step into the elevator and quickly turn around, pressing the close button as I see him rushing towards me.

Please close before he gets here.

"Mel," he calls out. "Keep the doors—"

"Have fun," I say bitterly before the doors close.

I let my back hit the wall and exhale hard, blinking away the wetness building in my eyes. I should have known Gabriel didn't want me. Maybe he did for a second, but… Lucy is the only he really wants. Not me. Why else would he be meeting with her behind my back?

He's leaving in less than two weeks anyway, if he ever finds an apartment to move into. I need to forget about him, and this whole mess of a situation I got myself into. I'm never going to be enough for him. Too bad I let myself believe otherwise.

Thirty Two

Gabriel

The last thing I ever expected to see this morning was my ex-girlfriend standing next to my current girlfriend.

Or that I'd be standing in nothing but a towel when my girlfriend rushed out of the door, jumping to the worst conclusions when she heard my ex was looking for me.

"Mel, keep the doors—"

My sentence is abruptly cut off as the elevator doors slam shut, and Melissa gets away from me.

"Fuck," I yell, my fingers frantically clicking the elevator button repeatedly, praying that she hasn't gone too far, and I can still catch her.

"Keep it down." I turn my head, seeing an old white lady with a disapproving frown directed at me. The dim light of the hallway outlines the wrinkled lines on her face. "Some people are sleeping."

I lower my voice, offering an apologetic smile. "I'm sorry, ma'am. It won't happen again."

Her eyes drift down my body, widening when she takes in my form. The disapproval in her gaze intensifies. "And put some clothes on," she says, slamming her apartment door closed. I sigh, realizing I'm still standing in the hallway, with only a towel wrapped around my waist.

I tighten my grip on the towel, silently praying that I don't inadvertently flash anyone. The soft ring signals the elevator doors opening, and I hastily turn around, finding it empty. But as I glance down at my semi-naked self, a frown creases my forehead. I can't exactly chase Melissa down the street in nothing but a towel.

I raise my head, locking eyes with Lucy standing outside my apartment, an amused smile playing on her face. "That was quite the show," she remarks, crossing her arms as I step inside, closing the door behind me.

I clench my jaw, irritation running through me. "Cut the shit," I tell her. "I told you to meet at the restaurant. Why the hell did you come here?"

She runs her tongue over her bottom lip, avoiding eye contact. "I wanted to see her," she admits. "Thomas told me you moved in with her."

"I needed somewhere to stay after you kicked me out," I say, narrowing my eyes at her.

"I didn't kick you out," she says with an eye roll. "I told you to *get* out. And besides, Thomas said he offered his guest room."

I breathe out a sigh, pinching my nose bridge. "Thomas talks too fucking much."

She shakes her head, a scoff escaping her. "I was right."

"You weren't," I clarify. "Nothing happened between Mel and me while we were dating. She didn't even like me, Lucy. You knew that."

"And now?" she asks, lifting her head, her eyes locking onto mine. "You can't tell me that little show this morning meant nothing."

My jaw clenches as I glance at my side, choosing silence over a response. The answer is clear. She's always known how I felt about Mel.

"I knew it," she says, a bitter edge to her laughter. Her eyes narrow as she studies me. "How long did it take? A week? A day?"

"That doesn't fucking matter, and you know it. I told you the truth from day one. I've never lied to you."

"No," she concedes with a nod. "You didn't. I knew what we were. But… I thought things were changing."

"It was never going to change," I tell her honestly. "You know I could never love anyone else like I've always loved Mel."

She holds eye contact, her gaze searching for something in mine. A sigh escapes her lips. "She's really pretty."

"Yeah," I affirm, a soft smile playing on my lips. She's so more than *pretty*; she's the most beautiful girl I've ever seen. "But that's not the only reason why I love her."

"She seems nice, too," she comments, her head dropping to the side as she scans the apartment.

I almost laugh. Mel is always nice, to everyone except for me. But that all changed the minute I stopped fighting myself and my lips landed on hers. She opened up to me, let me touch her, kiss her, love her.

"Then why did you come here practically flirting with me, and make her believe something's going on?" I question.

She shrugs. "I met her once," she says, and my brows furrow in confusion. That's news to me. I always assumed Zaria told Melissa about Lucy. "And when I saw her, I kept thinking she's the one you really want. I was just the girl you settled for."

"We both settled, Lucy," I tell her, a tinge of regret in my voice. "We met because we were drunk off our asses, heartbroken over other people. We connected on that one thing, and decided to see if we worked. But we don't," I breathe out, wanting her to realize that we were a mess together. Lucy wanted her ex-boyfriend Ryan, and I wanted Mel. Maybe we were meant to find each other during that time, but we were never meant *for* each other. "We never did."

A couple of months after Christmas, I had come to my parents' house for my birthday, as I usually did. I was eager to see my family, of course, but there was an undeniable excitement about seeing Melissa. I shouldn't have felt that way, but I couldn't help it. Every time I entered a room, my eyes instinctively searched for her.

Except Melissa wasn't there. She always attended my birthday, even if she despised me. She'd call me an asshole, pretend not to get me a gift – which I knew was a lie because there was always an unnamed gift – and then she'd sing happy birthday. But she wasn't there. Because I went too far.

I was so fucked up out of my mind in love with her, not knowing how to navigate it that I pushed away the one person

I want the most. It didn't take long until I found myself on my fifth drink of the night at a bar somewhere, and that's where I met Lucy.

"I know," she sighs, her eyes dropping for a moment before meeting mine again. "We didn't work."

My shoulders settle. I shake my head, wondering if this whole idea is worth it. "If you really don't want to help me, then—"

"No, she cuts me off, shaking her head. "I want to. I'll still help you."

"Are you sure?" I ask, skeptically. "Because I can look for another restaurant somewhere. If you're only doing this because you think it will bring us closer, then it's not going to happen," I tell her with a serious expression. "Nothing will ever happen between us, Lucy, I need to make sure you know that. I'm in love with Melissa. I have been since I was sixteen, and I will be 'till the day I die."

Her lips curve into a genuine smile. "That's really sweet." A sigh leaves her lips. "I'm sure. I want to help you," she confirms, nodding toward the door. "Do you still want to meet with my dad?"

A laugh bubbles out of me, and I glance down at the towel still wrapped around my waist. "I should probably get dressed first.

Thirty Three

Melissa

I've always loved being around children.

Except on a day like today, when all I want to do is curl up in bed and cry over how stupid I was.

The usual joy I feel about teaching has become a distant memory by the end of the day, replaced by the struggle not to scream as I force a happy face for the kids.

So, when the bell rings, and I can finally go home, a sense of relief washes over me. I'll treat myself to a pint of strawberry ice cream, and devour it while I watch a few episodes of Love Oasis. But as the minutes pass, I begin to remember Gabriel will be there, undoubtedly wanting to talk about what happened this morning, and the knot in my stomach tightens.

I've been stuck on what happened this morning all day, unable to get it out of my mind. Honestly, I know I'm the only one to blame for this whole mess. When it comes to Gabriel and me, I don't know what I was thinking. It was dumb to believe he could want me, especially after seeing the kind of girls he's been with. Girls like Lucy.

I'm so mad at myself for letting him under my skin, for believing him, and loving him, and telling him everything I've kept to myself for years.

The idea of heading home right now is the last thing I want. I can't bear the thought of talking to him, seeing him, or listening to whatever excuses he might come up with. The undeniable look on his face when Lucy exposed him for meeting up with her is burned in the forefront of my mind. He wouldn't be so freaked out if it wasn't true. He's been talking to her, eager to meet with her, and I allowed myself to believe I was the only girl he had eyes for.

Who am I kidding? Gabriel has never been the kind of guy who does relationships. Why did I trick myself into believing that would change because of me?

"Hey, Melissa." My spine stiffens as Mason's voice catches me off guard from behind. "You seem to be in a bad mood today."

"I'm fine," I reply, glancing back over my shoulder. He lifts off his car, and starts to walk toward me. "Just... ready to get home," I lie, trying to hide how I'm really feeling.

"I actually wanted to talk to you," he says, approaching me. I hastily reach inside my purse for my keys, my fingers fumbling to pull them out. He's been keeping his distance since the staff party, only exchanging occasional words, so why the hell is he talking to me now?

"What about?" I ask, clutching the car keys tightly in my hand. The parking lot only has a handful of cars, and a knot tightens in my stomach when I realize it's just me and him out here.

"I was wondering about your boyfriend," he says, his eyes narrowing as a smile plays on his lips. "I haven't seen him around, recently."

"He works too," I murmur, not willing to admit to him that I don't have a boyfriend anymore. I don't think I ever did. "He's not exactly going to be hanging around a middle school."

"Hmm." He approaches me, trapping me against my car as he places his hands on it. "Really?"

"Yes," I swallow, my nerves tingling as I wonder what the hell he's doing. "I actually need to go. We're... going on a date."

"A date?" he repeats, his eyes darkening with suspicion.

"Yes."

He shakes his head, a laugh rippling out of him that uneases me. "See, I think you're lying to me." His accusation hangs heavy in the air as I try to swallow, my throat feeling tight. "I think he doesn't exist. I think you just wanted to make me jealous, make me to chase you a bit, didn't you?"

"No. That's not true. I really do have a boyfriend," I say, the words escaping in a breathless plea as I attempt to catch my breath. "I need to go," I repeat.

"Come on," he says, leaning down toward me. His proximity is suffocating. "We both know we'd be great together."

"Let me go," I seethe, frustration bubbling within me as I push at his chest. "I don't want anything to do with you."

He grabs my face, his fingers digging into my jaw. "Stuck-up bitch," he hisses, venom dripping from each word. "You think you're better than me? Everyone knows you can't keep your eyes off me. You've been teasing me ever since you started working here."

"That's a lie." My heart races, threatening to break free from my chest. His hot breath hits my face, and I wince when he lowers himself even more. "Get off me, Mason."

"You want me," he whispers, his eyes intensely fixated on my lips. "And I'm going to prove it."

"No. Don't. Let me go, please—"

I squeeze my eyes shut, feeling his hand tighten around my jaw. My breath hitches in my throat, unable to do anything as he holds me in place. But then I hear a strained groan as I sense his hands releasing their grip from my face. A hard thud of someone crashing onto the floor makes me snap my eyes open, and I see Mason sprawled on the ground, with a trickle of blood staining his lip.

"Fucking prick." I turn my head at the familiar voice, taking in the sight of Gabriel shaking his fist, his face twisted with anger as he glares down at Mason.

"Gabriel?"

He turns to face me, and his eyes soften as he reaches for me, scanning me from head to toe. "Did he hurt you?"

"What?"

"Did he fucking hurt you, Melissa?" he asks again. His hands cup my face, turning it gently from side to side as he searches for any signs of harm. Then, he locks eyes on my jaw, a flicker of concern in his gaze. "Are these red marks from him?" he asks me, his voice holding a mix of worry and anger.

"Yes," I admit, a gulp catching in my throat as worry settles over me.

With a grunt, he whirls around and seizes Mason by the collar of his shirt, slamming him against the door of another car. A furious punch lands on Mason's face. "If you ever put your hands on my woman again," Gabriel's voice rumbles, each word dripping with fury, "I will fucking kill you. If you touch her, look at her, if you even think about her, I will find you and make you taste death. You got that?"

Mason's breath comes out in heavy, labored gasps, blood dripping down his lips. He nods weakly at Gabriel, who releases his grip. "Now get the fuck out of here," Gabriel tells him. Mason turns around, unsteady on his feet, and fumbles his way into his car, tires screeching as he speeds off.

Gabriel turns toward me, his jaw clenching with a mix of concern and regret. "Are you okay?" he asks, his eyes searching mine.

I shake my head in confusion, wondering why he's even here when I made it clear this morning that I didn't want to talk to him, but feeling so grateful that he is. A stray tear escapes, tracing a path down my cheek. He gently brushes it away with his thumb, and I instinctively pull back, avoiding his touch. A jumble of emotions overtakes me when I look into his eyes. Comfort, desire, love, everything I thought was real between us. But I know that it was nothing but a lie.

Gabriel steps back, a trace of disappointment in his eyes as he releases a heavy sigh. "Come on, I'll take you home."

"My car's right here," I say, my tone laced with a touch of defiance.

"And mine's over there," he says, nodding toward the far end of the dimly lit parking lot where his sleek black Rover is parked.

I glance away from his car, meeting his gaze with a mix of curiosity and irritation. "Why are you here?" I ask him.

"Because you ran away from me this morning," he says, his tone edged with a hint of frustration. "And we need to talk."

"There's nothing I want to talk to you about." I turn around, determinedly grabbing my keys as I try to get my car door open.

His hand wraps around my wrist, and he turns me around. "Well, that's too fucking bad, because we're talking. Let's go." He tugs me away from my car, heading toward his.

"Gabriel. I really don't want to hear the breakup speech right now," I mutter, rolling my eyes, my heart thudding at the thought of it all being over. Thank god we didn't tell Zaria. There'd be no point in getting her worked up over something that's over. "I know you're getting back together with your ex. You don't have to sit me down to tell me."

He stops abruptly, turning around with his brows furrowed. "You are so fucking wrong. How could you—" He groans, running a hand down his face. "I'm not having this conversation with you here. Let's go, Mel."

"My car's right here, asshole. I can't just leave it here."

Gabriel's mouth lifts into a smile at the use of the insult I used to call him when I still hated him. He shakes his head, his smile slipping. "We'll come and get it later. Now get in, Melissa," he urges, gesturing toward the passenger side of his car.

I cross my arms over my chest, refusing to move. He releases a heavy sigh, an exasperated expression crossing his face. "Trevi, get your ass in the car, or I'll put you in myself."

I scoff, knowing I'm provoking him. "I'd like to see you try."

Gabriel chuckles, lifting his shoulder in a nonchalant shrug as he strides toward me. He gets so close that I have to lift my head to meet his gaze as he towers over me, waiting for a moment, but when I don't move, he turns around and opens the car door with a sigh. "You're a pain in my ass," he mumbles, effortlessly picking me up and dropping me into the seat.

I flop down on the seat with a thud, frustration coursing through me. "If I'm such a pain in your ass, then why are you here?" I ask, glancing down at him. How did so much change from the moment we woke up to now?

He smirks, his gaze lingering on me for a moment. "I guess I like to torture myself," he quips.

I roll my eyes. "So I'm torture now?"

He lets out a laugh, staring at my lips. "You have been since I first met you, sweetheart."

With that, he closes the door, and smoothly eases into the driver's seat beside me.

Thirty Four

Melissa

"I don't want to talk to you," I tell him, forcefully inserting my keys into the door and rushing inside. Gabriel trails behind me, his fingers wrapping gently around my elbow when I attempt to close the door behind me. "I don't care if you're mad at me right now. Love me or hate me, sweetheart, you're not shutting me out," he asserts, narrowing his gaze on me. "We're talking, and that's final."

My breath comes out in heavy bursts as I turn to face him. "Fine," I huff, pulling my arm away from his touch. "Talk."

He exhales, running a hand down his face with a "I met Lucy earlier this year," he begins, causing my heart to drop to the pit of my stomach.

"I don't want to hear how you fell in love with your ex, Gabriel."

"Can you just let me finish?" he asks, a touch of frustration evident in his voice. I sigh in response, not exactly thrilled to hear about his ex, but also a little curious about why he's so insistent that I hear him out.

"We met on my birthday," he continues. "The one you didn't attend." I lick my lips, guilt coursing through me. I always attended the Andersons' gatherings, whether it was for a birthday, or the holidays, or simply for a meal together, but this year, I stayed away.

"I was mad at you," I tell him. "After Christmas—"

"I know," he nods, a flicker of understanding in his eyes. "I didn't realize how much I had hurt you until you didn't show up that day. I never meant to make you feel like that, Mel. It really stung when I realized you weren't coming, and I felt like shit for being the cause behind it." A heavy exhale escapes him. "I ended up getting drunk in some bar downtown, and Lucy also happened to be there."

My stomach churns at the mention of her name, but I keep my eyes fixed on him, waiting for his explanation. "She was upset about her ex dumping her, and I…" He shakes his head, sighing. "I was upset about you." *About me?* "Going home was always great, I loved seeing my family, of course, but... I was always excited to see you too."

My head spins, trying to make sense of his words. "But… you hated me."

"I told you, sweetheart," he says, taking a step closer. "I could never hate you." His hand reaches out, brushing my cheek in an affectionate way that makes my eyes flutter from his touch. "I've wanted you since the day we fucking met."

My eyes snap open, widening at his words. "What?"

He chuckles. "What did you think I meant when I said I'd been thinking about this for a long time, baby?"

The term of endearment makes my stomach flutter, and I shake my head, my heart beating so fast I can hear it. "I don't know," I admit. "I thought you meant a few weeks."

He scoffs, tilting my chin up to look at him. "I meant a lot longer than that, Mel."

"Then… why?" I don't need to elaborate as to what I mean. Gabriel can read me like a book.

"Because I was a fucking idiot," he admits with a shrug. "Because I didn't want to hurt Zaria if I went after you. Because I thought you deserved better than me. Pick one; they all apply."

"That's such a dumb excuse," I retort, narrowing my eyes.

"Like I said, I was a dumb teenager. I thought if I pushed you away, then it would be easier," he confesses, his throat moving as he swallows harshly. "You were Zaria's best friend, and I was still so young. I didn't think you'd be that important to me. I thought it was just a stupid crush." He shakes his head. "But it was so much more than that. You were always on my mind, always the first person I would look for. You were the only girl I ever wanted."

My brows furrow in confusion. "Because I didn't want you back?" I ask, wondering if that's the only reason.

"I know you had a crush on me when we met," he smirks, a playful glint in his eyes. Embarrassment washes over me, and I attempt to look away, but he gently lifts my head to make me meet his gaze. "Don't be embarrassed. It was cute as hell."

"I'm not admitting to anything," I say, defiantly.

"That's fine. We both know I'm right," he says with a laugh. "I just wanted you to know that's not the reason. I know you wanted me too, sweetheart, and it was so hard trying to convince myself I couldn't have you."

"Then what's changed now?" I question, wondering what made him change his mind about us. If he was so adamant about not being able to be with me, then why did that change?

"I got careless," he says, running his thumb over my lips. "Seeing you every day and not being able to kiss you was torture enough. But then when I saw you get dressed up for another guy…" He shakes his head, a regretful look crosses his face. "I couldn't handle seeing you go on a date with someone else when they could never love you like I do."

My lips part on a gasp at his words. "You… what?"

"I love you," he repeats, a smile on his face. "I've been out of my head in love with you since I can remember. I was a coward for pushing you away, I know that, but I guess I didn't want to admit to myself that no one else came close to how I feel about you."

"Lucy did," I say, swallowing down the jealousy coursing through me.

"No, sweetheart. Lucy and I were in love with other people. Her with her ex, and me with you," he clarifies. "We got into a relationship for the wrong reasons and decided to see if we were a good fit. But we realized that we weren't. At all." He sighs. "I was so tired of wanting someone I couldn't let myself have that I was trying to get over you. I moved in with her thinking it would help, but Lucy and I were always better off as friends than an actual couple." He swallows, licking his lips. "That relationship ended because of you, actually."

"Me?" I ask, my eyes blinking in surprise.

He nods. "Lucy knew I was in love with you from the very beginning, but I guess she thought I was getting over you as time went on," he says with a subtle shake of his head. "When she found me looking through your pictures, she knew my feelings for you would never change. We had a huge argument, and I realized the longer I stayed with her, the more we were hurting each other We ended it that night."

"And then you moved in here," I finish for him.

He nods. "I'm not going to lie to you and say it was the only available place I could have moved into, but I guess… I just wanted to see you."

I remember how I used to believe that Gabriel wasn't too keen on the idea of living with me. But now, I know how far off I was from the truth. "Even though you told yourself you couldn't have me?"

"Even then," he confirms. "I thought I'd be able to handle it. I had done for a long time, but when I got here, I found out how hard it was to be around you all the time," he says with a laugh. "You were even more beautiful than I remembered, and even when we argued, I wanted to kiss you."

"You did?" I ask, a flutter in my chest.

"Every single day," he says, holding my eyes. "You were constantly on my mind."

I want to believe him. I do. But… "What about what Lucy said this morning?" I ask, doubt filling my mind. "Why have you been meeting with her?"

His jaw clenches, and he shakes his head. "Lucy got a little jealous," he explains, a trace of frustration in his voice. "She knew how much I wanted you, and I guess she felt embarrassed about it. But what she said wasn't a complete lie." My eyes drop, and Gabriel smooths his thumb over my cheek. "Let me finish, Mel. It's not for the reason you're thinking."

"Then why?" I ask, lifting my head to look up at him.

He sighs. "Remember when I told you I wanted to open up a restaurant?" I nod. "Lucy's dad owns the building I want to purchase for the restaurant," he reveals. "It's in a good place, big, beautiful, and something I could afford. I asked her to meet with me to go over the deal with her father."

"A restaurant?" I ask.

"Yes," he affirms. "The chef at the restaurant I work for isn't giving me the role anytime soon, and he knows opening my own restaurant is something I've wanted for a long time."

"So you're not getting back together with her?"

"How many times do I have to say this, Mel? You're the only girl I want. You're the only girl I've wanted since I was fifteen. I love you, baby. I'm in love with you."

My heart soars hearing those words, but doubt creeps into my mind at the thought of being enough for him. "I'm nothing like Lucy," I tell him.

He smiles, a reassuring warmth in his eyes. "Believe me, that's a good thing."

"I mean I'm not like her, or you," I say with a frown. "I don't like to go out or socialize with people. I'm not fun or loud. You even said all I do is stay at home. Why would you ever want someone like that?"

His jaw clenches, and he shakes his head. "I wish I never said that. I was just trying to tease you. I never meant to hurt you or make you think there's something wrong with you,

Mel." He cradles my face, rubbing his thumb across my cheek as he stares deep into my eyes. "I love you as you are. Exactly as you are."

I shake my head, tears welling in my eyes. I don't even love myself sometimes. How could he?

"I know it's hard for you to love and trust," he continues, brushing away the tears. "I know your mother made you believe you weren't worth it, and she messed with your self-esteem, but you're all I've ever wanted since for ten years, and all I want is to love you with everything I have."

My lips part, and I blink away the tears, staring up at his warm eyes. "I love you too," I breathe out, my gaze locked on him.

He grins, a twinkle in his eyes. "I know," he says with a chuckle. "I'm pretty lovable."

I playfully roll my eyes, giving him a gentle push on the chest. "You just ruined that."

His laughter fills the air as he leans in, capturing my lips with his. "I love you, baby," he murmurs against my mouth. "And I'll make sure you know just how much every single day of my life.

Thirty Five

Melissa

"I can't believe you're finally mine," Gabriel whispers, his hands holding my hips as I straddle him on the couch.

"Took you long enough," I joke, smirking as his eyes narrow playfully. "I thought you had game."

"You don't think I have game?" he asks, his tone filled with amusement.

I shrug. "It took you ten years."

He chuckles, tightening his hold on me before my back drops to the couch, and Gabriel hovers over me. "You want to see game?" he asks, grinding his erection against me, pulling a moan from my lips. "I'll make you come so hard you'll forget your own name."

"Gabriel," I gasp.

He shakes his head, his lips trailing a path down my body. "What about now, baby?" His lips skim the edge of my leggings, and I breathe out a sigh, my body feeling like a furnace. "Hm?"

"Yes," I huff. "Fuck, I take it back."

His laugh vibrates against my skin, and my body shivers with pleasure, wanting him so badly I can hardly breathe. "So needy," he murmurs, running his hand over my thighs. "You're moving your hips, like you're searching for my cock." He presses his lips against my inner thighs. "I bet you've soaked your panties."

A soft whimper escapes my lips, and he laughs, gently pulling me up until I'm once again straddling him. I wrap my arms around his neck. "Please, I beg him, rotating my hips over the thick bulge in his pants. "I want you."

He stills my movements, gripping my hips in place. "I know you do, sweetheart," he says, his voice strained. "I want you too, but Zaria's going to be home soon, and if we start, I won't be able to stop until you come on my cock."

As much as I love the sound of that, my smile is wiped clean at the reminder of Zaria. My lips tug into a frown, and a wave of guilt washes over me, knowing I'm betraying her. I hate the sneaking around, and the secrets, and I hate that I'm doing all of this behind her back. I want to tell her, but I'm scared of how she'll react.

"It's going to be fine, Mel," Gabriel says, his voice pulling me out of the whirlwind of my thoughts running through my mind.

"You don't know that," I reply, worry seeping into my veins. "What if she hates me?" I ask, my lip wobbling at the thought of that happening. "What if she resents me for lying to her, for getting in between you two?" I shake my head. "I'll never forgive myself if that happens." Their family bond has always been strong, and I can't bear the thought of being the reason it falls apart.

"That won't happen," Gabriel reassures me, his hand cradling my face gently. "Zaria loves you, Mel. She might be a little upset we hid it from her in the beginning, but she won't hate you."

I really want to believe him, but the fear of hurting my best friend lingers in the back of my mind. "We need to tell her."

"Yeah," he agrees with a sigh. "We do. Maybe we can do it this weekend," Gabriel suggests. "At my parents' house. We'll tell them too if you want." He grabs my hand in his, intertwining our fingers together.

"Are you sure?"

He nods. "I'm ready to tell the world you're mine. I've wanted this for so long, I don't want to hide how I feel anymore." His smile etches into my mind, and heart. "I want to take you out on a real date. I want you to wear that sexy little dress of yours that drives me fucking crazy," he groans, grabbing my ass with his other hand. "I want to walk in with you on my arm. I want to kiss you whenever I want. I want to spend the whole night talking about anything, and everything."

Everything Gabriel's saying is exactly what I want. I want someone to want me. I want someone to love me, but I don't just want *anyone*. I want him. "Yes," I whisper with a nod. "I want that too."

"Good," he replies, a warm smile playing on his lips. "I'll take you out tonight."

"Tonight?" I ask, my eyes widening. "But what about—"

"We'll sort out all the details later. Just… please kiss me for a while, before we have to keep our distance again."

I chuckle, leaning down until our lips are stacked. "I love hearing you beg." Our lips meet in a soft kiss, quickly turning into a heated make out when his tongue slides in my mouth, his hands pushing my hips over his. "God yes," I breathe out, feeling his length over the thin material of my pants.

"So fucking beautiful," he murmurs, kissing down my neck. "I love you."

The three letter words makes me whimper as I grind down harder, needing him closer. I never want to leave his body. I want his lips, hands and everything else on me all the time.

"What the fuck?"

Zaria's voice echoes through the room, and it's like a bucket of cold water, making us jump apart. My heart sinks when I see her at the door, blinking in confusion, trying to process what's happening.

No. No. She wasn't supposed to find out like this.

"Zaria," I gasp, running a shaky hand through my hair. Her face, a mix of betrayal and disappointment, twists something inside me, guilt churning in my stomach.

Zaria shakes her head, her voice sharp. "What the hell did I just walk into?"

"Please," I mumble, taking a step toward her.

She lifts her hand, signaling me to stop, sadness in her eyes. "Don't," she says, her voice tight.

"Zaria, let's talk about this." Gabriel gets up from the couch, but Zaria's eyes flick to her brother, and she shakes her head again.

"I don't even know what to say right now." Her hand drops, balling into a fist at her side as she looks from me to Gabriel. "I don't know if I feel more betrayed by my brother or my best friend."

Her words hit hard, like a punch to the gut, and tears stream down my face. I should never have lied about my feelings for Gabriel, or when we finally got together. I should have told her.

"Z, I'm so sorry," I choke out, tears blurring my vision.

"I just… I need to get out of here," she says, hurt dripping from her voice.

Zaria turns around and walks out of the apartment, the door closing behind her with a thud that echoes through the room.

Thirty Six

Gabriel

I never thought I'd find myself standing here, knocking on the door of the guy who's hooking up with my sister. Trying to maintain the delusion where my little sister is still innocent is impossible. Being Zaria's big brother, I can't escape it, especially when she insists on oversharing the details of her love life.

My sister has a carefree vibe, and usually, It's something I admire. But when it comes to her spilling all the details about the guys she's seeing, it's a bit more than I signed up for as a big brother.

The door swings open, revealing the guy my sister's seeing. My eyes widen at the sight of his shirtless chest, and I quickly shift my focus to his face. The subtle lines on his face hint at the fact that he's definitely a few years older than both her and me.

I don't usually care who my sister dates. It's none of my business, but this guy has got to be almost ten years older than her.

"Yes?" he answers, blinking behind his glasses.

"Is my sister here?" I ask him,

"Zaria?"

I nod, crossing my arms over my chest. "That's the one."

"Yeah, hold on a sec." He turns away, calling for Zaria. "Hey, your brother's here," he calls.

"My brother?" Zaria's voice, a mix of confusion and annoyance, grows louder as she strides forward, positioning herself between me and her boyfriend – or whatever they are. Her brows furrow, and she shoots me a look. "How did you even know where to find me?" she asks.

Her boyfriend hesitates, his eyes briefly meeting mine. "I'll leave you two to talk," he says, giving a brief nod before making his way past Zaria.

"You're into older guys?" I tease with a smirk, attempting to joke around. my

She rolls her eyes, a clear expression of annoyance. "You're giving me a lecture about who I'm seeing, really?" My playful smile drops, and she lets out a weary sigh. "What are you doing here, Gabriel?"

"I'm here to talk."

"How did you even find out where Dominic lives?" Zaria's eyes flicker with suspicion.

"I asked Mel." I admit.

Her face stiffens, and she shakes her head. "I don't want to talk about this right now." Zaria turns away, attempting to shut the door.

I intercept her, standing my ground and glaring down at her. "Don't be like this, Zaria. We've never been the type to argue. Don't ruin that now."

"I'm not the one ruining it." Her response holds a mix of defiance and frustration, and she narrows her eyes at me. "You two are." The accusation lingers and I shake my head.

"How?" I ask. "Because I love her?"

Her eyes widen, caught off guard, her mouth dropping open. "You… what?"

"I love her," I say again, hoping she can see the sincerity on my face. "Did you really think I'd take the risk just for a hookup? Zaria, I've loved Melissa for years."

"What?" she asks again, confusion racking through her. "How?"

"Why does everyone act like this is crazy?" I mutter, shaking my head in disbelief. "I know Mel and I had a few arguments, but—"

My sister scoffs. "A few? You two hated each other."

"She definitely did," I affirm. "But I never hated her. Not once."

Zaria groans, burying her head in her hands. "This is too much for me to take in, right now," she mumbles into her hands. Zaria lifts her head, confusion painting her expression. "I don't understand. If you didn't hate her, then why were you always teasing her? You were constantly doing things you knew would make her hate you."

My jaw clenches, and I take a deep breath before admitting, "It was because of you,"

She blinks, her eyes widening in surprise. "Me?"

"Do you remember what you told me the day you brought Mel home from school?"

"No," she says, her brows knitting together in a frown.

I tilt my head at her. "You warned me not to go near her, Zaria. The minute she left, you turned around and pointed a finger at me and told me not to dare go near her. You told me there were plenty of other girls." I shrug, remembering that day like it was yesterday. "You must have seen a look in my eye or something, I guess. It was just a childish crush by then, nothing more, so I stayed away, tried to forget her."

"But you couldn't?" she guesses.

"No," I say, shaking my head. "I ended up really fucking liking her, and since you told me not to do anything, I kept my promise. I tried to forget about my feelings for her. I *really* fucking tried, Zaria."

She sighs, crossing her arms and lets her gaze fall to the ground.

"I didn't mean to fall in love with her, it just happened, and I couldn't hold it in anymore." My sister lifts her head, peering at me. "And now my girlfriend is in bed crying because she thinks her best friends hates her."

My sister frowns. "I don't hate her."

"I know," I say. "But she thinks you do. You haven't come home, or answered any of her texts in the last two days. She's gone through three cartons of ice cream, Zaria. Three."

"I needed some space," she says. "It was a lot to walk in, seeing you two kissing and..." Her face scrunches up in disgust.

"I know. We didn't mean for you to find out like that," I tell her. "We were actually going to tell you, mom and dad on Sunday. We wanted to do it together. Trust me, that was the worst way you could have found out."

"I agree," she says, she shivers at the memory. "I'm traumatized." I let out a laugh, the tension momentarily broken, and Zaria's phone rings in her pocket. She pulls it out, swallowing when she sees Melissa's name on the screen. "It's her."

"Don't shut her out," I tell my sister. "Please. Mel loves you. She never wanted to hurt you. I can't help that I fell in love with her."

"Does she love you too?"

I chuckle, running a hand over my beard. "Come on. Everyone loves me."

She rolls her eyes, her usual smile back on her face. "I don't know how Melissa's going to deal with you."

"Don't worry. I come with perks," I joke.

My sister, however, doesn't find it as funny seeing as she slams her hands over her ears. "Ew. Ew. Nope. You're not allowed to make sexual jokes about my best friend ever again. I don't want to hear it."

"Fine," I say with a laugh. "Just make sure you call her."

Thirty Seven

Melissa

My head lifts in anticipation as the door creaks open, hope fluttering in my chest, but my heart sinks as Gabriel walks in instead of Zaria.

"Hey, baby," he says, a warm smile on his face, leaning over to plant a gentle kiss on my forehead. "I'm sorry I took so long." He holds out a tub of strawberry ice cream, and hands me a spoon.

"It's okay," I murmur, opening the lid, staring down at the ice cream, and dig in without hesitation. "She didn't answer again," I mumble, my words slightly garbled as I stuff a spoonful of ice cream into my mouth.

Gabriel sighs, dropping down on the bed beside me. "She will, Mel. I know it."

My head droops, tears brimming in my eyes. "She hates me," I whisper, my voice barely audible as I let the tears flow freely.

Gabriel shifts closer, wrapping his arms around me. "She doesn't hate you, sweetheart, I promise." His presence makes this feel a little more bearable. "She's just processing it."

"It's been two days," I mumble into the crook of his neck.

"I know," he sighs, a hint of remorse in his tone. "I'm so sorry, Mel. This is exactly what I was trying to prevent during all those years I forced myself to stay away."

"I know I probably should, but I don't regret it," I say, my voice slightly shaky as I pull back to look at him, catching the glint of understanding in his eyes. "I don't regret us."

He smiles, a tender expression softening his features, and his thumb gently rubs my cheek. "I don't regret it, either, baby. I just regret the way she found out."

I groan, the memory of Zaria catching me straddling her brother on the couch hitting me hard. We had a plan, and it wasn't supposed to happen like that.

"What if you talked to her?" I suggest. "She won't be too mad at you, right? You're family."

"You're family too," Gabriel says, gently pulling me toward him. "I promise everything will be solved soon."

I let out a sigh, doubt clouding over me. Zaria and I had never argued before. Ever. And while I have my boyfriend beside me, right now, I really need my best friend.

My head jerks at the sound of my ringtone, and I quickly lift off the bed, reaching for my phone. "It's her," I say, my eyes widening when I see Zaria's name on the screen.

"Answer it," Gabriel urges me.

"Z?" I say into the phone, hastily wiping away the lingering tears on my face.

She sighs on the other end. "You want to watch the new episode of Love Oasis?"

My smile widens, and genuine laughter bubbles up. "Are you serious?"

My bedroom door swings open, and I turn around, spotting Zaria, who's holding her hands over her eyes. "I guess since you're my brother's girlfriend now, I need to start knocking or I'll see something I don't want to see."

I laugh, shaking my head. "Nothing's going on. Open your eyes," I say, hanging up the call.

She gradually peels away her hands from her eyes, her gaze shifting from me to Gabriel. "So... you two, huh?"

Gabriel wraps his arms around my waist, and he presses a gentle kiss to the top of my head. "Yeah," he says, his voice dripping with affection.

"Is that okay with you?" I ask her, feeling my heart beat quicken.

"Of course it is," she says with a warm smile. "I'm really happy for you, M. I know you've struggled in the past with trusting people, and if my idiot brother makes you happy then..." She shrugs. "All I want is for you to be happy."

"I am. I'm really happy."

She smiles, but then a sigh escapes her. "I'm sorry I didn't answer your calls. I guess I felt betrayed," she says. "My best friend and my brother were lying to me, while they were sneaking around behind my back." Her face drops. "I didn't take it well. I needed some time."

"I understand," I say, closing the distance between us and take her hand in mine. "I just didn't know how to tell you. I love you, Z. I never wanted to lie to you or betray you in any way. And I never wanted you to resent Gabriel because of this."

She shakes her head. "That would never happen. If I can forgive him for burning my Bratz dolls when I was six, I can definitely forgive him for this, and for making fun of Dominic's age," she says, narrowing her eyes at him. "And I forgive you too, M. That's what family does. They argue, they make up, and all is fine again."

Hearing her acknowledge me as family hits me deeper than words can express. She has no idea how much that means to me.

"So… you love my brother?" she asks, a genuine smile playing on her lips.

I exhale a relieved breath, my chest shaking with laughter. "Yeah. I do."

She shakes her head, a scoff escaping her. "It's going to be so weird to see you two all lovey-dovey after witnessing your arguments." The corner of her mouth quirks up.

"We'll still argue," I tell her with a laugh, glancing over my shoulder at Gabriel. "We'll just make up after."

He grins, walking up to me and lays a kiss on my lips, soft and teasing.

She groans, her frustration evident in the way she shakes her head. "Nope. I'm not ready," she says, slamming her hands to her eyes. "This is worse than I thought it would be." With a dramatic flair, her hands peel away from her face, and she squints an eye open. "We need a rule. No making out while I'm near you."

"C'mon," Gabriel groans. "We've had to keep our distance for so long. The point of telling you was to be able to be together now."

Zaria narrows her eyes at her brother. "You can still kiss her, just don't," she gestures with her hands between us, a disgusted look on her face, "maul her right in front of me."

"We won't," I assure her, chuckling when Gabriel groans again.

"Baby," Gabriel whispers, his brows tugging together in desperation. "Please don't tell me we're actually going to have to stay away from each other again."

I look up at him, a mischievous smirk curling on my lips. "I'll make it up to you when we're alone," I promise.

Gabriel's eyes widen in realization, and he leans in, capturing me in another kiss. I yelp into his mouth as he spins me around, wrapping his arms around my waist, his tongue sliding in my mouth.

"You broke that rule in ten seconds," Zaria groans. "You know what? I'm out. Have fun."

"We will," Gabriel mumbles against my mouth once Zaria closes the door.

"You're going to traumatize your sister," I say, laughter bubbling up when his lips leave mine, planting kisses down my jaw.

"Believe me, she's traumatized me enough with her own stories." Gabriel's hands grip my waist, pulling me even closer. "Now shut up, and let me kiss you, baby."

His lips find mine again, and he kisses me deep. The intensity of his touch makes all my thoughts evaporate.

"Thank you for talking to her," I whisper against his lips.

He pulls back, his brow furrowing with confusion. "How did you know?"

My shoulder lifts in a shrug. "Zaria mentioned you made fun of her boyfriend," I say with a playful smile. "I thought it was weird since you've never met him, but then I remembered you asking me about him yesterday."

A sigh escapes him. "I just wanted you two to get through this," he confesses.

"Thank you," I whisper again, feeling the warmth of gratitude in my chest as I wrap my arms around his neck. "You don't know how much it means to me."

"Of course I do, sweetheart. She's my sister, but she's your family, too." His thumb gently caresses my cheek. "And I know how much family means to you."

A soft smile plays on my lips as I tease, "I'm so happy you got jealous that night."

He laughs, shaking his head as he looks deeply into my eyes. "I'm happy I finally get to love you for the rest of my life."

Thirty Eight

Gabriel

"Can you stop ogling me, Mel?" I say to my girlfriend, who's currently drooling over me.

"Hmm?" she mumbles, keeping her eyes on my bare chest.

A smirk pulls at my lips. I love how unashamed she is when she checks me out now. I still remember seeing her do it when I first moved in, and how adorable she was when she tried to deny it.

"I'm supposed to be teaching you, sweetheart."

"You are," she says.

I lift an eyebrow. "Then what are am I cooking right now?"

Her lips part, but no answer comes out. She groans in defeat, rolling her eyes. "Fine, I wasn't listening."

I chuckle, dropping the wooden spoon on the counter as I make my way to Melissa, wrapping my arms around her waist. "As much as I love when you check me out, I'd rather you not burn down the kitchen when I move out next week."

The thought still makes my stomach sour, knowing I won't be ten seconds away from her. I won't be able to sneak into her room in the middle of the night, or kiss her when I wake up, or cook for her.

"Then maybe you shouldn't move out," she suggests.

"Or… you could move in with me?" I ask her for the tenth time this week. She shakes her head, a teasing smile on her lips. Mel isn't ready for that step yet, and I understand. We did only just get together, but I've been gone for this girl for a lot longer than she has, so I try not to push. I sigh. "Fine. Then you need to learn to cook. You can't order takeout all the time. It's expensive, and unhealthy."

"And what if I never learn?" she teases.

I scoff, looping my hands around her hips to grab her ass. "Then I'll have to bring food over for you every night," I murmur, leaning down to kiss her jaw.

"That sounds like a much better deal," she jokes.

I chuckle against her skin. "I'm not trying to pressure you. I just don't want you eating that crap. I want you to live a long, long life with me."

Her breaths come out harsher and breathier than normal. I chuckle, knowing how much my words affected her, but everything I'm telling her is something I can't stop thinking about, especially since I finally admitted to her that I love her. I want a life with her. A future. Marriage, kids, maybe a pet. I want everything with her.

"You sound like Zaria," she says, rolling her eyes when I pull back. "She's always talking about the sodium content and threatening to check my blood pressure."

"I can't help it," I say with a shrug. "My dad's a doctor. He's been instilling this into us for years."

"Fine," she says with a sigh. "What are you making?"

"I figured a stir fry would be easy enough."

Intertwining our fingers, I tug her toward the stove, showing her how to season the vegetables, and chicken and she copies me, nearly cutting off a finger in the process. After a while, she gets the hang of it, and I sit back, watching her.

"Like this?" she asks, looking behind her shoulder. A laugh escaped her when she catches me staring at her ass, fucking guilty as charged.

I nod, smiling back as I approach her, grabbing her waist with one hand as I place the other on top of hers, over the wooden spoon, our hands moving together.

I press into her from behind and she gasps when she feels my hard length press against the thin material of her leggings. Her breathing becomes labored as I kiss her neck, tugging the skin with my teeth, tasting her like a man starved. I've been denied this for ten years, and I'm not going to hide how much I want her anymore.

"What about dinner?" she mumbles, a low moan leaving her pretty little lips.

"Fuck the stir-fry. You can just sit pretty and watch me cook instead," I spin her around, wrapping my arms around her waist, pushing her into me as my lips meet hers. Her hands run through my hair, wrapping on the crook of my neck. "Fuck, Mel," I groan, two seconds away from picking her up and throwing her on my bed.

"Ew. Gross."

We pull away from the kiss, glancing at Zaria standing outside of her bedroom door, her face contorted in disgust. I laugh, seeing my sister's expression. It's been over a week since she found out about us, and while she knows, she's still not used to it, which means we still have to sneak around a little.

"Don't fuck in the kitchen, please," she says. "It's where we eat." Melissa and I look at each other, a smirk on my lips, knowing that rule was broken a while ago. Zaria groans. "You already did, didn't you?" She holds a hand up. "You know what… don't answer that. I'm going over to Dominic's. Don't binge watch the new season without me," she warns Mel.

"I don't know if I can do that," Mel replies, a teasing smile on her lips as she glances my way. "Your brother's a big fan now."

"I'm not," I lie. Mel raises her brow at me, knowing I'm lying and I sigh. "Fine. I got hooked on that stupid show."

"Well too bad. Watch something else. Love Oasis is mine and Melissa' tradition. I know you're dating now, but I'm still her best friend. We need time together."

"Fine," I sigh, knowing she's right. As much as I wish I could just be with Mel all hours of the day, I know that's not possible. Zaria was her best friend long before Mel was my girl.

Zaria chuckles, shaking her head. "You're acting like a sad puppy."

I shoot my sister a glare. "Weren't you leaving?"

She laughs as she heads toward the door, leaving the apartment until it's just me and Mel.

She moves toward me, wrapping her arms around my neck and I lift her up into my arms, wrapping her legs around my waist. "God, you're so beautiful," I murmur into the crook of her neck, burying my lips in her skin.

Mel moans, throwing her head back. "I want you," she says. "Fuck me, Gabriel. Please."

A groan rumbles from the back of my throat. Melissa used to be so shy when it came to talking about sex. She could hardly tell me what she wanted when I first kissed her, but she's no longer shy. She lets me know exactly what she wants for me, and where she wants me.

"You're driving me crazy, baby. I can't wait to feel you." Dropping her on the couch, I tug her leggings off, throwing them to the side until I can see the triangle of lace covering her pretty little pussy. My fingers graze the cloth, feeling it drenched. "So wet, baby. Have you been this wet the whole time?"

She nods, a whimper escaping her. "I need you so bad."

My head spins, all the blood rushing to my cock from the sight in front of me. "Take off your top, sweetheart. Let me see those gorgeous tits."

Lifting onto her elbows, she grabs the hem of her t-shirt and tugs it over her head, freeing her breasts. "Now you," she says, licking her lips as she gives me a once-over.

I grin, tugging my sweats off until I'm in nothing but a pair of black boxers. "Is this what you want?" I ask her, grabbing my junk over my boxers. "You want my cock inside you?" I pull my boxers off, my dick bobbing free.

Her eyes widen at it, and she nods, a whimper letting loose as her hips start to buck.

I feast on the sight of her, and lean down to tug at her panties, pulling them down until she's bare before me. "Fuck, look at you, baby," I murmur, staring at her pretty, pink pussy dripping, and eager for my cock.

"Gabriel," she breathes out, her tits rising with each breath. "Please."

My hands wrap around her waist and I pull her down, until my cock nudges her entrance. I grab my cock in my hand and slide it over her pussy, pressing the tip against her clit. Melissa's beautiful moans make my cock leak as I keep thrusting between her lips, coating my cock in her arousal.

"Put it in," she pleads. "I want to feel you."

"You have no patience," I tease, chuckling at how she moves her hips, wanting me inside her.

"I need you."

Pleasure rolls through my body at her words, and I position my cock at her drenched hole, and push in. "Fuck," I groan at the feel of her tightening around me. "So good, baby. You always feel so fucking good."

"Deeper," she begs, tilting her head back.

I pull back until only my tip is inside of her, and thrust to the hilt, pulling a delicious moan from Melissa. It isn't long until I'm moving faster, harder, gripping her waist to pull her down onto my cock.

The feel of her is too fucking much, and to save myself embarrassment, I pull out of her and bend her over the arm of the couch, her beautiful ass in the air. I slide back inside of her, gripping her chin in my hand as I kiss her deeply. "You feel too good," I grunt, thrusting inside of her. "I need you to come, Mel. Drench my cock, baby." I play with her clit, rubbing little circles over it, until she drops her head.

"Don't stop," she begs, her pussy clenching around my cock. "I'm… fuck."

"That's it." Her legs shake uncontrollably as I push inside of her again, and again as the orgasm hits her. "Fuuuck," I grunt, spilling inside of her, my own orgasm crashing against me.

Her body melts into the couch as she comes down from the high. I fucking love how she looks after I make her come. I pull my spent cock out of her, groaning when I see my cum dripping out of her pussy. The thought of filling her up with my kids one day makes me fucking crazy.

"Are you okay, baby?" I ask her, turning her over.

Her eyes flutter closed drunk with pleasure. "Hmm," she mumbles cute as shit.

I laugh, dropping down on the couch and pulling her into my arms. "I didn't go too hard?" I press my lips to hers, holding her body to mine.

"No," she says, smiling as she wraps her arms around my neck. "It was perfect. It's always perfect."

"I love you," I murmur catching her lips with mine. I can't ever get enough of her. I still can't believe this is real. After spending ten years of my life thinking Mel and I would never happen, we managed to make our way to each other, and I thank God every day that she's finally mine.

"Love you," she mumbles against my lips. Her face scrunches up as she sniffs the air. "Is something burning?"

Melissa's eyes widen at the same time as mine, and she lifts herself off my lap, running to the stove. I quickly put on my sweats, joining her.

"It's burnt," Mel says with a frown as she glances at the blackened vegetables in the pan.

I laugh at the sight, knowing I got distracted by Mel as soon as I was alone with her. I can't help it. After next week we won't be having these moments together as often, and I need to take advantage of the rest of the time we have. "It's ok, sweetheart. I've had my dinner," I tease, my eyes roaming over her beautiful naked form. "I know what you really want is dessert, anyway," I say, grabbing the ice cream container from the freezer.

"You don't mind?" she asks me, slipping her clothes back on. "You really wanted to teach me."

"No," I affirm, spooning some into a bowl for her. "All I wanted was to spend time with you, Mel. Sure, I would prefer if you could make yourself some actual food, but—"

"I do know how to make actual food," she says with a frown.

A laugh bubbles out of me. "Grilled cheese doesn't count, sweetheart." When she sighs, I smile, so in love with everything she does. "I'll cook for you," I tell her. "Now eat."

"You're not having some, too?" she asks, sitting down on the stool.

My face screws up, shaking my head. "It's disgusting."

She lifts an eyebrow, licking the spoon. "If I remember correctly, you said it was the best thing you've ever tasted."

I lean in, holding her chin between my fingers and lick her plump bottom lip, cleaning up the ice cream that dribbled down. "It wasn't the ice cream I was talking about, sweetheart," I whisper, grinning when I see her eyes widen.

All the little moments she remembers before are completely different to me. She thought I hated her, when in fact, it was the complete opposite.

"Are you happy?" I ask her, rubbing my thumb over her cheek. All I've ever wanted was to love her, and now I can do that without a problem, knowing the love of my life loves me too.

She smiles, her head bobbing up and down in a nod. "The happiest."

Epilogue

Gabriel

"Where the hell is she?"

"Calm down," my dad says. "She'll show up."

"She should have been here an hour ago," I groan, pulling out my phone again. No messages. Not a damn one.

"Don't worry. You know she'll say yes," my mom reassures me, affectionately tapping my cheek. "She loves you, Gabriel. No matter where or when you ask, she'd say yes."

I know.

I know Mel loves me, but I want this to be perfect for her. I want the sunset to paint the sky over the ocean when I ask the love of my life to marry me. I want our family there to celebrate when she says yes. I want to kickstart our journey together. I want to marry her. Right here, right now. I want everything with her.

The last two years with her have been amazing. A grin spreads across my face when I think about everything we've been through. How I opened my restaurant, and she cried when she found out I named it *Visano's* after her. How she sold her dad's house, and we bought a new one for us. How she tried to learn how to cook, and nearly burnt down said house trying to surprise me with birthday pancakes. How the first words she said to me when she found out she was pregnant were, "Why couldn't we be seahorses?"

Melissa has ruined me since the moment I laid eyes on her. I'm hopelessly in love with her, and every day, that love deepens. I don't regret a single moment in my life. The good and the bad, the arguments, and the years it took me to finally go after Melissa – they all led me straight to this very moment. Honestly, if I had to do it all over again, I'd gladly face every hurdle, savor every joy, just for the chance to end up with her.

"You ok man?" Dominic asks, tapping me on my back.

I reach up, wiping the sweat off my forehead. Fuck. Why am I so nervous? Probably because this has been twelve years in the making. Ever since I saw her at my house twelve years ago, it's all been leading up to this.

"Yeah. I'm just… nervous."

He nods, understanding exactly what I'm going through. Dominic and my sister got married a few months ago, and I remember how nervous he was when he asked my dad and I for permission.

We laughed in his face, Zaria didn't need our approval. Her love for him was clear, and no amount of resistance from us would have changed that.

"Where are you taking me?"

My eyes widen at the sound of my beautiful girlfriend, walking toward me, with a blindfold over her eyes. I turn around to look at her, and my breath gets caught in my throat when my eyes dip to the flowy pink dress she's wearing, her beautiful belly round, and swollen with our daughter.

"You'll see," my sister says, smiling at me. I don't even bother asking her what took her so long, because Mel's here. That's all that matters.

Taking a step closer to her, I approach with a gentle grip on her hands. She inhales sharply at the touch. "Gabriel?" she asks. "Why are we on a beach? Can I take my blindfold off now?"

I chuckle, my heart thudding with anticipation. I pull off the blindfold, and Melissa blinks, adjusting to the light. She's fucking breathtaking. Pregnancy has made her even more beautiful, and I can't help smiling at the thought of my little girl in there.

"Hi," I whisper, cupping her face as I bring her lips to mine, kissing her soft and slow. We have all the time in the world.

Her eyes flutter closed when I pull away from the kiss. "Hi," she mumbles, her warm smile making my heart thud even faster. Her smile drives me crazy. I'll never get over how she looks at me, how she smiles, laughs, kisses me. I love being the source of her happiness.

Her eyes widen as she looks around, spotting the candles and roses surrounding us. Our first date was at the beach, and I figured it was the perfect place to ask her to spend the rest of her life with me.

It took me so long to realize there was never going to be anyone else who made me feel the way I felt for Melissa, but it was only ever her. I want every day with her until death, and every day after that. She's the love of my life, and the only girl who will ever make me this happy.

"Mel," I whisper, brushing away the tears spilling down her face. "Ten years ago, I fell in love with you, and two years ago, I finally went after what I always wanted, and now that I have you, I don't ever want to let you go."

I take a deep breath as I reach for her hand, lowering down to one knee. A smile tugs at the corners of my lips at the sound of her surprised gasp. Another tear rolls down her cheek, and I fight to contain the swirl of emotions in my chest. "You're the only woman who has ever owned my heart, and the only one I want to spend my life watching those reality shows you love so much with." Her laughter fills the air, blending with the tears streaming down her face.

I reach into my pocket, and pull out a black velvet box. Her hands fly to her mouth, and more tears fall down her face when I open the box and she sees the gold ring. She makes no attempt to wipe them away, too enraptured by this moment to do anything else. Zaria helped me pick it out a little over five months ago before we found out Mel was pregnant. I thought about waiting until the baby was here, but I made the mistake of not going after what I want once, and I'm not doing that again. I want Mel to be my wife.

"I promise to make you smile every day," I start, my throat clogging with emotion. "I promise to make you as happy as you make me. I promise to love you more and more every day, and I promise to cook for you so you don't endanger our lives." Her laugh escapes through her tears. "I promise to love you when we argue, because I know I'm the only one who you allow to see that side of you."

I stroke her beautiful, round belly. "I'll love you when you bring our baby girl into this world, and I'll love you when we're old as fuck, and you can't walk without a cane."

I look into the eyes of the love of my life, wishing this moment could stretch into eternity. But the anticipation of our shared future pushes me to continue. "I want you with me every day, for as long as we live. Will you be my wife, my partner, my life, Melissa Trevisano?"

"Yes," she cries out, wrapping her arms around my neck. Lifting myself off the ground, I wrap my arms around her waist as her lips crash into mine, resisting the urge to wrap her legs around my waist.

"God," my sister mumbles, holding the camera as tears spill down her face. "You're going to cry when you see this video, M."

Mel laughs, turning back to face me. "I'm going to rewatch it so many times."

A wide grin spreads across my face. I know how much she loves watching proposal videos, so I was determined to make ours just as memorable for her. "I love you," I mumble against her lips, pulling back slightly to slide the ring onto her finger.

She lifts her gaze up to me. "I love you so much," she says. "I can't wait to spend the rest of my life with you."

My girl. Twelve years, and a lot of tribulations, but we're finally here. Together.

The End

Author's note

To all you wonderful readers who read and loved the first edition of Love Me or Hate Me, my heartfelt gratitude goes out to each and every one of you. When I started this journey with my debut book, I never imagined it would reach as many people as it did. But you guys proved me wrong. Your support and enthusiasm have truly been the driving force behind this journey.

As time went on, so did my growth as a writer. I felt like it was necessary to revisit and enhance the story that started it all. Many people also asked for Gabriel's POV, and I couldn't resist the opportunity to delve deeper into his perspective, and their love story.

Returning to the world of Melissa and Gabriel was so fun, and I loved revisiting it so much. Their love story holds a special place in my heart, and I really hope you guys love it too.

Thank you so much for being a part of this journey. Your continuous support means the world to me, and I can't wait for everyone to read the new, and updated version of Love Me or Hate Me.

If you enjoyed Love Me or Hate Me, please leave a review as they're important, and very helpful for indie authors.

About the Author

Stephanie Alves is an avid reader and writer of smutty, contemporary romance books. She was born in England, but was raised by her loud Portuguese parents. She can speak both languages fluently, though she tends to mix both languages when speaking. She loves to write romantic comedies with happy endings, witty banter and sizzling chemistry that will make you blush. When she's not writing, she can be found either reading, or watching rom coms with her two adorable dogs cuddled up beside her.

You can find her here:
Instagram.com/Stephanie.alves_author
Stephaniealvesauthor.com

Printed in Great Britain
by Amazon